gather the sentient

Sevens Prophecy Series
Book Two

gather the

the

sentient

AMALIE JAHN

BERMLORD PUBLICATIONS

Whispering Hope, song lyrics written in 1868 by Septimus Winner.

ISBN-13: 978-0-9910713-4-0 (BERMLORD)
ISBN-10: 0-9910713-4-4

Library of Congress Control Number: 2016908734
BERMLORD, Charlotte, North Carolina

First Edition, July 2016

Typeset in Garamond
Cover layout by Amalie Jahn
Author photograph courtesy of Mary Ickert of Mary L. Photography

For Laura,
who helped to develop the background for Jose's narrative
while we lazed around my back porch together
one warm, summer afternoon.

Thanks for the inspiration, not only for *Gather the Sentient's*
main character, but for the way you approach life
with such drive and perseverance.
You'll always be my hero.

Acknowledgments

To my internet service provider for the lightning fast service I used to research (and research and research) many facets of this book: the Democratic Republic of Congo, domestic violence, gang violence, the prevalence Chinese body shaming, the name for the part of your nose between your nostrils, and the best place to sing karaoke in Fells Point these days.

Heartfelt thanks also go out to:

The women who told me their stories of abuse, raw and unfiltered. Thank you for sharing your truths so I could bring Andrea's story to life.

My editor, Anne Zirkle, for agreeing to continue this journey with me, for understanding that sometimes it *is* possible to edit via text message and emojis, and for helping me see the holes that needed filling along the way. You're always the voice of reason. Can't wait to collaborate again on book three!

The beta readers near and far who volunteered their time and their eagle eyes, flushing out typos, spelling mistakes, and grammatical errors so the book would go out into the world free of any embarrassing blemishes.

And to my family, for the pride I hear in your voices when you tell people I'm an author. Thanks for always believing in me.

"Borromean rings are three rings which are interlocked in such a way that removing one ring causes the entire structure to fall apart. This is an illustration of what is known as a Brunnian link, a situation where no two loops in a figure are directly connected.

Borromean rings are extremely ancient. They appear in Buddhist art from thousands of years ago, for example, and they can be seen on Viking rune stones, in Roman mosaics, and in an assortment of other places. People appear to have an enduring fascination with the phenomenon of Borromean rings, and they appear especially frequently in religious artwork from a variety of cultures.

When used in religious artwork, coats of arms, logos, and crests, Borromean rings are meant to symbolize strength in unity, a living illustration of what happens when one link in a united element is removed. The rings are named for the Borromeo family of Italian nobles, who famously used them in their family coat of arms, popularizing the three interlocked rings."

Source: www.wisegeek.com

gather the sentient

MANCHU

Monday, March 21, 1955
Central Africa

Manchu wasn't used to the heat of Sub-Saharan Africa. Although the summer months were always warm living in Shanghai, the oppressive intensity of the jungle heat stopped the young man where he stood, bent over and struggling to catch his breath.

"It's thick out here, isn't it?" his graduate professor and travelling companion, Dr. Yueng Wei asked as he slipped briskly past him, expertly cutting through the dense foliage with his machete.

Manchu swatted at a biting fly which had somehow found its way under the cool, damp bandana he'd tied around his neck. "I don't know how people live here," he said, forcing himself to continue on, following the crude path his mentor left through the brush.

"People do and have for thousands of years. Evidence of their existence is all around us. Evidence is what we're searching for today."

When Dr. Yueng had approached him earlier in the semester about accompanying him on a research trip to Africa, Manchu had been told they would be going to Angola to archive antiquities housed at their Natural Museum of Anthropology in Luanda. He'd assumed there would be accommodations – beds, fans, running water. What he'd discovered instead, upon his arrival, was that his professor had no interest in archiving antiquities. Instead, the true purpose of their trip was to document and research the origins of an ancient prophecy.

The Sevens Prophecy.

According to Dr. Yueng, the prophecy was as old as man himself, passed down from generation to generation, foretelling of a time when the fate of the world would be decided by a chosen group of gifted psychics, ushering in an age of goodness or evil. Should the light prevail, seven 'children of the light' would lead those living at the time to work together as equals for the betterment of all mankind, producing a utopian society. The darkness would fall away and wars would end. There would be no more famine. No more poverty. It would be an age of charity, humility, and grace.

Conversely, should the dark prevail, a hedonistic society would arise, led by the seven 'children of the dark.' They would come to rule the earth's citizens as unchallenged dictators, exploiting the world's riches for their own personal gain. It would be a time of gluttony, greed, wrath, and lust.

Dr. Yueng had been explaining all of this to Manchu on their month long trek together through the most remote parts of central Africa, which he believed to be the birthplace of the prophecy. They were searching for clues as to the timing of the end of days; clues Yueng felt sure could be found in the Congolese jungle. The untimely death of the man's own mentor 30 years before had tasked him as a 'keeper,' and the professor had spent the better part of his adult life searching for signs of the world to come.

"A keeper," Yueng clarified as they continued through the thick brush, "is one who is commissioned with the noble task of searching for both the light and dark psychics with the ultimate goal of assisting the light and stifling the dark. It is also my job to conceal the prophecy's existence, systematically eliminating it from society's collective conscious to preventing the world's darkest people from seeking one another out in the hopes of fulfilling the prophecy themselves."

Manchu thought about the worst cases of genocide and wondered aloud how one could know for sure that the prophecy hadn't already been fulfilled.

"There have been many times throughout history when keepers were certain the end was at hand," Yueng said. "When men committed atrocities so evil there was certainly no other explanation than the final alliance of the dark psychics. In fact, as long ago as 40 AD, keepers were convinced the age of darkness had arrived, when Rome's third emperor, Caligula, ruled with a hand so malevolent, he was known for saying, 'I wish Rome had but one neck, so that I could cut off all their heads with one blow!'"

Dr. Yueng shared many stories of the times keepers were convinced the age of darkness had certainly come to pass. Accounts of men like Nero, who not only murdered every member in his family, but also poisoned, beheaded, stabbed, burned, boiled, crucified and impaled thousands of Roman citizens. Men like Maximilien Robespierre who was so obsessed with the guillotine, he incited a reign of terror in which tens of thousands of French citizens had been beheaded.

The list went on and on with names which were both familiar and unfamiliar to Manchu. Names like Genghis Khan, Attila the Hun, Tomas de Torquemada, Ivan the Terrible, Adolf Hitler, and Joseph Stalin.

"Just when we thought all was lost during the reign of each of these tyrants, a light would always appear. Some voice of reason. A coalition of goodness to overthrow the evil. In fact, here in the Congo, when King Leopold II of Belgium mutilated and slaughtered millions of Congolese, he was finally thwarted by a world-wide human rights movement inspired by literary works such as Joseph Conrad's *Heart of Darkness*, Mark Twain's *King Leopold's Soliloquy*, and Arthur Conan Doyle's *The Crime of the Congo*. Eventually, international opposition motivated by these good men's works caused the Belgian parliament to compel the King to cede the Congo Free State to Belgium in 1908."

5

Yueng paused, taking a sip of water from his canteen before continuing up an especially steep section of terrain. "We keepers know, however, that a time will come when the work of a few good men will not be enough to overthrow the darkness. Which is why we must do whatever we can to protect both the secret of the prophecy and the light psychics as they are drawn to one another."

Manchu was still pondering the strangeness of the prophecy, wondering if it was something he could actually believe when he heard his professor crying out up ahead.

"Manchu! Come quickly and bring the newsprint! I believe I've found an etching about the prophecy."

Manchu dug through his ruck sack for the ream of paper, one of half-a-dozen means of replication he'd been hauling around, and tried to ignore the briars tearing at his face and hands as he made the final ascent to where Dr. Yueng was waiting near a cave at the top of the hill. Together they unrolled the paper against the wall of the cave, and Yueng began coloring over the inscription on the rock face with a smooth piece of charcoal.

"What does it say?" Machu asked as the last of the symbols appeared on the parchment.

The professor made one final pass with the coal across the inscription and tossed the remaining nub to the ground. He stood back, admiring his work and with a tremor in his voice replied, "'Seven light to save the earth. Seven dark to destroy it.' The prophecy has been known here, Manchu. I'm certain now. We're on the right track."

CHAPTER

1

MIA

Wednesday, August 24
Baltimore

Mia slipped into the back of the courtroom unnoticed. The door groaned behind her, but no one turned to glance in her direction as she slid into one of the last remaining seats in the far corner of the gallery. She hadn't stepped foot in the courthouse since the two days she'd spent on the stand at the beginning of the trial. Since then, she'd watched the remainder of the case unfold on TV, as the state presented a solid case against the accused. All that was left was to announce the verdict.

Several rows in front of her were Lera, Anya, and Svetlana, three of the trafficked women she'd been imprisoned with in the basement of the warehouse. When the donation money from the precinct began pouring in, most of the other rescued girls returned home, but the three who sat before her made the conscious decision to stay, thanks to specially granted permission from the government. And, as it turned out, their testimony had been the most compelling, and damning, of the trial. It was no wonder they'd become social media darlings, heralded for their bravery and dedication. Mia wondered what life held in store for them now that the trial was going to be over.

She was still imagining their futures when the jury members filed into the box one at a time. Twelve solemn faces, not a one conveying the slightest indication of their decision. Their souls were light, revealed to her by the brightness of their auras, just as they'd been when they listened to her testimony several weeks before. She was comforted knowing it was their nature to see justice served, but she was also aware that even the purest of souls could be deceived.

As they settled themselves in their seats, Mia turned her attention to Dalton, the man who had somehow worked his way up numerous chains of command to become Baltimore's police commissioner. Her stomach churned, digesting the memory. Highly regarded, with a seemingly spotless track record, he took over command of the city, much to the delight of her father, Chief Carlos Rosetti. He'd been blinded, along with everyone else, by Dalton's glowing credentials. She wondered if his embarrassment was keeping him from the courtroom today, or if he simply couldn't be trusted to share the same space with the man who nearly killed her. Seeing Dalton now, sitting smugly beyond the multitude of spectators, she wished she'd had the courage to trust in her abilities from the beginning. Perhaps, she thought, if I hadn't questioned myself, we could have arrested him sooner, and Kate would still be alive.

But of course, it was all in the past. She pressed her eyelids closed, forcing herself to hold it together. She couldn't express her emotions. Not here. Not now. Today, of all days, she would be strong.

Just before court was scheduled to convene, she felt the bench shift beside her. She didn't have to look to know who it was.

"Hey," Thomas whispered, his fingers discreetly brushing the polyester of her uniform just above her knee. "How ya holding up?"

He was in a Flaming Lips concert t-shirt and Levis, which she often teased was his uniform. "You're a sight for sore eyes," she said, leaning into him. "But I thought you had orientation this afternoon?"

The bailiff announced Judge Garrison's arrival, and Thomas shrugged as everyone stood while she entered the chamber. "What's there to know? I go to class. I learn. I go home. Who needs orientation?"

Returning to their seats, the last thing Mia needed was to be reminded of just how much of a spectacle the trial had become. It wasn't a stretch to say that the entire country had spent the better part of six weeks glued to their newsfeeds, watching to see what would become of the highly-decorated commissioner, accused of spearheading one of the world's largest human trafficking operations. The media circus they'd been embroiled in was nothing short of surreal. After everything she'd witnessed and everything she'd been through, she didn't know how she would react if he was acquitted.

"I feel Kate here with us, you know?" she said, meeting his gaze. "I just hope, if she's watching from somewhere, she'll be proud of all we've accomplished here."

Before he could respond, the gavel sounded and the foreman was asked to read the verdict. Mia could hear the woman in front of her snapping her gum nervously on the back of her teeth. She could hear the second hand marking the time on the wrist of the man to her right. She could hear Thomas' shallow breathing just over the pounding of her own heart inside her chest. She closed her eyes.

Thomas wrapped his hand around hers where it rested on the seat between them. Clearly, he understood the reading of the first verdict was going to have a powerful effect on her, one way or another.

Because, of course, the first verdict pertained specifically to her.

"We the jury, in the case of the state of Maryland versus Roger M. Dalton, on the count of attempted murder in the second degree, find the defendant guilty."

Cheers erupted from the gallery, and she opened her eyes, taking a huge gulp of air into her oxygen-deprived lungs. Only then did she realize she'd been holding her breath since the gavel had sounded moments before. Relief washed over her and she melted into Thomas' shoulder, knowing she had successfully convinced the jury he'd intended to murder her in his foyer the morning she confronted him about his involvement with the trafficking.

"That'll put him away for a while," Thomas grinned, obviously thrilled at the prospect.

Her eyes were now fixed on the back of Dalton's skull. "I don't want him to go away for a while," she replied. "I want him put away forever."

The foreman wasted no time announcing the remaining verdicts. "On all 46 counts of conspiracy to kidnap, we find the defendant guilty. On all 46 counts of third-degree sex offence, we find the defendant guilty. On all 46 counts of second-degree sex offence, we find the defendant guilty. On all 46 counts of second-degree conspiracy to commit rape, we find the defendant guilty."

More cheers filled the courtroom, but the foreman continued to the final verdict, as if the burden of holding in the last of the sentencing was too much to bear. "On all 46 counts of first-degree conspiracy to commit rape, we find the defendant…" He paused, glancing at Dalton in a motion so slight, Mia sensed perhaps only she had observed it. Half a second later, he cut his eyes to the paper trembling in his hands and continued. "Guilty."

Thomas leapt from the bench in an uncharacteristic display of revelry, scooping her into his arms. "You did it!" he cried, as he pressed her face into his chest.

She had done it. She'd played an instrumental role in securing Dalton's arrest and subsequent conviction, but the outcome was still bittersweet. As the courtroom erupted into chaos around her, a small but concentrated point of apprehension smoldered deep in her gut. Because while the experience taught her a valuable lesson about trusting her abilities as well as her intuition, she also knew Dalton was merely a cog in a much larger machine. The buck certainly didn't stop with him. Someone higher on the food chain was running the show.

She pulled away from Thomas, trying to convince herself she didn't need to take one last look at Dalton. He'd caused so much turmoil in her life – plowing a rift between her and her father, imprisoning her along with the trafficked women, and nearly strangling her to death. She should be happy to never have to gaze upon his face again, and yet…

Thomas tucked her under the crook of his arm, almost as if he could sense what she wanted to do, but in the end, she couldn't keep herself from glancing toward the front of the room where Dalton was being led away by the bailiff.

He was facing her, shrouded in an opaque darkness as clear to her across the room as it had been during their first meeting. Their eyes locked and a small smile played at his lips. And then, without a hint of irony, he winked at her, mouthing the words 'see you soon.'

The courtroom was clearing out, people pushing and shoving into the hallway. "Let's go," Thomas said, steering her into the flow of spectators being corralled toward the exit. If he had seen the exchange, he didn't let on. Her mind exploded, imagining why Dalton thought they would ever come face to face again.

CHAPTER

2

PATRICK

Wednesday, August 24
London

Patrick looked up from the book he was reading, startled by a subtle shift in the universe. He never tired of Nietzsche's *Die fröhliche Wissenschaft* and was loath to set it aside, but upon looking at his watch, he realized immediately what event had just transpired.

His colleague, Roger Dalton, had obviously just been sentenced. The difference in time zones between London and Baltimore meant that although the sun was setting just outside the window of his Compton Avenue estate, it was only 1:00 pm on the east coast of the US. The timing was just about right.

He set his book face down across the arm of the settee and closed his eyes, pulling at the periphery of his subconscious. There was no mistaking the surge of Roger's anger and disappointment flooding into his system, an obvious indication of the direction the jury had decided. Patrick didn't linger in the astral plane and quickly pulled back into himself.

Reflecting on the sentencing, he felt a twinge of sadness for the loss of his associate, but quickly shook it off. Roger had no one to blame but himself for his arrest and subsequent fall from power. In Patrick's opinion, he'd been far too lax in screening the men he invited into the ring, as well as those he relied on to run the operation. There had been too many loose lips. Too many loose ends. And to have kidnapped the woman officer who knew too much instead of killing her outright was just plain sloppy. It was no wonder the whole undertaking blew up in Roger's face. If there was any silver lining to the whole ordeal it was that there were no direct lines linking them to one another.

Patrick made sure of it.

He was no fool.

It was a shame though, to lose Roger from his inner circle. He was one of the few allies outside the prophecy who was a true nihilist - who understood what it meant to be free of the universal moral law.

He took a sip of his tea – no sugar, extra milk - and let the warmth of it melt away any lingering regret. He wouldn't allow losing one man to derail his agenda. The mid-Atlantic trafficking operation was but one small cog in his vast empire.

Onward and upward. That's what his father had always said.

That was, until Patrick had him eliminated.

With his evening of relaxation disrupted, his mind wandered. He placed a tasseled bookmark between the pages of *Die fröhliche Wissenschaft* and returned it to the mahogany floor-to-ceiling bookshelf on the far wall of his library. Beside him, laid out on the table in the center of the room, were the scrolls and faded parchment which had become the obsession of his adult life. Without making the conscious decision to pause beside the desk, his fingers traced the edge of the closest worn document. And then, as if powerless to stop it, he succumbed to the allure of the one focus which could always calm his nerves and hold his interest – the prophecy.

Patrick had been a perceptive child, splitting his time between his divorced parents – his mother in California and his father in South Africa. He didn't mind being shuttled back and forth, like a prized possession, though seemingly less valuable than the collection of Chinese antiquities they also fought over until he left for college. He was fully aware neither of his parents enjoyed spending time with him, and that he was merely a pawn in the pageantry of their lives, leveraging him at every turn to spite one another. However, unlike most children who would have been traumatized by this insight, it didn't bother him in the least. In fact, he took great pleasure in the fact that he was a constant source of turmoil between them.

Regardless of whether he was in the US or Africa, he was never a priority to whomever he was with and he knew it. The best part about being a throwaway child was it gave him plenty of free time to pursue his own endeavors, which from the time he was a teen included researching the Sevens Prophecy.

As he sat now at his desk, rereading the prophetic message which had been passed down from scribe to scribe through the ages, he felt the same sense of overwhelming pride he always felt in its presence. For he was as certain now as he had been as a teen that its words pertained directly to him.

Septuagent Prophecy

Lo, I say to you, who doth wait with great fear and longing for the great tribulation. An hour shall pass at such time in which seven seers of light and seven seers of darkness will be sent down upon the earth from the bosom of the heavens, charged with resolving the fate of all who walk the earth. Mystical powers from the creator shall draw them nigh, one to another, until such time that each shall join together, light to light, dark to dark. Shall the light prevail, making great haste in their assemblage, all glory and honor shall reign upon the earth. And woe to the earth, shall the dark prevail, as anguish and servitude will perpetuate forevermore.

By thirteen, Patrick had already identified his ability to sense what other people were thinking and feeling from great distances as clairvoyance. But instead of assuming he was going mad, with unsolicited access to other people's thoughts and emotions, he embraced his gift for what he assumed it was – something which made him superior to everyone else.

He scanned a list of names, written in his fluid script, beneath the prophecy. His name, Patrick Meyer, was at the top. Below his were names of the four other men and women he'd confirmed were also foretold of in the prophecy. Beneath their names were two empty spaces.

Two empty spaces, which were not only the focus of his days, but also the cause for his recurring insomnia at night. He felt certain he was close to finding the fellow psychics who would usher in the End of Days, changing the world as he knew it.

Changing it for the better.

At least for Patrick.

He was examining a detailed spreadsheet – a meticulously compiled record of the thousands of people around the world who were born on his birthdate, February 17th. It was an extensive list, but not fully comprehensive, as there were many people whose births were never recorded due to any number of circumstances. For this reason, among others, Patrick employed a team of researchers whose purpose it was to discover the last two dark psychics while eliminating any potential light psychics they encountered along the way. Better to kill off any potential threats if their loyalty was in question. Prudence was Patrick's middle name.

That several months had passed without any new developments frustrated him to no end. Every day his seven remained apart was a day the others gained to gather themselves. He shuddered to think. Fortunately, he'd heard mention of a new discovery earlier in the week, and was relieved when minutes later, the doorbell's deep gong announced his fellow psychic, Javier, had arrived for their weekly dinner meeting to fill him in on the team's progress.

"The beef looks delicious, as always," Patrick told Elsa, one of the small army of servants he kept on staff. "Please give my compliments to Mrs. Drury in the kitchen."

"I certainly will," Elsa replied, backing out of the room. "Let me know if there will be anything else."

He waited until the door latch clicked behind her, and as soon as they were alone, Patrick began grilling Javier about the lead on Number Six.

"She's Brazilian, as we expected," Javier announced in his thick Spanish accent, after taking a sip of his wine and tucking a lock of his shoulder-length hair behind his ear.

"So it is a woman after all? Eshanti's drawings are correct?" He was intrigued. Before the discovery of the Brazilian, he'd been speculating about the abilities of the latest addition to their group, a girl they'd discovered in India, who had the capacity to subconsciously inscribe words and drawings, giving valuable insight to future events. When he discovered her, she'd shown him dozens of drawings of his likeness scattered around her room. She'd predicted his arrival with her art. "That's truly remarkable considering this latest find in Brazil wasn't even on the list."

Javier chewed and swallowed a bite of his Wellington. "Apparently Eshanti's psychographic ability is stronger than we imagined. Using her drawings of the girl and her surroundings, Wesley was able to track her down, questioning locals along the way. She lives in an isolated portion of the Amazonian river basin. And you wouldn't believe some of the pictures the team sent back. Talk about primitive living. Houses built on sticks. Thatched roofs. Like a National Geographic special. They don't even speak Portuguese, so Wesley had to find a local translator to communicate." He took another bite and glanced up from his plate, a mischievous look in his eye. "They told him her name's Akantha. It means 'burning sun.'"

Patrick instinctively reached out into the astral plane in an attempt to connect to her, but he could not. Her location was far too remote. Or at least that was the reason he allowed himself to use as an excuse. "What does she do?"

Javier didn't look up from his plate. "Pyrokinesis."

"You're kidding," he gasped, imagining the good fortune of having someone with the ability to manipulate fire at their disposal. "And her birthday checks out?"

Javier nodded, setting his fork down for the first time, clearly enjoying his role as the messenger. "As far as we can tell. She's the right age, and she was born in the summer, most likely February, based on the crops being harvested at the time of her birth, as well as her parents' accounts."

Patrick chewed on this information but was leery of allowing himself to get too excited. They'd found others before who had seemed promising but hadn't proven to be part of the prophecy in the end. "And we're sure she's one of us?" he asked finally, accentuating her relation to their group.

Javier lifted his wine glass and smirked. "When Wesley found her, she was locked in a rudimentary metal cage in the center of a large clearing. Apparently she kept burning down houses. And sections of the forest."

"On purpose?" Patrick interrupted, raising an eyebrow at the possibility.

"It seems that way," he replied.

Patrick's pulse quickened at the prospect of discovering the sixth member of the prophecy. "Where is she now?"

Javier dipped his final bite of beef in the au jus. "Wesley told the girl's family he was a doctor who could help with her affliction. The plan was to bring her here, unless you'd prefer we take her somewhere else."

Patrick's uneaten food cooled on his plate as he contemplated his next move. It was typical for Wesley to bring the men and women they found to him for questioning. He'd been chosen for the job because of his gargantuan stature, as he was an imposing force most chose not to oppose. But Akantha was an anomaly. She didn't speak a known language, much less have the ability to communicate well enough for their standard interview. And it seemed she might not be impressed by Wesley's stature in the same way others had been in the past.

Their interrogation process was developed by Patrick and Javier in the early days of their pursuit. They'd met as teenagers, while Patrick was visiting the Mediterranean city of Marbella, on what was supposed to have been a family holiday during the summer of his fifteenth year. However, instead of sightseeing with his mother, who chose to devote her days to boutique shopping and sunning herself poolside, Patrick cast off on his own to explore the seedy underbelly of the city without her. Which is where he met Javier, in a back alley running a small gambling operation. He was drawn to the boy immediately.

"Do you remember the day we met?" Patrick asked him now, changing the subject. "How smart you thought you were, using your ability to bamboozle all those poor tourists."

Javier chuckled. "I made more money with that stupid ball and cup gag as a kid than some people make in a lifetime," he boasted.

"It helps when you can move the ball from under the cup with your mind," Patrick teased.

In response, Javier raised his glass as if to toast, without the use of his hands. "That it does," he replied, before taking a sip. "I couldn't figure out for the life of me how you were able to guess where it was every time."

"It helps when you can sense where the ball is, even when the bozo running the show keeps moving it." Patrick laughed, and then regarded his associate more seriously. "I'm glad you trusted me enough in those early days to share your secret with me. Look at everything we've built together since then. And now this… finding Number Six. It's like a dream come true. We're so close to the end."

"So close," he repeated. "But first we need to figure out what to do with Akantha. She could be tough, especially since she seems intent on burning things up. Worse still, we don't have a good way to communicate with her. It'll be hard to explain who we are and who she is with regard to the prophecy."

Patrick considered their options. It seemed as if there was only one solution. "I think it's time to bring in Lillian."

CHAPTER

3

JOSE

Thursday, August 25
Phoenix

The hospital was as quiet as hospitals ever can be, which is to say there was still a modicum of chatter from the nurses' station and muted clicks and beeps could still be heard coming from patients' rooms if you listened carefully. Beyond that, the halls were silent, as no visitors were allowed in the ICU overnight.

Jose passed through the ward on his way to the ER and gave a nod to Selma, one of the nurses who also worked the graveyard shift. The two had been out together several times but no relationship ever developed. This bothered Jose if for no other reason than he had always been drawn to the warmth of her smile. She waved to him, barely making eye contact, and quickly returned to her conversation with the others.

He slowed his pace once he was past their line of sight and scanned the patients' names on the doors as he strolled down the hallway. He was familiar with all but two, who he assumed had been brought in since his shift the night before. Their files hung on wall hooks just outside their rooms, and after glancing back down the corridor to be sure he wouldn't be seen, he snatched Chloe Hall's clipboard from the wall and stepped inside her room.

The lights were off and except for a faint overhead light in the doorway and the eerie glow of the machinery monitors, the room was dark. He peered into the dimness and could barely make out the shape of a figure asleep under the sheet. Chloe appeared tiny and her chart confirmed that she was only 17 years old, hospitalized as the result of a traumatic head injury – a horseback riding accident was listed as the cause. Jose crept slightly further into the room until he could see the steady rise and fall of her chest and the green halo of the ventilation machine. Wisps of hair peeked out from beneath the gauze around her head and he imagined what she'd looked like the day before, atop her horse soaring across the Sonoran Desert, the wind chasing her down.

Without a word, he reentered the hallway, cautiously replaced Chloe's chart, and entered the room of the other newcomer to the ward, Matt Mulhaney. A quick scan of his chart revealed the reason for his admission – a front end collision with a dump truck early that morning. He'd spent all day in surgery having his arms and legs bolted back together, and while there was only a slight threat of internal bleeding, the doctor's notes indicated he remained in the ICU because of his lethally high blood pressure. Framed by the light from the hallway, Mulhaney appeared to be a sort of prehistoric arachnid, his limbs suspended around him as if he was caught in a web of his own construction. Jose wondered if the man's family was waiting somewhere in the building or if they'd relented and gone home after a full day of weeping and praying. He envisioned the man's small children climbing over waiting room furniture, no longer satisfied with broken crayons and daytime TV, unable to comprehend just what 'critical condition' really meant.

Jose left the second patient's room more confused than when he entered, and after confirming he hadn't been seen, made his way through the double doors and into the elevator which delivered him to the emergency room where he was expected for work. The glaring brightness and cacophony of the ER was a stark contrast to the intensive care unit on the second floor. Vanessa, the head nurse, spotted him cutting through triage on the way to the break room and stopped him before he even had a chance to drop off his bag.

"Have you clocked in?" she called, pushing an elderly man in a wheelchair through the waiting room.

"I was just on my way," he replied, motioning toward the door.

She shook her head. "I'll have Gloria swipe your card. I need you to take Mr. Fletcher here to the restroom to get washed up. It seems he's had a bit of an accident."

The stench coming from the man indicated what kind of accident he'd had and it wasn't the type which involved a motor vehicle. Although he initially balked, Jose quickly remembered his job as an orderly was a means to an end. Changing the old man's pants now was the only way he would have access to the others later, so with that in mind, he left his bag behind the triage desk and hurried Mr. Fletcher to an unoccupied restroom.

He cleaned the man quickly and proficiently, redressing him in a pair of standard issue scrubs while avoiding both eye contact and small talk. When he began working as an orderly right after high school, tasks involving human waste often made him consider other career options, but six years later, he knew he could never leave. The access it gave him to complete his life's work was unsurpassed, so he quickly learned to overcome his squeamish tendencies.

After returning Mr. Fletcher to his wife in the waiting room, he was immediately called to help restrain a new arrival who was hopped up on hallucinogens and threatening to tear an examination room apart.

"He thinks we're trying to kill him," one of the shift nurses told him. "And he's seriously strong, so be careful. Dr. Unger's already in there and has been calling for back up, but I didn't know where you were."

Without the slightest hesitation, Jose hurried past the support rooms toward the treatment area where he heard the man screaming obscenities and threatening the staff. The room's door was no longer closed for privacy and exposed the scene inside as he approached.

"Listen, Kirk, no one is trying to hurt you," Unger was telling the patient when Jose rushed up behind him. "Just set down the scissors so we can find out what's really going on."

Kirk, a formidable looking teenager, stood against the far wall wielding a pair of surgical scissors he'd obviously scavenged from a drawer somewhere in the room. The terror in his eyes convinced Jose the kid truly believed his evasive actions against hospital personnel were necessary for his survival and that there would be no reasoning with him. Mascara stained the cheeks of a pretty brunette pleading quietly from the corner of the room for him to stop, while Vanessa and Gloria stood behind Unger, positioned to flee if necessary.

"Come on, baby. Just chill out, okay? Please?" the brunette begged. "Let's just forget any of this ever happened and I'll just take you home."

"NO!" he screamed at her, "you're in it with them! All of you together! You're all trying to kill me but I won't let you!"

Jose immediately wished there was another man in the room. He knew with Unger's help he could restrain Kirk, but the adrenaline surging through the kid's veins made him unpredictable. There was no telling what he would do if they provoked him further.

Unger turned to Vanessa. "Has security been called?"

She appeared poised, but did not take her eyes off the boy. "Yes, of course, but someone said they were outside dealing with a fight in the parking lot. Who knows when we'll see them."

Kirk's eyes darted around the room and Jose sensed he was planning to make his escape. Lives would be in jeopardy if he was allowed to leave the room and there was no telling what type of chaos would ensue. He took a step closer to the teen.

"Hey, border bandit," Kirk sneered. "Stay away from me. I'll kill you if I have to! Nobody will care if there's one less Sanchez in the world!"

The words sliced a nick in Jose's composure – no one ever cared he was a fourth generation American of legal descent, but it wasn't enough to provoke him into action prematurely. He ventured another step forward with Unger by his side.

"Ready?" Unger whispered.

"Yeah," he replied.

The men tackled the boy in one fluid motion, Unger on his left side and Jose on his right, pinning him against the wall. Vanessa fumbled for a set of zip tie cuffs in the bottom drawer of a cabinet as Kirk wrestled to free himself. Once she found them, she ran to Unger who quickly strapped his left hand into the tie while Jose continued to restrain Kirk as best he could, cautious of the scissors which were dangerously close to his body.

"Get off me, Chalupa!" Kirk spat as he thrashed his head in sheer defiance. "I'll kill you, I swear it!"

After securing the boy's left hand, Unger slid behind him in an attempt to reach his other side, but as he lessened his grip, Kirk seized the opportunity to lunge forward, stabbing the scissors into Jose's thigh. He cried out but didn't release the boy, jamming his shoulder securely into his chest. Within seconds, Unger slipped the tie over Kirk's right hand and pulled tightly on the restraint, forcing him to the ground.

"Oh my God, Jose," Gloria cried out, noticing the blood pooling in a ring on his scrubs.

He brought his hand to the wound, testing to see how deeply he'd been pierced. "It's nothing," he replied, as she hurried to his side. "I don't think it even needs stitches."

Security arrived as the police were being called and Gloria led Jose into an adjacent room to look at his injury.

"Seriously, it's fine. I'll just change my pants and put on a Band-Aid," he said.

Gloria slipped on a pair of latex gloves. "Nonsense," she replied as she carefully began cutting a hole in his pants to expose the wound. "Just let me make sure that little punk didn't do any serious harm."

He allowed her to examine him as it gave her peace of mind, but he knew there would be no lasting damage. As she cleaned and dressed the puncture, prattling on about how they didn't get paid enough to deal with crazy people, he allowed his mind to wander to the new ICU patients. It was always hard when he had to make a choice and tonight he could only choose one person on the floor. To choose more than one would be far too risky. He couldn't chance exposing his intent. By the time Gloria finished, he'd weighed all his options and made his decision. He hoped it was the right one.

The police were escorting a subdued and restrained Kirk out of the ER as Jose sought out Vanessa to tell her he was going on his break. He slipped unnoticed through the lobby to where the elevators carried him back to the second floor.

It was still peaceful there as he crept down the hallway, hugging tightly to the wall so he could duck into an alcove if one of the nurses made an appearance. When he arrived at the room of the patient he'd selected, he wasted no time getting straight to work.

Chloe Hall lay before him, sleeping soundly as she'd been when he first looked in on her earlier in the evening. Selecting her out of all the possible ICU patients wasn't an easy decision, but he knew in his heart she wasn't going to make it and that he was the only one capable of putting an end to her suffering. He gently brushed the wisps of hair across her pillow, whispering a simple prayer for her soul, and then Jose placed his hands upon her chest and surrendered himself to what he knew needed to be done.

4

Friday, August 26
Baltimore

"Is he expecting a mistrial? Does he think I'm gonna visit him in prison?" Mia raked her fingers through her auburn hair, securing it into a messy bun with the rubber band from her wrist. "I just don't know why he would say he's going to 'see me soon.'"

Thomas stood up from his mother's kitchen table, where the three of them had just finished eating five-bean casserole for supper. "Are you sure that's what he said?" he asked as he cleared away her plate.

"I'm positive."

He watched her gnawing on the cuticle around her thumbnail the way she always did when she was deep in thought. It bothered him she was still preoccupied with what she thought she saw Dalton say to her from across the crowded courtroom. It wasn't like her to waste time dwelling on something so arbitrary.

Thomas' mother, Mildred, spoke up as she loaded the silverware into the dishwasher. "You know, dear, 'soon' is a relative term. Maybe he didn't really mean 'soon.' Maybe he just meant 'later.' Like 'see you later.'"

Mia narrowed her eyes and shook her head slightly. "Uh. He chose all three of those words for a reason. 'See' meaning he's actually going to physically set eyes on me. 'You,' as opposed to anyone else. And 'soon' signifies in the immediate future – not 50 years from now when the penal system grants him compassionate release." She finished off her can of soda and carried it over to the recycling bin across the room. "There's no question that he said what he did for a reason. I just have no idea of what that reason might be."

Mildred returned to her seat at the table, resting her hands on the chipped green Formica while Thomas washed the casserole pan at the sink. "Now don't you go borrowing trouble," she said, in the motherly tone she typically reserved for him but had begun using more frequently with Mia as well. He wondered if Mia felt comforted by his mother's growing affection for her as he scrubbed the last stubborn beans out of the dish. "That evil man is going to be locked up in a federal prison for a very long time. No sense worrying about him anymore. You did your job. There's nothing more to do."

Although the two women had bonded quickly while holding vigil together at the hospital following his gunshot wound to the head, there was a lot Mildred still didn't understand about Mia. Looking at her now, brow furrowed, stewing about Dalton, there was no doubt he still had a bit to learn about Mia himself.

He set the dish on the counter to dry. "You think there's something more going on?"

She peered up at him, brooding beneath her lashes. "Maybe."

"You talked to Jack about it? Or you wanna run something past me?"

He didn't mind sharing her with her partner, Jack. They were more like siblings than coworkers, and he was certainly no threat to their relationship, especially considering he and his wife, Stella, were only weeks away from having their first child together. The truth was, he felt safer knowing Jack was looking after her out on the streets, day in and day out. Not that she needed protecting, but there was always safety in numbers.

Mia pushed back from the table. "I think I might need some fresh air. Wanna go for a walk?"

He knew this was code for 'I'd like to talk privately, away from Mildred,' which probably meant she wanted to talk openly about their abilities.

"Sure," he told her. "Lemme grab my shoes."

He met her on the front sidewalk. Her chin was cocked, eyes closed, soaking in the last rays of evening sun.

"Still kinda muggy out," he said, opening what he was sure was going to be a heavy conversation.

She kicked a rock into the street and shrugged. "Summer in Baltimore. When isn't it muggy?"

He chuckled, taking her hand in his. He liked that she was less reserved at his mom's house, out of uniform. "So, let's talk. What's going on inside that head of yours?"

"You sure you wanna know?"

He wanted to know everything about her. "Of course. You haven't been yourself since the verdict. There's gotta be a reason why. It's almost like you're not satisfied with how it all turned out."

She sighed heavily, dropping his hand in favor of stuffing them into her own pockets. It was a bad sign.

"There's something we need to discuss, and I need you to keep an open mind."

His heart sank. Maybe her sour mood didn't have anything to do with the trial after all. "Is this about moving in?"

Since her roommate Chelsea was getting married in November, in order to save money, Mia had agreed to stay with Thomas and Mildred once her lease ran out. As much as he knew it was a matter of convenience for all of them, he also hoped she was excited at the prospect of living together. He certainly was.

She shoved a shoulder into his arm. "It's not about moving in," she groaned. "How many times do I have to tell you we're solid?"

"I have abandonment issues," he deadpanned.

"No kidding," she replied, rolling her eyes playfully.

They waited at the street corner for the light to change before he continued. "So if it's not about living together, then what is it I need to keep an open mind about?"

She'd picked up the pace and he was having trouble keeping up. Clearly she was nervous about something.

"So remember when we figured out you, Kate and I all have the same birthday?"

"Yup."

"And we also decided we all have some sort of ability – my auras, the way you sense impending danger, and how Kate made stuff happen."

"Yup." He wondered where this was going and how their abilities had anything to do with Dalton's conviction.

"Since the whole commissioner thing went down, I've been doing a bunch of research about abilities. About what we can do and about other people like us." She gazed across the street at a bulldog barking at them as they passed. "Actually, that's a lie. I've been researching people with psychic abilities since I was a kid."

This didn't surprise him. Mia was nothing if not relentless in her quest for information, serving her well in her line of work. That she was unable to keep her inquisitive nature from her personal affairs made perfect sense. And although her disclosure resulted in more questions than it did answers, he chose to simply ask her why.

She shrugged. "As a kid, it was a way to lessen the isolation I felt, since my family insisted I keep my abilities to myself. I guess I just wanted to feel connected to other people who knew what it was like to be different." She paused, lifting her chin so their eyes met for the first time since leaving the house. "But now, my research is about something more."

His jaw tightened but he didn't interrupt.

"I've been reading about a prophecy."

"A what?" He was incredulous and he resisted the urge to groan.

"Ugh. I knew you would have this reaction, which is why I didn't really want to bring it up. But now, I don't think I have a choice."

Images of his third foster mother bubbled to the surface. A medium who swindled unsuspecting patrons out of their hard-earned money, Madame Freakshow had often spoken of prophecies and powers.

And Madame Freakshow was a fraud.

"I don't think I want to have this conversation with you," he said.

She stopped dead, planting her feet as if they'd been cemented to the sidewalk. "Thomas, I love you. And I know it makes you uncomfortable to even talk about this stuff, much less consider the possibility it might be true and that you might be a part of it. But I need you to be all in. Because I don't think I can let this go." Tension strained between them as she stared him down. "The last time I didn't see something all the way through, someone died."

It pained him to know she still felt responsible for Kate's death when, all things considered, he was far more to blame. And the fact that she was making an emotional scene right in the middle of the street meant he was going to have to get over himself. Mia needed to be heard.

Awash with resignation, he straightened his back and squared his shoulders. "Okay," he said. "I'm listening."

In an instant, her demeanor changed, as if a dam had burst within her. She grabbed his hand and began dragging him down the street. He ran along beside her, just short of a jog.

"When I met you and couldn't see your aura, it freaked me out. Like, big time. Because I'd never experienced any problems with my abilities until that point. And then, when I saw a dark aura around Dalton, I was sure there was something wrong with me. I started researching to see if I could find other instances of psychics experiencing changes in their abilities, and I stumbled upon a prophecy." She glanced at him from the corner of her eye, presumably assessing his reaction to the word. He remained stoic, despite feeling as if he was being kicked in the gut. Evidently, she equated his silence as acceptance and continued. "The more I think about it, the more I'm convinced it's real. And the more I'm convinced we are two of the fourteen people it describes."

It was Thomas' turn to freeze where he stood. "You think you and I are part of some prophecy?"

She didn't reply immediately, but instead slipped her phone from her back pocket and began scrolling through her browser. Then she held it out to him. "Here. Read it for yourself."

Seven Light - Seven Dark - Seven Sins
The Sevens Prophecy (With Regard to the End of Days)
There will come a day when seven psychic children of the light and seven psychic children of the dark will be born. From the moment of their birth, strong powers will be in place to bring the seven light together and the seven dark together to form two separate but equally powerful groups. The first seven to gather all in one place will seal the fate of the world – dark for hell, light for heaven. At that point the seven deadly sins will take over the world or cease to exist.

He read it. And then he reread it.

It was preposterous.

"You're not serious about this?"

She snatched her phone and stuffed it back into her pocket. "I'm completely serious. I don't think I can afford not to be. And I don't think you can either."

Maintaining his composure was taking every bit of strength he had. Mia's revelation rekindled the disappointment and anger he felt when she'd first revealed her gift to him. But he called to mind Mildred's wisdom. *Faith*, she'd often told him, *involves believing in things you cannot see. And sometimes it involves believing in people.*

She'd been right about that.

Standing on the sidewalk as the sun began to set, he decided perhaps the same wisdom could apply to this as well. Because maybe he wasn't ready to believe in the prophecy, but he could definitely believe in Mia.

He softened.

"So, I'm assuming you and I are part of the light. Because if any of this turns out to be true, I need to be one of the good guys, Mia."

Her face split into a smile. The smile that made everything okay, even when nothing else was. "You're the best good guy," she said.

CHAPTER

5

JOSE

16 Years Ago
Phoenix

While taking a shortcut on their way home from school, nine-year-old Jose, his sister Sabina, and a few other neighborhood kids discovered a pigeon fluttering on the ground in the abandoned lot behind the liquor store.

"It's spazzing out," Mateo said, kicking at the bird with his sneaker. "Let's throw it in the dumpster."

"No!" cried Sabina. "It's just a baby!"

Doug reached down and poked at the bird's wing with his pencil. "It's not a baby, stupid," he said. "But it's as good as dead. Which one of you wants to stomp on it to put it out of its misery?"

Jose couldn't take his eyes off the pigeon, because although theoretically it was the same as every other pigeon scuttering about on his walk to and from school each day, there was something intriguing about this particular bird. This one wasn't pecking absentmindedly at the ground. This one wasn't lined atop the roofline with the rest of the flock, awash in a sea of grey plumage. This one wasn't staring at him with its beady, prehistoric eyes.

This one was dying, its misshapen wing contorted beneath its body, which instigated the bizarre flapping behavior as the bird attempted to right itself.

Jose thought of his mother, cursing about the pigeons which frequented his family's restaurant. Less than a month before, the health department shut down their outdoor patio seating until they could get their 'vermin problem' under control. He'd watched in horror from the kitchen window as his mother attempted to poison them, setting out bowls of seed laced with rat poison, but for every one she successfully eliminated, another showed up in its place. Here, just a block from the restaurant, was an opportunity to help her in her crusade against the winged scourge of his family.

"I'll do it," he told the others, kneeling beside the bird to scoop it into his hands.

He could feel his friends watching as he turned the bird over, caressing the broken wing between his fingers. It was strange to hold a bird, a creature which, by all accounts, should never be touched by human hands. It was both heavier and lighter than he expected it to be, and the pigeon attempted to flap its healthy wing in opposition to its confinement. Jose closed his eyes, unable to ignore the ferocious thumping of the pigeon's heart inside its tiny chest. His own heart sped up, as if to mimic the panic seizing the bird, and he knew in that moment he could not wring its neck as he'd intended.

Warmth spread from his hands into the bird in much the same way as hot water when it is added to an already cooling tub. The pigeon stilled for a moment, shocked into submission by the heat, and when at last it began to stir again, Jose knew instinctively to open his hands toward the hazy, afternoon sky.

And the bird knew instinctively to fly away.

"What the hell, Jose?" Mateo hushed, backing away until he bumped into the wall of the store.

Jose shrugged, as confused by what had just transpired as the others. "I don't know. I guess maybe it was just pretending to be hurt. Animals do that sometimes, don't they?"

Doug shielded his eyes from the sun as he gazed up, still following the bird's path. "You mean like a possum or something?"

"They play dead, idiot," Mateo said, already recovering from the shock of what he'd witnessed as he turned on his heel in the direction of his house. "They don't fake being hurt. It just must not have been hurt that bad."

Jose fell into step behind Mateo, and Sabina raced up beside him, her knapsack thudding noisily against her back. "I'm glad you didn't kill it," she whispered up at her brother. "I'm glad you fixed it, even though Momma doesn't like them birds."

As he and Sabina crossed the street and made their way down the alley between Monterey and Cheery Lynn, he thought about the sensation of the heat traveling from his hands into the bird and was suddenly embarrassed. He shoved them hastily into his pockets, as if hiding them would prevent him from having to think any more about the stupid bird. Had he healed it? Had he fixed the bird's wing without even knowing what he was doing?

Although he fully expected to be questioned further, the others didn't bring up the incident again. Not on the walk to school the following morning. Not as they strode through a flock of pigeons on the way to the ball field Saturday afternoon. It was as if they hadn't given the bird's resurrection a second thought.

Jose, on the other hand, hadn't stopped thinking about it.

Which is why, when the others headed to the Dairy Freeze after shutting out the Padres in a 7-0 victory, he peeled off from the rest of the team and snuck behind the deserted bowling alley, where he knew the homeless people set up camp. He'd been there before, in their makeshift city of cardboard boxes and weather-beaten tarps. He knew he should probably be scared, because he'd overheard on the news about how a man was murdered there once, but he wasn't afraid. He'd followed a dog there many times before, and the dog always made him feel safe.

It was the dog he was searching for today.

As he wove between a dumpster and a makeshift lean-to, constructed of rotten pallet lumber and a sheet of torn construction plastic, he spotted Baxter. He was curled up against a filthy blanket, the laceration on his left flank, oozing and raw – worse than it had been the week before.

"Hey, Bax," he called cautiously to the dog as he drew near, crouching to make himself small in case the canine should feel threatened in his weakened condition. "Didn't I tell you to stay away from that mean, old Doberman? That dog's nothing but trouble. I hope you got a piece of him too."

Despite the pain of the infection, the dog's tail beat madly against the ground at the sound of the boy's voice. Baxter strained, hoisting himself up on his haunches. Typically, the pup raced to greet his friend, but today, he only managed a weak scoot in his direction.

"It's okay, boy," Jose said, inching closer on his hands and knees. "I'm here to help. I'm just gonna give you a pat."

Baxter lifted his head as Jose reached out to massage his snout and scratch behind his ears. The fur felt matted and coarse along the dog's protruding spine, and Baxter whimpered when the boy's hand approached the wound.

"I brought you some scraps from the restaurant," he murmured, "but if you want 'em, you gotta be a good boy and let me touch it, just for a minute."

As if he could understand what was about to happen, the dog acquiesced and relaxed onto the ground, allowing the boy full access to the gash.

After spending the better part of two days doubting himself, Jose remained hesitant, his palm hovering above the wound. After feeling the warmth and watching the bird fly from his hands, he'd convinced himself that surely, it wasn't what it seemed. That there was no way he could have mended the bird's broken wing simply by touching it.

There had been no miracle. Just nature playing tricks.

And yet, there he was in the homeless village, bent over the only injured soul he knew, his own curiosity compelling him forward.

If he was correct in his assumption that the pigeon was simply a fluke, then the dog would continue to suffer and he would return to his life, full of baseball practice and bike riding and fourth grade. However, if he was wrong…

"I'll do my best, but I really don't know what I'm doing," he confessed to Baxter quietly, as he finally worked up the courage to place his hands on his friend's festering skin.

The sensation overtook him instantly. Warmth radiated from his palms, and the dog's head fell limply onto the blanket, his eyes shutting tightly. For a moment, Jose was sure he'd killed the dog, but then, just as the heat from his hands became almost unbearable, Baxter opened his eyes and the pain retreated as quickly as it had arrived. He lifted his hand to gaze at his palm, because he didn't yet have the courage to look directly at the wound. Where there should have been blood and fluid, there was nothing – only the pale smoothness of his own skin. Upon seeing this, he forced his gaze to Baxter.

Where there was no mistaking the wound was gone.

CHAPTER

6

LANYING

Sunday, August 28
Shanghai

Lanying scanned the confirmation email from the airline on her phone, outlining her itinerary from Shanghai to Baltimore where she was scheduled to attend an obesity seminar the following month. She'd already dragged her rolling luggage from her family's storage closet in the basement of their high rise apartment building and as it lay zipped open on her bed, she wondered what she should pack.

Although her trip to Baltimore was still over a week away, her excitement about leaving the country for the first time in her life couldn't be squelched. She was attending the seminar as part of her graduate degree program to become a certified obesity counselor. Her career choice was not a decision she'd taken lightly or one she'd fallen into accidentally. Lanying was no stranger to obesity or the body shaming that frequently went along with being overweight, especially in the urban Chinese community in which she was raised.

In a culture where young women were encouraged to post online images of themselves successfully completing tasks like the A4 challenge, posing behind standard sheets of

A4 paper to prove how tiny their waists are, Lanying was an anomaly. Instead of embracing the notion that she should be able to completely hide her knees behind a six inch iPhone or wrap a 100 Yuan bill around her wrist, she wanted to challenge the ideology that the body images revered in her culture were healthy or attainable. More than that, she wanted to help those individuals struggling with actual obesity to establish and maintain healthy lifestyles.

As she scanned the contents of her closet, contemplating possible blouse/skirt combinations for the conference, her mother appeared at her open bedroom door.

"What's all this?" she asked, puckering her face into a disapproving scowl.

Lanying flinched at the critical sound of her mother's voice. It was the same tone she always used when speaking with her, but it's frequent recurrence didn't make it any less demoralizing.

"I'm, uh, just trying to get things ready for my trip," she told her mother, sliding the closet door shut with her foot.

"Do they make appropriate apparel in your size?" she asked in her characteristically passive-aggressive way. "I assume you're going to be expected to wear something more sophisticated than those baggy jeans you're always schlepping around in."

Lanying balled her fists and forced herself to take a deep breath. She wouldn't let her mother offend her. Still, it frustrated her to know that although she'd lost over 70 pounds in the years since being diagnosed with polycystic ovarian syndrome, better known as PCOS, her mother remained quite obviously embarrassed and ashamed of her appearance. That a disorder had incited Lanying's sudden and uncontrollable weight gain at the age of 13 was inconsequential to her mother. All that mattered was the shame she'd brought to her family.

"I have plenty of appropriate apparel in my size, thank you for asking," she said finally. "I was actually more interested in making sure my luggage is large enough to hold a week's worth of clothes."

Her mother scoffed. "Well, it's certainly big enough to hold a week's worth of *my* clothes," she said. "But if all yours don't fit, you're welcome to borrow your father's bag. His is considerably larger."

She thanked her mother for her generous offer and watched her retreat down the hall before returning to her closet. Moments later, as she selected a teal dress, holding it across her hips to confirm it still fit, the periphery of her eyesight began to grow cloudy. She prepared herself for what she knew was about to happen, managing to take a step backward toward her bed before the vision overtook her. She wondered whose life she would be observing this time. A neighbor? A classmate? A random stranger?

It turned out to be someone else entirely, and as her sight cleared she found herself in a relatively familiar place. She'd witnessed the man seated at the piano in this living room many times over the years.

He was young and attractive and distinctly American, in both his speech and his mannerisms. As she entered the vision now, he was playing an upbeat selection she didn't recognize but was excited to continue listening to just the same. She settled in, enjoying her private concert; just she and the man she'd dubbed 'Billy Joel' since he was the only real piano man she knew.

As she watched his fingers fly across the keys she recalled the first time she'd visited him through a vision - he'd been a sullen child in those days, and she as well. Another time, another house, another piano.

Same boy.

Her visions of him had been increasing during recent months, and she wondered if there was a reason behind the surge. She certainly wasn't complaining. Far better to enjoy being serenaded than ridiculed or ostracized when other's thought she couldn't hear them. She never knew when a vision was going to be pleasant or distressing, and sadly, for most of her life, the scenes she encountered were more nightmare than daydream – one of the worst being the day she witnessed a girl she considered her best friend calling her a beached whale while laughing with other classmates about her size.

There was less ugliness in her visions these days and she was grateful. Listening to the man's performance brought her peace, welcome respite from her mother's constant disparagement and her father's seeming indifference. As the vision ended and she pulled back into her physical self, the image of the man and the piano fading, she had the sudden inclination to thank him for being a part of her life. It seemed silly and perhaps unrealistic, but there was no denying the beauty he'd infused into her woefully glum existence.

Maybe someday, she thought. *Maybe someday I'll even learn your name.*

Monday, August 29
Phoenix

"I'm scared, Dad," the sandy-haired boy whispered from his prone position on the gurney. His worried father walked beside him, clutching the boy's hand which peeked out from beneath the thin sheet draped across his torso.

"You're gonna be fine," he responded, glancing at Jose for validation.

Jose stopped just beyond the nurses' station and pressed the button to call the elevator to take them to radiology. "Oh, yeah," he confirmed. "You're gonna be better than fine. We get half a dozen broken bones through here every day, so they get lots of practice putting legs back together. I bet they'll have yours fixed up in no time." The elevator doors opened, and he wheeled the boy inside, carefully maneuvering over the gap in the floor so as not to cause any pain. "I broke my arm in seventh grade and had it x-rayed right in the room where we're headed. And look at me now," he added, holding up his left arm. "Good as new."

The boy smiled and returned his attention to his father who shot Jose an appreciative glance. "If I need a cast, can we get some metallic Sharpies so everyone can sign it?"

His father raised an eyebrow at Jose as the doors slid open on the fourth floor. "Breaking your leg seems like a pretty extreme way to get those markers you've been asking for, don't you think?" he teased.

"Dad! I didn't fall off my bike on purpose," he said, rolling his eyes, and then added without missing a beat, "but can we?"

Jose laughed along with the boy's father as the radiology technician met them in the hallway.

"Good luck," he called to them as they rounded the corner out of sight.

Although they were expecting him back in the ER, instead of going back to the ground floor right away, he decided to take a short detour via the ICU. As the car descended to the second floor, he couldn't keep himself from smiling about the boy. Helping patients feel safe and comfortable was an unexpected perk of his job. In addition to giving him unprecedented access to the ICU, being an orderly also provided daily interaction with average patients each day. He'd learned over the years how to quickly build a rapport with them, not only to gain their trust, but also to ease their anxiety over being hospitalized. Now, however, it was time to get down to business.

He usually didn't venture to the ICU during the day, but he wasn't scheduled for a night shift until much later in the week, and he was afraid if he waited until then, he wouldn't get a chance to see Chloe before her release.

After healing her the weekend before, he'd kept tabs on her improving condition and had only recently discovered her attending physician was preparing for her discharge. He considered visiting the patients he cured a narcissistic indulgence, but try as he might, he couldn't keep himself away. He felt drawn to them and couldn't bear not knowing how his decisions played out. Had he chosen the right person? Did they realize the value of the gift they'd been given? This desire to follow up had all started with Baxter, who, after many nights of not knowing where he was or what he was doing, was finally adopted by Jose's family, after he convinced his parents the dog deserved more than a life on the streets. Since then, Jose had always felt the need to see things through to the end.

He strode confidently off the elevator into the ICU, a clipboard tucked under his arm. He found carrying a clipboard made him look official, and other staff generally left him alone when he had it. The hallway was deserted and no one stopped him as he ducked into Chloe's room.

She was lying in her bed, under a tray covered with magazines and empty snack wrappers. She was watching something on the television, but cut her eyes to the door as Jose crossed the threshold.

"Hi," she said warmly. "Are you here to take vitals because Selma was just here about 10 minutes ago and said everything looked good."

A bandage still covered her temple, concealing what Jose assumed was the remains of the gash to her head from the fall. The ventilation machine was no longer in the room, and Chloe's cheeks were flushed with life. He approached, settling into the chair beside the bed with the hope of confirming his assumptions.

"Oh, yes. Everything's fine," he said, preparing to recount the same liturgy he always used on his chosen patients. "I'm just here to ask a few questions about your medical care here at the hospital before your release. Is that something you feel like you could do?"

"Of course," she replied, straightening herself up against the headboard and turning off the TV. "What is it you'd like to know?"

He pulled his clipboard out from under his arm and plucked his pencil from behind his ear. He asked her several questions about the nursing staff and the quality of the meals. And then he got to the actual reason for his visit.

"What do you think aided in your healing process the most?" he asked, pencil poised above the paper.

She paused for a moment, considering the question while she eyed him skeptically from the bed.

"Is that really a question?" she scoffed.

He held his hands up, shrugging. "I don't write 'em, I just ask 'em," he sang, although he couldn't help but be impressed by her astute observation.

"Okay, then," she said thoughtfully. "I guess I was in really rough shape when I came in. They tell me I was in a coma, and I overheard my mother telling my aunt on the phone yesterday the doctors told her when I got here they thought I was going to die. So one minute I was dying, and the next minute I was awake and recovering. That was it. Apparently I haven't been experiencing any of the symptoms typically associated with a head trauma. They keep asking me about headaches and checking my speech. They keep doing this eye thing with a light and asking memory questions, as if I wouldn't know what year it was or what my brother's name is." She rolled her eyes. "Anyway, it seems to me that what aided my healing process was a miracle, you know? I don't think anything any of the doctors or nurses did made me better. They just kept me alive and then, boom, I wasn't dying anymore."

Jose smiled at her, letting the truth of her words wash over him.

"Are you going to write that down?" she asked.

He shook himself out of his trance. "Oh, yeah. Of course." He jotted down a few random notes – 'miracle,' 'alive,' and 'recovery.' As he finished, she spoke again.

"Do you believe in miracles?" she whispered.

He lifted his eyes from the paper and gazed into hers. The joy was unmistakable.

"I do," he replied.

She ran her hand absentmindedly over the gauze on her head. "I'm really happy to be alive. I watched a TV show once about a man who cheated death and then he vowed to use his life in the service of good." She paused and began to pick at the edge of the bandage on her arm where her IV had once been. "Maybe that's what I'll do too. You know, help feed homeless kids or try really hard in science class so I can find a cure for cancer."

He slipped his pencil behind his ear and stood up, satisfied Chloe wouldn't waste her second chance. "I think you should get back on your horse and make the best of your life," he told her. "Thanks for answering my questions and be careful out there, okay?"

She waved at him. "I will," she laughed.

CHAPTER

8

PATRICK

Monday, August 29
London

Everything was in place for Patrick's first communication with Akantha. Knowing she was wildly misunderstood in her own community, he hoped to inspire a sense of peace and understanding with regard to her assimilation into his group. For the prophecy to be fulfilled, they would have to be together, each of the seven, in the same space. This meant fostering her commitment to their cause and defusing her anger, at least as it pertained to them.

"It's been too long, Patrick," Wesley said as he strolled into the conference room on the 32nd floor of the Heron Building in London's financial district, the space which served as headquarters for Patrick's bevy of global corporations.

"Good to see you." He rose from his chair to greet Wesley with a handshake, overcome as always by the Australian's massive frame.

"Any hostility from the Brazilian Beast today?"

Patrick wasn't amused by Wesley's moniker for the newest member of their group, but chose not to make it an issue. He'd learned early on he could take the man out of Australia but couldn't take Australia out of the man. "Since

I've been able to hone in on her location and track her emotions, she's been pretty stable. We can't be too careful though. Let us not forget the unwieldy brute from Cambodia."

Wesley scowled. "I remember that monster. That bloke nearly tore my head off. I still can't believe he didn't turn out to be one of us, but I can't say as I'm disappointed. I definitely didn't mind offing him though." He rubbed the back of his hand under his chin against the scruff of his week-old beard. "Seems as though we might be nearing the end of our search now though. If this girl's really the one, we'll be down to finding Number Seven. Next thing I know I'll be out of a job and all we'll have left is ruling the world."

"All we'll have left?" Patrick snapped, leading Wesley to the seats at the far end of the conference room table. "Ruling the world will be just the beginning." He was growing tired of Wesley's short-sightedness and it was grating on his nerves. For the sake of the day's mission, however, he tried to squelch his annoyance and move on. "I sense Lillian is on her way?"

"She's in the building."

"And Javier too?"

"Yes. Just down the hall. You think this is gonna work?"

Patrick had been asking himself the same question for three days, wondering if Lillian's abilities would be enough to keep her safe from Akantha's pyrotechnics. The Brazilian girl's family had made it very clear she wouldn't hesitate to maim or even kill if she was provoked. Between their horror stories and the drawing Eshanti produced weeks ago of Lillian suffering from third degree burns, it was only natural for him to be concerned. He only hoped Lillian would remain unharmed, for if she were to perish, the prophecy would surely fall to the other side.

Before he could respond to Wesley, Lillian herself materialized in the doorway. It wasn't unusual for the others to wonder which version of her they were seeing – the actual physical presence or the otherworldly version she was able to project at will.

"Howdy, boooy-eeeez," she sang in her thick Texan drawl, as if the word was comprised of half a dozen syllables. "Y'all miss me?"

Hearing her voice, Patrick was transported to the moment he'd first heard her speak. The way he'd known immediately she was part of the group before ever setting eyes on her face. She was Javier's and his first find. She was Number Three.

"We always miss you," Patrick crooned, crossing the room in great strides to kiss her properly on each cheek. "How have you been, my dear?"

"Right as rain. Righter now that you think you found Number Six. I just hope she'll listen to me."

"About that," Wesley interrupted, greeting her with kisses of his own. "We saw Eshanti's drawing. Are you sure Akantha won't be able to harm you physically during the biolocation?"

Lillian threw back her head. "You mean is she gonna fry me to a crispy critter?"

"Yes. Exactly that."

She draped her coat across the back of the chair in front of her and smoothed her fitted pencil skirt, which Patrick had to admit hugged her in all the right places. "I can assure you, Gentlemen, as sure as the sun shines, I will be just fine. She'll see me and hear me, but she won't be able to touch me. You just gotta tell me what to say to that translator of hers to convince her we're on her side, and I'll take care of the rest."

Javier breezed into the office carrying a laptop and small projector. "Hola, Ms. Lillian!" he said, winking as he slid past her to deposit the equipment on the table. "Everything's set up in Belem. Akantha's in a concrete holding facility and the translator is behind protective glass. She's been civil with him so far, but there's no reason to take any risks. The last thing we need is to have to find another interpreter, especially knowing the difficulties you had initially, Wesley."

"No kidding," he sighed. "Finding someone who spoke fluent Bakairi outside of a tribal community wasn't easy. We can't let anything happen to him. We may need him for a while."

Within minutes the team was assembled at the table, with Patrick at the head and Wesley and Javier on either side. They positioned themselves with an unobstructed view of the video projection. Once they began streaming the live feed of Akantha and Lillian's encounter, Patrick planned to orchestrate their conversation. Lillian, for her part, sat by herself at the far end of the table, eyes closed, deep in thought.

"I'm ready," she told them.

Seconds later she appeared on the screen from the remote location in Brazil. She also remained with the others in London.

"She always freaks me out when she does that," Wesley whispered to Patrick.

"I can still hear you," Lillian quipped. "Remember?"

Javier widened the camera's focus and the group got their first look at the Amazonian woman they hoped to welcome into their group. "Ay Dios Mio," he swore under his breath.

Akantha's face was emblazoned with striking red paint, save for her eyes, which narrowed defiantly at the sight of Lillian materializing out of nowhere on the other side of the room. Her earlobes were pierced with large wooden cores and an animal bone protruded from her nose. Clearly not a woman to cross, Patrick was beguiled when instead of attacking Lillian outright, she lifted both hands in a defensive position, palms out in front of her chest.

"Tell her not to be scared," Patrick instructed, worrying just how much provocation it would take for her to light the place up. "Tell her you're not going to hurt her."

Lillian related the message through the interpreter, but instead of pacifying the woman, Akantha's hands began to glow like molten iron.

Patrick felt a rush of panic. "Tell her you know about her power to control fire and that you have a power as well. Tell her about your gift. About what you can do."

Patrick watched with the others from the London office as Lillian, who was both with them and 5000 miles away, lowered herself onto a metal folding chair directly across from where Akantha was standing in the center of the room. After positioning herself below her aggressor in a classic submissive posture, she lifted her chin and gazed at the Amazonian woman, doe-eyed, as she began her communication.

"I know what you can do with your hands. I know you are powerful and worthy of my admiration. But I'm here to tell you about the purpose of your gift. The truth of your destiny. You are part of something much bigger than yourself and we're here to help you reach your full potential."

Patrick held his breath while the interpreter shared Lillian's words, but with the aggressive reaction Akantha was having, it seemed as though something was being lost in the translation. The Brazilian glared at Lillian with all the hatred of someone who had never been truly accepted by another living soul.

"There are no words in her language to describe destiny or potential, as you're describing them," the interpreter lamented. "I'm having a very difficult time helping her to understand."

Patrick wished he could channel Lillian's power and bilocate himself to Brazil in order to safely manage the operation on his own. Accustomed to a position at the helm, taking a backseat to Lillian and the translator caused the involuntary twitch at the corner of his left eye to spasm.

He coached Lillian from the conference room. "You need to be more general with her. Remember, she's spent 25 years living in a tribe along the Amazon with no contact to the outside world. We need her to understand you're gifted too and you revere her for her power."

Lillian's face broke into a smile. "I've got it," she said. And then she vanished from the screen.

Patrick watched as Akantha reacted to her disappearance. She crouched low, squatting like a caged beast, her hands outstretched toward the spot where Lillian had been standing only seconds before. Her eyes were wild. Panicked.

"What are you doing, Lillian?"

"Trust me," she snapped.

Patrick's fingers balled into fists in an uncharacteristic show of fury. He hated being told what to do, especially by a woman. As Akantha began to growl, a guttural sound, more animal than human, he considered the possibility of aborting the operation. But just when he thought she was going to begin fraying at the seams, Lillian appeared again, in the farthest corner of the room, directly behind the interpreter.

Akantha screamed.

Lillian fell to her knees, tearing a wide slit up the back of her skirt as she genuflected before the Amazonian, immediately silencing her cries. She kept her eyes lowered as she addressed the translator who stood dumbfounded on the periphery of the room.

"Tell her she is a god. Tell her there are six other gods living here in the world, and I've been sent by the others to welcome her into our group. Tell her we all have great powers, and I can disappear and reappear at will, and that I know she can manipulate flame. Convince her I'm here to welcome her into our family."

Patrick could feel the tension pulsing off the other men and knew his own anxiety was palpable to them as well. None of them moved. None of them dared to breathe while the interpreter translated Lillian's message into a staccatoed gibberish only Akantha could understand. When he finished, the woman lowered her hands for the first time since Lillian had first appeared and spoke.

"She wants to see you go away again and then come back. She wants you to come close so she knows it isn't a hoax."

"It could be a trick to get you close enough to burn you," Wesley whispered.

"She can't hurt me," Lillian reminded him. "And besides, if you want her to join us, I've gotta try."

Patrick knew she was right. "Go ahead," he told her, asserting his authority as though it was warranted. He watched on the screen as she approached Akantha, cautiously, as a charmer nearing a snake. She hesitated just beyond her reach, and then Lillian dissolved into the air for the third time.

Akantha spoke.

"She's asking for you to return," the translator announced. "She wants you to bring the other gods."

Patrick glanced around the table as Lillian reappeared beside Akantha. "Tell her we don't have the ability to appear like you, but we'd like to meet her if she'll agree to come here to London. Tell her I'll send my 'magic' bird for her to fly on across the ocean."

As the interpreter translated the message, Akantha's demeanor shifted from hostile to curious. She reached out as if to touch Lillian but then pulled back, perhaps fearful of the potential consequences. Her face softened and she addressed her fellow psychic in a voice free of malice or fear. It gave Patrick hope.

"She says she'll go to London, to meet the others. She says she's always known she was a god - she's just been waiting for someone else to notice."

CHAPTER

9

JOSE

Monday, August 29
Phoenix

After his visit with Chloe, Jose returned to the ER and was immediately accosted by Vanessa.

"Where have you been?" she barked accusingly. "I've been looking all over for you!"

He motioned upstairs. "Took the little boy up to radiology."

She glared at him. "Twenty minutes ago!" After a beat, she shook her head and sighed. "It's fine. Really. We just got really busy, and I've got Andrea Morillo in three, covered in bruises, sporting a nasty looking black eye. It's gonna be a while 'til Unger can get to her, so while she's waiting I thought you could go in there and do that thing you do. And I'm warning you, it's worse than last time."

He was confused, worrying immediately she knew about his abilities. "What thing are you talking about, Ma'am?"

"Oh, you know," she called over her shoulder as she slid through the door into the hallway, "just go talk to her and see if you can get her to spill the beans. People trust you. Maybe you can finally get her to fess up about what's really been going on, cuz Lord knows she didn't trip over the cat again."

Relieved she only considered him a good listener and not a psychic healer, he quickly made his way to room three where he found a very battered looking Andrea Morillo sitting on the evaluation table hunched over her cell phone.

He tapped gently on the door. "Miss Morillo?" he said.

Without lifting her head, she raised her eyes to meet his gaze. Her left eye was almost completely swollen shut and blood had coagulated around a deep gash on her temple. "Yes?" she replied.

He crossed the threshold into the room and left the door open behind him. The last thing he wanted was for her to feel confined with him, not knowing the circumstances surrounding her injuries.

"I was sent in by the nursing staff to find out more about your..." He paused, searching for the right word. He didn't want her to feel worse than she already did. "Situation," he finished.

She lowered her face back to the phone screen, burying her chin into her chest. "I told them already, I tripped and fell in the kitchen. That's it. And I'm only here because..." She hesitated, staring at the blank screen. "Well, because when I woke up this morning I couldn't see out of my eye, and I checked Google and it said I should go to the doctor." She lifted her head now for the first time, practically staring him down. She pleaded with him, "Please, I don't want to lose my sight."

He could feel the fear emanating from every pore of her body, and he was relatively certain not all the fear was associated with potential vision loss. He ventured across the room.

"May I?" he asked, gesturing to the spot on the table beside her.

Without answering, she slid over to make room for him to sit.

He had seen his fair share of domestic abuse cases in his years at the ER and had learned quite a bit about its victims. More often than not, they felt as if they deserved to be battered - that their behaviors, however benign, warranted reprimanding. Other times, victims put up with being abused because they saw it as the only way to prevent loved ones from becoming victims themselves. Mothers protecting children. Siblings safeguarding siblings. And for many, it was almost as if their abuser was omnipresent, saturating every fiber of their lives. They wouldn't leave because they couldn't. There was often nowhere else to go.

He was quite certain this was the case for Andrea Morillo. According to her chart, in less than three months, this was her fifth visit to the ER sporting dubious looking injuries which the staff was convinced were the result of an abusive situation. Unfortunately, without her admission, there was no way to prove their suspicions.

Jose had treated her three times before – dressing a wound on her hand, assisting with stitches to her face, and cleaning up a laceration on her arm. Each time there had been other staff in the room with them. This was the first time they'd ever been alone.

"It's okay to be afraid," he said cautiously.

She didn't respond, but he could feel her body become rigid beside him.

"Love is a complicated thing," he continued. "It took my aunt Carla six years to leave my uncle Elias. Six years. She loved him so much. I was eleven when she came to live with us. Brought my cousins with her." He chuckled, remembering how they crowded into his tiny bedroom. Little people everywhere. "The funny thing was, Aunt Carla thought her life was normal. That she deserved to be slapped across the face when she was late coming home because of traffic. Or that getting burnt by a lit cigarette was a reasonable response for not remembering to pick up ice cream at the grocery store. She thought he was justified in punishing her since he was only trying to make her better. Because he loved her."

As he finished speaking, Andrea didn't move. She didn't blink. She didn't twitch. In fact, he could barely detect the shallow rhythm of her breathing. It was almost as if she was trapped deep within herself, tucked away from the reality of her situation inside a labyrinth of her own creation. His instinct was to continue, but he forced himself to wait, sensing perhaps, if he gave her time, she would come back. After several moments of awkward silence, she finally closed her eyes, took a labored breath, and then released her hushed confession.

"I don't have anywhere else to go."

He felt compelled then to touch her. To reach out and make a connection, one human being to another. He hesitated, but was relieved when she didn't pull away when his fingers touched her forearm.

"It's going to be okay," he told her, because it seemed like the right thing to say, even though he had no way of actually knowing for sure whether things would ever be okay. And for the first time in his life he wished he could do more than heal the body. He wished too he could heal the soul.

"There are places you can stay that are safe," he continued.

She shook her head solemnly. "He'll find me. He owns me. And besides, it would be wrong for me to go."

As much as he couldn't believe what he was hearing, it wasn't unusual for a victim to feel obligated to stay. "Wrong?" he asked, wondering why someone would choose to stay with someone who caused them so much pain.

She looked up from the hangnail she'd been picking and wiped the blood onto her jeans. "He took me in off the streets. He gave me a home. He put food in my mouth, and he never asked for anything in return. He never sold me out. Never forced me to do things I didn't want to do. All he's ever asked for is my obedience, and I'm so ungrateful I can't even give him that." She pulled her sleeves down over her hands and wiped her nose with her sweatshirt. "I can't believe I'm even saying any of this to you. Just another betrayal I suppose," she lamented as tears pooled in the corners of her eyes.

Jose leaned down beneath her gaze so he was sure she could see him. "There is nothing in the world he could give you or do for you that would ever give him the right to harm you in any way. I don't care if he gave you a million dollars and a trip around the world. You don't owe him anything. You can always walk away."

He could see her turning his words over in her head, attempting to reconcile his observations with the jagged reality of her situation.

She tilted her chin up and cocked her head to the side, a gesture he immediately recognized as surrender, not defiance. "Even if I had someplace to go, he would find me and drag me back." Her eyes pleaded with him. "He's got a network of people like you wouldn't believe. I'd never get far. He'd find me and drag me right back."

He considered the possibility that what she was telling him was true. He had no idea what sort of connections her boyfriend had at his disposal.

"Are you talking about a gang situation?"

Her shoulders sagged from the weight of the admission. "Wedgewood Chicanos."

Almost imperceptibly, Jose sucked in his breath. You didn't grow up in Phoenix without knowing about one of its oldest and most notorious gangs. Any optimism he'd felt for Andrea's situation suddenly seemed tragically overrated.

When he didn't reply, she managed a weak chuckle. "Yeah. I told you I wasn't going anywhere."

He considered the ammunition he had at his disposal in the form of the legal system. He could write up her statement. Send it to the police. Certainly someone in law enforcement could protect her from this thug.

"He can't drag you back if he's in jail, Andrea."

She smiled then. A painful looking grimace of a smile. "And who's gonna put him in jail. You? Me?" She put a hand to her face, testing to see if the laceration beside her eye was still there. She winced. "Besides, I don't want him to go to jail. I want him to go back to being the guy I fell in love with a year ago. I just know that guy is still in there, if I could just stop pissing him off."

Before he had a chance to respond, Dr. Unger appeared in the doorway. Jose could smell the disinfectant on the doctor's hands as he wrestled on a pair of latex gloves.

"Miss Morillo, I'm so sorry to see you back again," he said, glancing at Jose as if to get a read on the conversation he'd just interrupted. "Another accident? In the kitchen this time?"

Feeling frustrated and inflamed, Jose excused himself from the room, mumbling weak wishes for Andrea's recovery as he backed through the door. Given what he knew of her, he was certain she wouldn't confide in the doctor as she'd done with him, and that she would perpetuate the thinly-veiled narrative to explain the origin of her injury. This made him angry. Angry that she didn't value her life enough to see herself out of an abusive situation. Just the same, he hoped Unger could mend her eye and save her sight because without a plausible means of access to her in the coming days, he knew it would be impossible to cure her himself.

Impossible, unless of course the next injury she sustained at her boyfriend's hand landed her in the ICU.

CHAPTER

10

MIA

Thursday, September 1
Baltimore

"You wanna grab something from the Shake Shack for lunch?" Jack asked Mia as he eased their patrol car onto I-83 toward the station.

Instead of responding to her partner, she massaged her temples with the pads of her fingers. She had a splitting headache, and the thought of ingesting a greasy burger made her nauseous. Sleep had evaded her since the night of Dalton's conviction, and she blamed exhaustion for the way she'd been feeling in the week that followed.

"What's going on with you? Is it this case?"

Their latest assignment involved tracking down a local scam artist selling fake insurance policies to cancer patients. They'd spent the better part of two weeks interviewing men and women at chemotherapy infusion centers hoping to identify a pattern with regard to the origin of the calls. Without a single lead to go on, they started from square one, requesting personal information about physicians, clinics, and insurance companies. Luckily, most of the patients were happy to help. So far they'd discovered 18 patients who had been contacted by the bogus insurance company. And they felt certain it was no coincidence that the majority of them were being treated by a Dr. Frances Wu.

"It's hard being around cancer patients all day, isn't it?" he continued when she didn't reply for the second time. "Knowing some of them aren't going to make it. That some of them are going to go through all that treatment and heartache and are still going to die in the end?"

"We're all going to die in the end," she said, matter-of-factly.

"You know what I mean, Mia."

She did know what he meant, but it was the prophecy, not the case, that was upsetting her. She actually enjoyed talking to the patients - listening to their stories while she sat with them during their infusions. The truth was, finding the scam artist preying on the innocent patients gave her something to focus on instead of the prophecy.

Now, as she sat stewing beside her partner, her mind returned to ex-commissioner Dalton and his cryptic words to her at the end of the trial. She played the message over and over again in her head, certain she was missing something crucial. What had he meant by 'see you soon?'

And then it hit her.

She'd purposely erased that morning out from her memory. The morning back in February when she and Jack had gone to Dalton's house to confront him, to accuse him of his involvement in the trafficking ring. Now though, for the first time in many months, she allowed the man's words to come back to her. The last sound she'd heard before passing out had been the commissioner's voice whispering in her ear, "The end is coming, Mia. Soon the prophecy will be fulfilled."

Suddenly, it was all very clear. The people Dalton worked for were part of the prophecy. They had to be. It was the only thing that made sense. Dalton knew they were getting close to fulfilling it and the age of darkness was drawing nigh.

Her head throbbed even thinking about it. What were the chances of all of them being interconnected? It seemed highly unlikely, and yet, what other explanation could there be?

While Jack maneuvered effortlessly through the heavy traffic, she attempted to relax her face into a neutral expression in the hopes of avoiding having to talk to him about what was on her mind. Because although, in her opinion, he was the most trustworthy partner on the force, there were some subjects that were too complicated to discuss, even between the closest of friends. She wasn't ready to explain about the prophecy just yet.

As though he could sense her anxiety, he changed the subject, letting her off the hook. "I saw the letter on your desk from the law firm. Is it about the nonprofit?"

"Yeah. It went through. I meant to tell you. The Kate Malinov Foundation is finally official."

"That's terrific news," he replied genuinely, placing a hand on her shoulder. "I know how much starting the foundation meant to you."

While it was true that establishing the foundation in Kate's name had been a large step on the path of her recovery, there was more to it than that. It wasn't just about moving on. It was about not wanting to forget. "I called her family yesterday to let them know, and you wouldn't believe how emotional they were. I guess it's something of a consolation to know your daughter will always be associated with helping trafficked women get back on their feet."

"The foundation's gonna help a lot of people."

She looked out the window at a group of homeless men digging through the dumpster behind the 7-11. "I wish they didn't need the foundation's help," she told him. What she couldn't say was that she wished her only legacy would be the foundation and helping the trafficked women. But she knew, because of the prophecy, she had much more work ahead – she was destined to save not only the trafficked women, but the entire world. The burden was too great.

"Well, until the world is free of darkness, we need people like you, Mia. It just seems like every day, more and more evil makes its way to the surface. Scares me to death, bringing a baby into this world sometimes."

It wasn't the first time he'd voiced his concerns with regard to his fear of becoming a parent.

"She's gonna be fine, Jack. She's gonna have you and Stella to protect and guide her. Besides, I think there may still be hope for the world."

He shifted his focus from the road and cast a dubious glance in her direction. "Mia, have you met the people we deal with every day? It's like we're screening for roles in the upcoming apocalypse."

She had to laugh at this, picturing them together in an auditorium, choosing cast members based on who had the more dastardly performance.

"That pedophile PTA president from the case at the elementary school last week would definitely get top billing. Talk about a douchebag."

Jack chuckled despite himself. "See? That's what I'm talking about. I'm not even gonna feel safe sending her to kindergarten!"

"May I suggest slipping a tiny set of nunchucks in her Hello Kitty backpack?"

He glared at her. "Hello Kitty? Are you kidding me? Girl's gonna have a Black Widow backpack and a Buffy Summers' lunchbox."

"Not letting her eat school lunch?"

"Too many GMOs," he quipped.

At that moment she realized how much better she was feeling. Jack always had that effect on her. And the mention of food shifted her attention to her stomach. "Still interested in Shake Shack for lunch?" she asked.

"Thinking about a Mushroom-Swiss burger?"

"Sounds perfect," she laughed.

CHAPTER
11

PATRICK

Friday, September 2
London

Patrick felt Akantha's presence in the airspace above London before Wesley called with the news she'd landed safely at Heathrow. Since observing her via video during Lillian's biolocation, his connection to her had grown, further confirming she was indeed Number Six.

"I haven't seen you this excited in years," Javier commented as they sipped scotch together in his office, awaiting her arrival.

It was true. The last time he'd felt such a powerful bond to one of the others was with Lillian, just before he and Javier tracked her to a country music festival in Texas during the fall of his sophomore year at Oxford. After they discovered her birthday was a match, she'd infiltrated his dreams until at last he'd convinced Javier to travel with him to the US to track her down.

He pushed back his chair and crossed to the other side of the room where a wall of floor to ceiling windows provided a spectacular view of the medieval city, as well as the valet parking drop off directly below. There was a nervous anticipation to the moment, knowing he would soon be meeting another one of the chosen seven, explaining to her what it means to be one of them.

It was a question he'd spent many years considering. In the early days, as a teen, it had simply meant a life of freedom. Freedom to do what he wanted, knowing his life was more important than everyone else's. He determined his purpose far surpassed the simple, fruitless goals of other people - to live, to reproduce, to die. In that knowledge, he had lived a life without consequences, taking what he needed, when he needed it, from whatever source it could be attained. And he had needed many, many things. He'd helped himself to all the finest things in life, using his senses to assure he would never be caught stealing the things he desired – fine food, top-shelf alcohol, electronics, and brand-name clothes.

As he entered his twenties however, it wasn't enough just to steal what he wanted outright. Power became his prime motivator, and he realized he could get far more of the control he wanted through market share. He began fine tuning his abilities, seeking out markers which enabled him to sense shifts in the global markets.

He'd discovered the markers by accident as a child when he used the astral plane as a way to avoid his parents incessant bickering, which he found more annoying than upsetting. He escaped his physical body and set out to explore the world from his unique perspective, sensing the emotions of both individuals and collective groups alike. It was the reason he enjoyed high stakes sports gambling and had correctly chosen the winner of every European football match for over a dozen years. The secret was in simply sensing the emotions of the teams' players. While he acknowledged skill was a consideration in determining who won or lost a game, he knew the emotional state of the players was often the most influential factor. Sometimes all that mattered was who wanted to win more.

Those emotional energies, or markers, were visible on the plane, and it didn't take Patrick long to begin associating marker patterns with events taking place in people's lives. Stock market volatility was one of the first correlations he made, noticing fear markers were indicative of decline while confidence markers brought about positive gains. It seemed strange that people's emotions drove the economy and not the other way around, but he took advantage of the valuable insight the markers offered, directing him to buy and sell at the most advantageous times. Each day he would transfer his conscious onto the astral plane, prying into the minds of large stakeholders to get a sense of their emotional state with regard to their finances. Were they confident? Patrick would preemptively buy. Were they pessimistic? Patrick would sell before prices dropped.

Through this strategic investing, he amassed a financial empire in less than two years, but by the time he began swallowing up major corporations, including his father's, into his massive corporate conglomerate, even that wasn't enough power to satisfy him completely. He wanted more from life. He needed more. He longed for a life without limits, and that is when he fully realized what it meant to be part of the prophecy: he could control the fate of the world and thereby his own fate. According to the prophecy, a life without limits is what the dark prophets would usher in for the seven dark psychics.

Evagrius Ponticus, an early desert father from 300AD, was the first to identify and spread the idea that there were seven evils one needed to avoid – lust, gluttony, greed, sloth, wrath, envy, and pride. It was thought these evils lead ultimately to the moral decline of a man. This suggestion was laughable to Patrick in so much that he believed life was at its finest when each of the seven was embraced instead of scorned. For what other purpose was there but to indulge in all of life's pleasures?

What the religious called 'sin' and atheists called 'the moral truth,' Patrick called repression. As far as he was concerned, both dogmas were established by man for the sole purpose of avoiding chaos. But what if chaos was what made the drudgery of life worth living? It was accepted in modern society that murder was objectionable. But why? To oppose death one must inherently value life, which he did not. Therefore, if there were people whose lives he did not value, what should stop him from killing them?

That he was forced to live in a society in which he did not fundamentally belong infuriated him. Being required to obey laws he did not subscribe to was beneath him. Therefore, on his 25th birthday, he committed to redoubling his efforts in an attempt to locate the remaining dark psychics.

The result of those efforts was on her way now, and he knew it would be difficult to adequately describe to her how meaningful it was to be one of the seven dark psychics, just as he had done with each of the others at their first meetings.

He was still mulling it over when the town car arrived.

"She's here," he announced, clutching his hands together at his chest.

Less than five minutes later his personal assistant slipped her head through the doorway to announce Akantha's arrival. "Send her in," he commanded.

He wasn't prepared for the woman who now stood before him. No longer in her immodest grass skirt and tribal face paint, she was outfitted in modern attire – a pair of jeans and a red cotton t-shirt with the Manchester United crest on her chest. Although the bone had been removed, a gaping hole in her nose's columella remained, as did her wooden earlobe adornments. She was close to six and a half feet of pure sinew, which was clearly visible, outlined beneath the clinging cotton of her shirt. She towered over both he and Javier, rousing the slightest pang of inferiority in his carefully-crafted persona. He wasn't used to being at a disadvantage, physically or otherwise. He suddenly hoped Eshanti's portraits of their peaceful introduction were accurate.

Instead of crossing the room to greet her, he offered her a seat by the window, gesturing with his hands and slipping into the leather wingback furthest from the door. Sitting together, eye to eye, felt like the safest way to greet this woman who was clearly capable of becoming a formidable adversary given the right circumstances. The interpreter, a squat, bookish-looking Brit with a receding hairline and expanding waistline encouraged her, in what Patrick assumed was her native tongue, to take the seat across from him. When she obliged without so much as a moment's hesitation, he smiled to himself at finding such a suitable translator for the job.

"Hastings, is it?" he asked the interpreter, who took the fourth chair across from Javier in the semi-circle beside the window.

"Yes, sir," he replied.

Knowing Hastings would soon be privy to many of the prophecy's secrets, it was necessary to become better acquainted with him. "I trust your flight was uneventful?"

"Yes, sir."

"And Akantha was well-behaved?"

"She was visibly shaken during take-off, but rightfully so, and no worse off than most nervous first-time travelers."

She spoke then, a series of broken gibberish.

"She wants to know what we're discussing. She doesn't like being... excluded."

Patrick smiled warmly at Akantha, the same endearing smile he used to encourage would-be investors into his Ponzi schemes and women into his bed. From beneath his chair he produced a scroll. He unrolled it to reveal Eshanti's paintings of the Amazonian. Akantha leaned forward in her seat, reaching out as if to touch the canvas. She spoke.

"She's asking if these pictures are of her."

"Indeed they are. Tell her they were painted by another god of the prophecy who has the ability to foretell the future through her drawings. Explain they helped us to find her and convinced us she's one of the seven."

Akantha considered this and spoke again.

"She wants to know what it means to be one of the seven."

Patrick's heart leapt. The moment he'd been waiting for.

"To be part of the seven is an extraordinary thing," he began. "Based on my own interpretations of the ancient scrolls which reference the prophecy, I believe that once the seven of us are finally in one place, together we will rule the world. We will have authority not only over the remaining light remnant but also all of the people who, although dark, are inferior. We will be at the helm of a purely hedonistic society and we will make slaves of those who would challenge us."

He waited for Hastings to interpret his explanation, taking pleasure in the fear he saw in the man's eyes. When he finished, Patrick asked Akantha, "So tell me now, do you enjoy creating fire?"

"Yes," she replied.

"You enjoy using it to punish people you don't like?"

"Yes," she said again.

"It brings you pleasure to burn things."

She nodded.

"But the people of your tribe have always prevented you from burning as you wish?"

"Yes."

"I don't blame you for hurting your family when they prevented you from doing what you wanted. As a matter of fact, I admire that sort of initiative. Just between you and me, I had my own father killed years ago when he tried to prevent me from taking over his business. It didn't have to end as it did. He could have just let me do as I wished. But he refused to yield." Patrick shrugged. "And so I was forced to eliminate him. Such a pity."

He slid forward in his chair and their faces were so close he could smell the earthy huskiness of her skin. "What if I told you being one of the seven will ensure there will come a time when you will be allowed to do as you wish with your power without fear of punishment or repercussions."

He could sense Hastings, the interpreter, fumbling over the translation. There was terror in his voice.

Patrick smiled.

And Akantha smiled in return.

Then she set Hastings on fire.

CHAPTER

12

JOSE

Tuesday, September 6
Phoenix

Andrea's eye remained swollen, but the surrounding skin was no longer black. In the days since Jose had last seen her, the bruise had faded into a vivid shade of green, like the sky just before a rare desert storm. He stood above her now, watching the rise and fall of her chest, considering the loveliness of her features and the stubbornness of her spirit.

While cleaning the floor in exam room three, he'd heard the EMT's call come in from the ambulance about the 22-year-old female with a crushed pelvis, collapsed lung, and internal bleeding. He'd watched a team of doctors and nurses race her lifeless body through the emergency room straight to the OR, where after eight hours of grueling surgery, they'd managed to stabilize her.

Now, as Andrea lay sleeping in the hospital bed, he wondered how she would explain away her life-threatening injuries when she finally came to. Would she admit her boyfriend had been the one behind the wheel of the car which careened into her at over 30 mph? Would she try to convince herself that she deserved to be run over by a moving vehicle? Or would she finally recognize that pain is not a part of love, no matter how you try to force the misshapen piece into the heart-shaped puzzle?

She stirred fitfully, and his stomach dropped as he glanced at the bank of machinery monitoring her vital signs. If any of the machines alarmed, the nurses' station would be alerted and there was a good chance he wouldn't be able to make it out of the room unnoticed before someone arrived. He couldn't allow himself to be caught loitering in a patient's room, especially outside of the ER, but when the beeps and clicks remained steady, his breathing calmed and he convinced himself to stay.

In all his years of healing, he had never felt a stronger need to cure. He let his fingers brush against her bare arm, swollen with IV lines and crisscrossed in surgical tape. He considered doing it here, now, without her knowledge or consent as he had always done with others, but as he contemplated the true source of pain in her life, he reconsidered. Although her damaged body was in dire need of his intercession, she needed more from him. She needed a way out of her current life.

When his Aunt Carla made the decision to leave her husband, she'd locked herself away for several months at his parents' house. Jose remembered Uncle Elias pounding on their front door late at night, crying out for Carla like a braying mule. Disturbed from his own sleep, he'd watched porch lights flicker on up and down the street from his bedroom window as neighbors peeked out their front windows to see who was causing the ruckus. After several weeks, when it seemed his uncle's midnight tirades were becoming a habit, his father called the police and had Elias arrested right on their front lawn for disturbing the peace.

Not long after that, Aunt Carla packed up most of her family's possessions in the back of her F150 and headed east with her children, not knowing where she was going or what she would do when she got there. Three months later Jose discovered a letter under a stack of bills on the kitchen table postmarked from Baltimore with no return address. Curious as to his cousins' whereabouts, he read the letter but was disappointed to discover that although they were all fine, Aunt Carla hadn't divulged their precise location.

Jose had never seen them again.

As he crouched beside Andrea, steadying himself on the bed's metal rail, he knew her gangster boyfriend wouldn't be satisfied with middle-of-the-night door pounding as his uncle had been. It was obvious now, based on the injuries she'd already sustained at his hand, that he wouldn't hesitate to kill her if he didn't get his way.

If she ever wanted to be safe, she would need to disappear. Just like Aunt Carla.

"I'll be right back," he whispered to Andrea as he crept out of her room, back into the harsh glare of the hallway. He wasted no time descending the emergency stairs and racing outside, to where he always had the best cell reception behind the cafeteria dumpsters. He glanced at the time as he powered on his phone. With the three-hour time difference it was already almost 11pm in Baltimore, a detail which caused him to hesitate momentarily. Was it too late to call? He quickly decided it didn't matter and scrolled through his contacts until he found her number.

She answered, somewhat groggily, on the third ring.

"Aunt Carla? It's me. Jose."

She sucked in air, and then, her voice came out strained. "What is it, Jose? Is everything okay?"

"Oh, yes. I'm fine. Mom too. We're all fine."

"Ay! Don't scare me like that, calling so late!" she scolded. "There must be something!"

He leaned against the side of the dumpster, trying to ignore the stench of decaying food scraps permeating the air. "Yes, there's something, but it doesn't involve the family. There is someone else though."

She sighed heavily and he could imagine her collapsing onto her bed, too tired from the day's endeavors to continue standing. "What's going on?"

"There's a girl, here at the hospital. Her name is Andrea, and she's been in and out of the ER a handful of times the past few months for a bunch of different injuries. Lacerations. Contusions. A black eye. A concussion. Today an ambulance delivered her after being hit by a car. She's barely alive."

There was a beat of silence before Carla spoke. "It's a man, isn't it?"

"Yeah."

There was more silence as Jose allowed his aunt to draw her own conclusion about the reason for his call.

"What do you want from me, Jose?"

"She needs a place to go."

She scoffed. "And I'm the one you call?"

He felt his loosely contrived plan sifting through his fingers like the sand at the playground when he was a boy. He'd always hated playing in the sand. To spend so much time creating the perfect castle only to have some other kid delight in trampling it down.

"I thought of all people, you'd be the one to understand." There was an unintended edge to his voice, and he hoped he wasn't being too harsh, but he didn't know of another viable option. He needed to convince her to take Andrea in. "He's going to kill her, and I have to do something to help."

The back door to the hospital kitchen swung open and one of the staff tossed a garbage bag into the dumpster behind him, resonating with an echoing thud.

"How long 'til she's recovered enough to travel?" Carla asked.

He considered how quickly he could heal her without raising suspicions, especially from his aunt. "A few weeks. Maybe less if she's lucky."

His aunt was quiet. Was she reconsidering?

"She'd have to stay on the couch. I only have one bedroom. And she'd have to get a job and earn her keep, you hear me? Just because she's being abused doesn't mean

74

she gets to freeload off of me, you understand? I'm no dishrag."

"I understand." His mind began to race with the possibility of getting Andrea safely out of Phoenix. It certainly wouldn't be easy, starting with simply convincing her to go. "Thank you, Aunt Carla. You won't regret this."

She conceded, chuckling nostalgically into the phone. "You always had a big heart. Could never just stand back and watch something bad happen, could you?"

"I guess not," he acknowledged, remembering the time he stood up for his cousin, Jorge, on the bus when he was being teased for his wardrobe full of hand-me-down clothes.

He said goodnight to his aunt and ended the call, realizing he only had eight minutes left of his half-hour break. If he was going to finish with Andrea, he needed to work quickly.

Although it went against his practice of never telling the patients about his abilities, there was only one sure way to guarantee she would agree to his plan. Back at her bedside, Jose placed his hands on either side of her face and closed his eyes, allowing the heat to spread beneath her skin. However, instead of waiting until the warmth subsided on its own, he pulled away, rocking himself backward against the magnetic attraction of his power. He had never attempted to interrupt himself before but knew he couldn't afford to heal her completely since the promise of her full recovery was his only bargaining chip. He expected the little energy he gave her would be enough to rouse her from the coma and into full consciousness by the end of his shift, when he would return with the hopes of convincing her to agree to his plan.

CHAPTER
13

MIA

Tuesday, September 6
Baltimore

On Tuesdays, after her shift was over, Mia picked up Thomas at Towson University, where he was enrolled as an undergrad in their education program with a concentration in instrumental music. She'd convinced him to apply for admission in February, after his brush with death during the search for Kate's sisters - reminding him life was too short not to follow his dreams. By spring however, most traditional incoming freshmen had already applied and were being accepted, so because of the timing, Thomas had been waitlisted. Luckily, a spot opened up for him in July, along with a sizable financial-need scholarship.

In the end, the only real challenge had been persuading him to go.

As Thomas tossed his messenger bag into the back and slid into the passenger seat of Mia's sedan, she leaned across the center console to give him a kiss.

"Aren't you glad I convinced you college was a good idea?"

"Are you gonna ask me that every time you pick me up?" he countered, rolling his eyes.

Mia turned over the engine and eased the car out of the parking lot beside the Center for the Arts. "Maybe," she said. "I'm just glad you got over being so nervous about going back to school. I knew you were going to be amazing."

"I'm not amazing," he told her. "I'm above average at best. But yes, I will concede, college was a good idea. In fact, I met with my advisor this morning, and she thinks I'll be able to pick up enough credits during the summers to finish in three years."

She mentally calculated how old that would make him at graduation. "So you could have your own classroom by 28?"

"And be running my own studio by 30," he added. "As long as we can figure out the finances."

Money was only part of the reason she'd agreed to move in with Thomas and Mildred when her lease was up. Every hour he was in class or working on assignments was an hour he wasn't earning a paycheck, so since Mia had been the driving force behind his return to academia, she felt obligated to make sure they all kept a roof over their heads.

And, of course, she was looking forward to waking up beside him every day.

"We'll figure out the money," she assured him. "Besides, I think I'm going to be put up for a promotion before the end of the year."

He spun around to look at her. "Really?"

She'd been holding on to this bit of information as a way of easing him into a discussion about the prophecy. She figured there was nothing like good news to distract someone from an uncomfortable conversation.

"Yeah. Really. My dad mentioned my name was on a memo circulating around the brass, so we'll see." She paused, considering the best way to broach the subject and finally decided to throw out some bait. "Hopefully we'll get a chance to see all this stuff pan out."

Thomas jumped right on it. "Why wouldn't we? I thought you said everything was under control?"

She shrugged, acting abstruse. "I dunno. It's just the world is a crazy place, and you never know when things could get weird."

"Weirder than you're being right now?"

If there was one thing she'd learned about Thomas in the months since he'd quite literally stepped into the lineup that was her life, it was that he would eventually come around. Getting him on her side wasn't always easy, but he always got there in the end. And that's why she decided the best thing to do now was to just come clean.

"I think we need to start being proactive about the whole prophecy thing." She called to mind Dawson's warning and her intuition about his link to the prophecy. "Because I think, assuming this prophecy thing is real, the dark psychics' influence and power may be far more widespread than I'd initially imagined. And if we're part of it, then I don't want to stand back waiting for the bad guys to get their act together before we do." She paused, carrying her train of thought all the way to its inevitable conclusion. "If they haven't begun finding each other already."

Thomas studied her from the passenger's seat. "We're doing this now?"

"You wanna get out?" she asked, nodding out the window toward the guardrail speeding by.

He shook his head in annoyance, but she couldn't help but notice the way the corner of his lip curled into a crooked smile.

"So that's your MO now? You trap me in your car, luring me in under the pretense of a free ride, and this is what I get?"

She could tell he was only partially serious. And she was trying not to get aggravated.

"Yes. This is what you get. I know you think I've lost my mind, but this is something I need to do. It's like a spiritual calling."

He raised an eyebrow.

"Stop doing that! I can't explain what's happening. I dream about it at night. I worry about it all day. It's consuming me from every angle, and I think the only way it's gonna get any better is if I just give into it and start searching for the others."

"The other what?"

Instead of snipping at Thomas, she took out her frustration on the car in front of her, laying on her horn after being cut off.

"The other people," she explained, as calmly as she could. "The other good guys. If we are one and two, we need to find three through seven. And this feeling in my gut tells me we have to find them soon."

He was silent for a moment, fiddling with the angle of the air conditioning vent. "I reread the prophecy online," he said finally. "And I've been doing a little digging of my own."

She couldn't believe what she was hearing. Thomas willingly participating was almost the last thing she would have expected. "You have?"

"Of course I have. If it's important to you, it's important to me. That's how relationships work, right? We help each other out?"

If she hadn't been driving 60 miles per hour on the beltway, she would have leaned over to kiss him right then. Instead, she reached over to touch his cheek, brushing the coarseness of his day-old stubble under her thumb.

"So what do you think? About the prophecy? How do you think we should go about finding the other people?"

"Do we need to actively search them out? I mean, the prophecy itself says powerful forces will bring everyone together. It already brought us together, right? And Kate too?"

Mia blanched at the mention of her name. Although months had passed since her death, calling her to mind still tore at the thinly scabbed wound which remained. As she walked across the thin tightrope of her life, thinking of Kate now stirred the breeze around her, causing her to falter.

"You're still convinced she's one of the seven light psychics? We're not even positive she had a power," Mia scoffed, trying to persuade herself more than Thomas there was still a possibility she wasn't.

He nodded. "I was there, Mia. I watched her will a random stranger, who just happened to be walking by, to open the door of that police car for her. She didn't say a word, and I don't know how she did it, but there's no doubt in my mind she made him open that door with the power of her mind."

Mia considered his assessment of Kate's abilities and reflected for the hundredth time on her own observations during their time together in the basement. All the times she spoke cryptically about making things happen. There was no denying the verity of his theory.

"She was born on our birthday, wasn't she?" This came out as more of a confession than a rhetorical question.

"Yeah," replied Thomas. "She was number three, Mia. That's why she was brought here. The prophecy."

A wave of nausea overtook her and she merged into the far right lane and onto the exit ramp toward Mildred's house. As soon as she was off the beltway, instead of taking a left, she pulled into the first parking lot past the light.

"Wendy's? I thought we were eating at home?"

She shook her head and thrust her foot heavily against the brake, bringing the car to a rapid stop. "I need you to drive," she told him breathlessly, unfastening her seatbelt before wresting open the door. By the time she made her way to the other side of the car, Thomas was already climbing out of the passenger side. He stood before her, gathering her into his arms.

"What's the matter?" he asked, resting his chin on the top of her head.

She wrapped her arms around his waist and melted into his chest. Subconsciously, she'd known all along Kate was one of the seven light psychics. From the moment she began putting the pieces of the puzzle together in the hospital with Thomas – the birthdays, the abilities, the prophecy. If only she had taken the proper precautions to assure Kate's safety after they were rescued. If only she'd been more focused on guarding the innocent people she vowed to protect instead of being so hell-bent on getting to Dalton instead. Kate would be there now, with them, to help usher in the light. But instead, she was gone, and Mia was left to face the stark reality that she'd failed. Failed Kate and failed the entire world. The dark was going to prevail.

Eventually, she pulled back, straightening her tank top over the top of her shorts.

"It's just that if Kate was number three, then there's no sense in going on. Since she's already gone, the fate of the world is sealed, and no matter what else happens, the dark seven will gather first because the light can't gather at all."

Thomas gazed at her, but not with the look of concerned desperation she was expecting. In fact, he was smiling.

"I thought the same thing. At least initially. And then I realized, the fate is only decided once they're all together." He kissed her gently, and she allowed the warmth of his touch to soothe her. He tucked a loose strand of hair behind her ear and turned toward the open driver's side door. Then he called back to her over his shoulder. "That just means we need to keep them apart. So let's find them before they find each other."

CHAPTER

14

JOSE

Tuesday, September 6
Phoenix

"Jose?' Andrea said as he entered the room.

"Hey." The hallway was empty and although he was visiting the ICU outside of his working hours as a friend and not an orderly, he was still nervous. Old habits die hard.

He was relieved to see her awake and immediately inquired about her condition as he sat in the visitor's chair beside her bed.

"Everything hurts so much. They've got me on IV pain meds, and it's making my head all fuzzy. I guess they were expecting me to be in the coma for a lot longer so I could heal without feeling the pain, but I woke up," she explained, her voice raspy from the recently removed intubation tube. "The doctor said I'm pretty messed up."

He felt an immediate pang of guilt for causing her to experience undue suffering, but he consoled himself with the knowledge it would be short lived. "You got hit by a car, Andrea. You're lucky to be alive."

She lowered her eyes, obviously not wanting to speak about the accident.

"It's not your fault." He reached out to touch her hand. Her fingers were like ice.

She shifted uncomfortably beneath the sheet, but he refused to let her pull away. "It was actually all my fault," she said at last. And then she met his gaze. Her lids drooped under the weight of the medication. "I told him I was done."

Jose couldn't hide his anger, crying out far louder then he'd intended. "So he hit you with a car?!"

She yanked her hand away then, the beeps from the heartrate monitor on the wall increasing in speed.

"I knew how he'd react, and I still took your misguided advice to leave. I'm not at all surprised this is where I landed." She looked down the length of the bed at her mangled body. "It would probably be better if I was dead."

He didn't like listening to her speaking so matter-of-factly about her own demise and knew he needed to intervene. "What if I could take away the pain? What if I could make you better?"

She scoffed. "Last time I checked you weren't wearing a white coat, Jose."

He'd never shared his secret with anyone else. Not his parents. Not his sister. Not his best friend. He wasn't sure he wanted to share it now, but he couldn't think of any other way to save Andrea's life. And although she probably wouldn't believe him initially, she would realize he was telling the truth once she was cured.

"When I was nine, I found a bird and unintentionally saved its life by simply holding it in my hands. Then there was this hurt dog I completely cured just by touching it. After that, I healed everything I could find – animals hit by cars, my family's cuts and bruises while they slept, homeless people in the park. I don't know how it works, and I don't know why I can do what I do, but when I say I can heal you, believe me that I can."

She studied his face, as if to distinguish whether he could be trusted. "Bullshit," she said.

He shrugged, not the slightest bit offended by her disbelief. "Why do you think you came out of the coma? It's because I needed to talk to you."

"Oh, fabulous. Thank you. I'm so much better now that I'm not blissfully unaware of how much pain I'm actually in. You're a terrific doctor." It was obvious by the sarcasm in her voice that she didn't believe a single word he'd said.

He scooted his chair a few inches closer to the bed and took her hand again. She surprised him by not pulling it away. "I'm sorry you're in pain and I can make it go away, but only if you promise me you're going to let me help you get out of the abusive situation that keeps landing you in the hospital."

She squeezed his hand condescendingly, the way an overbearing adult might do to a naïve child. "Listen, Jose, I don't know why you're even here. Is it because I confided in you the other day and now you think you're going to swoop in and rescue me? Because let me be the first to tell you, I don't need another knight in shining armor. I already had one of those, and he ran me over with a car."

He was starting to lose confidence. Maybe convincing her to take his help was going to be harder than he thought. Maybe there wasn't anything he could do to change her mind. He would continue to see her month after month in the ER. Until she showed up one last time in a body bag.

And that wasn't an option.

"I don't want to save you. I don't think you need a man to ride in on a white horse and rescue you. I just want to offer you a way out. An alternative to where you are. That's it. No strings attached."

She turned her face away. "There are always strings attached."

"Not with me."

She considered him then, for a moment, and it occurred to him that she was having trouble staying awake. She needed to rest and he needed to make his point, but before he could continue, she spoke.

"Why?"

"Why what?" he asked.

"Why would you do this for me? What makes me so special?"

He thought about making something up. Something about being drawn to her by some cosmic connection or about Fate bringing them together. Something about seeing himself in her. Something about how he was secretly in love with her. Or that he was secretly Batman. And then he decided to tell her the truth.

"There's nothing that makes you any more special than any of the other people I've been able to help with this thing I can do." She looked crestfallen and he knew immediately he'd chosen his words poorly. He rubbed the back of his neck with his free hand and tried to explain it to her another way. "It's not that you're not special, it's just that I think everyone's pretty special, in their own way. So if everyone's life is valuable, I should try to help out when I can. So I can cure your body without any problem, but it would be a waste for me to do it if you're just going to allow yourself to get hurt again. I need you to work with me on this. Promise you won't continue to put yourself at risk and will agree to the second part of my gift."

"Which is?"

"Going to Baltimore to stay with my aunt while I try to get things figured out back here with your knight in shining armor. The one with the dented front end."

She was hanging on his every word now. "What do you mean by 'figuring things out?'"

As was typical of every abuse victim he'd ever known, Andrea cared more about her boyfriend than herself. She moved right past the part about moving across the country to the part about what was going to happen to her abuser.

"I'm going to have him arrested. I'm going to send him to prison. I'm going to make sure he's locked up so he can't keep hurting people. And you are going to help me, but from far away where he can't find you." He stood up then to indicate he was done talking. It was time for Andrea to make up her mind. "I'm sorry I'm forcing this decision on you, especially in your condition, but there are others who could use my help up and down this hall. If I choose you, then I can't choose them. I have to know you'll go."

"To Baltimore? With your aunt?"

"Yes."

"Until it's safe to come back?"

"Exactly."

The corners of her mouth lifted ever so slightly, forming tiny dimples in her cheeks which were peppered with cuts and scratches from broken glass. "That's all well and good," she said. "But what will I do after that?"

Friday, September 9
Baltimore

The downtown bus was practically empty. Except for a mother and daughter, leaning in close and engrossed in conversation, Thomas was the only one on the number eight line into the city. And for that, he was grateful.

His Fundamentals of Musical Theory lecture notes were spread out on the seat beside him, and he was about halfway done with the week's assignment. He was hoping to finish before reaching the hotel, but it didn't seem there was going to be enough time. It was shaping up to be a late night.

When adjustments to his schedule needed to be made at the beginning of the semester, keeping his Friday gig at the hotel wasn't a tough decision. It was never a windfall, but the tips he made there on a good night often determined whether they were able to make the mortgage payment. He hoped tonight's haul would help keep them in the black.

For Thomas, walking through the front doors of the Tremont Plaza Hotel felt a lot like stopping by the home of his childhood best friend. He never needed to knock. He knew he was always welcome. And he could always count on someone to appreciate him. Tonight was no different.

His friend, Bill, the concierge, made a beeline in his direction when he noticed Thomas setting up at the piano.

"It's a good thing you got here early tonight," he whispered conspiratorially, perching his elbow atop the Baby Grand. "All these foreign doctors are coming in from China and Europe and all over for this obesity conference. The hotel is totally booked for the week. Every room. And I'm betting they have tons of money to throw your way."

Thomas set his tip jar beside Bill's elbow. "That'd be great," he said. "Money's tight right now."

"I hear ya," Bill agreed, frowning. "I wish they'd let me set up a 'gratuity welcome' sign over at my desk. You entertainment guys get all the luck."

Thomas laughed. In his experience, there was very little luck to be had as a pianist. Pure talent put bread in his jar.

A large group of wayward travelers rolled their luggage through the front doors. Bill scooted off across the lobby to man his station, lest they find themselves in need of dinner reservations. Alone now, with his back to the chaos at the check-in, Thomas began to play.

One of the things he loved most about the piano was it forced his mind to focus. He found he was only able to concentrate on one other thought while he was playing, unlike most other times when his attentions ricocheted all over the place, like a pinball in a machine. Tonight, as he sank into a familiar concerto he'd known since childhood, he allowed his thoughts to settle on Mia's prophecy.

After careful consideration, he still didn't completely buy it. Much like his mother Mildred's fervent Christianity - which he wanted to embrace but held at arm's length with a modicum of skepticism - he was having trouble fully accepting the possibility that supernatural powers were controlling the fate of the world. Reconciling the more well-known biblical 'end-of-days' predictions with the Sevens Prophecy was proving rather difficult. Why hadn't he heard of it before? Why weren't more people concerned about these seven dark psychics getting together? Surely, if other theologians knew, he and Mia wouldn't be alone in their search.

And yet, why couldn't it be true? If it was, then knowing what he knew, he was obligated to be proactive and do what he could to protect the fate of the world. And if it wasn't true, would pursuing some leads cause any real harm? Maybe a little time wasted, but besides that, there were no real negatives to following the path they were on.

While hammers continued to strike the piano's strings at the bequest of his nimble fingers on the keyboard, he decided once and for all that he would help Mia in her search for the other members of the prophecy. He would use the resources available to him at the university to begin tracking down the names of people born on his birthday. He would work with her in the evenings, comparing notes and leads.

Whatever it took, he would see the process through until Mia was satisfied with the outcome.

Pleased with his decision, his mind returned to the present and he scanned the lobby which was now teeming with guests. A few bills and a handful of loose change lay in the bottom of his jar, and he ramped up his song selection in the hopes of eliciting some larger donations. As he transitioned seamlessly into Song of Newsboy by Nie Er, a petite Chinese woman with soulful eyes and a friendly smile approached the piano.

"Of all the songs you could be playing, this is one of my favorites," she told him. "My grandfather used to play it when I was a child."

Thomas tried to keep conversations to a minimum while he played. "I'm glad you're enjoying it," he said politely, returning his attention to the keys. He expected her to move on, hoping maybe she would leave some change. But she didn't.

"This is my first trip to the United States," she admitted, as if she was sharing one of her deepest secrets with him. "I'm here for a conference about obesity. I'm an obesity counselor. Or actually, I'm studying to become one. I'm here with some of the other students in my Master's degree program."

He couldn't tell if she was nervous or just lonely, but something compelled him to respond, despite his stance on banter. "I'm a student myself," he told her.

"Oh, you are!" She beamed at him, clearly grateful for the connection. "What are you studying?"

"Music," he replied as he continued to play.

She looked away then, embarrassed. "I should have guessed. Although it seems like you could be the professor. You play so well."

Now it was Thomas' turn to feel self-conscious. "Thanks, but I'm actually studying to become a teacher. A music teacher. And I've got a lot to learn."

She took a step closer and boldly sat on the piano bench beside him. "I can relate. I've got a lot to learn about becoming a counselor, even though I know a lot about being overweight."

"How's that?" The woman didn't look the slightest bit heavy to him.

Her shoulders fell, almost as if she was being deflated. "I was overweight for most of my life. People said a lot of mean things about me behind my back. Depression set in and there was no one around to help me. That's when I knew I wanted a career helping young people struggling with weight management."

"Sounds like a terrific plan. And it seems like you're well on the way to realizing your dreams."

"I made a commitment to myself on my eighteenth birthday, and I've been working hard to achieve my goals ever since." She thought for a moment. "It's hard to believe I've been at it for seven years already."

Thomas lost himself in the piece for a moment, stumbling over a few notes as he calculated her age.

She was 25.

He did a mental head slap, already hating himself for what he was about to ask. But he couldn't help himself – he had to prove that sometimes a coincidence was just a coincidence.

"That's funny," he laughed. "I'm twenty-five too. When's your birthday?"

"It's February 17th. When's yours?"

At that point, his fingers could no longer keep their place within the music. Between the conversation and the atomic bomb, the woman had just set off inside his head, his only option was to stop playing – something he had never before done in a public venue. He turned to her.

"Why did you stop?" she asked, hastily returning to her feet. "Did I say something wrong? Am I being impolite?"

Strong powers will be in place to bring the seven light together...

The words of the prophecy replayed over and over in his head like a Vine video.

He composed himself, taking a deep breath, and then patted the bench beside him to encourage her to sit.

"It's not you. I promise," he chuckled. "It's just that, believe it or not, I'm 25 years old and February 17th is my birthday too."

"Really?" she gasped. "We were born the same day? What are the chances?"

He actually knew the answer to this, thanks to some preliminary research of the other psychics. "About 1 in 355,000, give or take," he said. "There are a lot of us out there. Still, the chances of us meeting are pretty small."

"But here we are," she said.

"Yes. Here we are."

The woman looked anxious now, as if she was afraid the conversation had reached its culmination. She adjusted her purse on her shoulder and began to stand. But Thomas couldn't let her walk away. Not without first finding out more about her.

Not without first finding out if she had some sort of psychic power.

"My name's Thomas," he said abruptly. "And my girlfriend's name is Mia. She was born on February 17th too." He knew he sounded like a crazy person, but he continued anyway. "I know she'd love to get to know you so I was wondering if you'd like to meet up for drinks, maybe just here at the hotel if you have some time?"

"Drinks with you and your girlfriend?"

Oh, God, he thought, realizing it sounded as if he was suggesting something racy. She probably thinks I'm some sort of pervert. He attempted to save face.

"Yes, just drinks, and I promise my intentions are pure. I'm a total gentleman." He ran his fingers through his hair, positive he was blowing it as she stared dumbfounded at him. "It's just that Mia has a thing for finding people who share our birthday, and I know she'd love to hear your story. Please say you'll join us."

She lowered her chin and closed her eyes. "I came here thinking, hoping, maybe I could make a new friend. I won't miss out on an opportunity to do just that." She held out her hand. "My name's Lanying. My session's over at five tomorrow. We can meet back here in the lobby at six if you'd like?"

He took her hand, shaking it firmly. "Sounds great. I know Mia will be thrilled."

CHAPTER
16

PATRICK

Saturday, September 10
London

Patrick woke with a start. He could sense a shift in the astral plane, like a ship cresting a wave just seconds before thundering into the foamy sea below. He knew immediately, before ever opening his eyes, that another light psychic had joined their growing ranks, bringing their number to four.

In the years before, he hadn't given them a second thought, never sensing they were on a path toward one another. Now he thought of them with great frequency, since in just over eleven months he'd felt their connections growing. First two. Then the third. And now the fourth. It did little to ease his mind, knowing the dark psychics already numbered six, since statistically it had taken them significantly longer to find one another. At the rate they were going, it would be months, not years, before all seven light psychics came together. He knew twilight was setting on the prophecy, as was the time he had to locate Number Seven.

Without looking at the clock, he pressed the call button beside his bed. His assistant answered almost immediately. "Sir?"

"I need you to get Eshanti on the phone for me right away."

There was a brief pause. "It's quite early in India, sir. Only a little after 6am. Perhaps it can wait?"

"Perhaps you can get her on the line this instant or you will see yourself into another line of work. Something that requires fewer of your opinions. Like digging ditches."

Less than a minute later Eshanti's heavy accent broke the hanging silence. "Good morning, Patrick," she said thinly.

"I need to know of your recent work. Have there been any new insights?"

"No. Nothing of consequence."

"I should probably be the one deciding whether something is consequential or not, don't you think?"

She sighed into the receiver. Patrick didn't care whether it was out of annoyance or exhaustion. "I'll email you photos of my latest work," she replied. "As I said though, I don't think any of it will be helpful. Mostly just landscapes."

Her attitude aggravated him, that she could know more than he did about what was best for the search. "The photographs won't be necessary. I'll have Javier apport them here to London so Wesley can examine them himself firsthand. Because while you may be unable to ascertain anything about our final member from your work, his abilities may be better suited for the task."

Until that point, he'd felt comfortable allowing her to determine when to notify him about possible leads from her paintings, but as more of the light psychics came together, his need to control every facet of the search grew in intensity. He could leave no stone unturned.

He hung up on the Indian woman without saying goodbye and wasted no time in having his assistant contact both Javier and Wesley on a conference call.

"For Christ's sake, Patrick, it's one in the morning. What's so important?" Javier said.

"There are four of them together now. That leaves only three."

"Light psychics?" Wesley asked. "Did you sense it?"

"Yes. Just a bit ago. So we can't afford to be resting on our laurels now that their numbers are increasing so steadily."

Wesley chuckled. "I'd hardly call what we've been doing 'resting on our laurels,'" he said. "We have paid a staff of over 100 people searching databases for them every day. We have another two dozen attending psychic conventions and expos around the world hoping for a lead. We're using every psychic ability at our disposal. I don't know what more we can be doing."

A spark of indignation ignited inside him, and it was a struggle to keep from lashing out at the man he'd considered an ally for so many years. Not long after discovering Lillian in Texas, he and Javier detected a birthday match in one of their databases, directing them to a medium working the carnival circuit just outside Brisbane. Although it seemed strange for a man to be working in such a profession, Patrick was able to connect with Wesley over the astral plane from London and could immediately sense his sinister intent. But it wasn't until they arrived in Brisbane to watch him in action that they were able to confirm he was truly one of them.

From a distance, Patrick and Javier loitered along the edge of the side show exhibits, just outside the tent Wesley used to conduct his séances. Patrick was able to listen in, using his own clairvoyance, to the way Wesley used what he saw about each customer to belittle them, often eliciting tears. When a woman confessed she was concerned about the health of her unborn baby, Wesley was quick to point out she had every right to be, given the drugs and alcohol she'd consumed since his conception. A man had also approached, curious as to why he seemed to be so unlucky in love. Without hesitation, Wesley rightly pointed out it was because of the man's annoyingly pretentious personality and greasy complexion. Patrick could feel the joy it brought

Wesley, causing emotional pain to the patrons who entered his tent, as without fail, he was able to find something personal about each of them to cause distress.

From that moment, he'd admired Wesley for the way he took personal pleasure at the expense of others, but he'd been unimpressed by his lack of drive and ambition. Now, many years later, Wesley's laissez-faire approach to their search was beginning to grate on his nerves.

"You won't mind then, if the light gather first and everything we've dreamed of never comes to pass? Because that is what will happen. Instead of choosing whichever woman you like to fulfill your wanton desires, there will be only chastity. All the wealth we've amassed will pass away in the interest of charity. The gluttonous feast will be tempered and any pride you feel now will be suppressed by humility. Instead of doing as you please, you will live to please others." His voice rose now, in a fevered pitch. "Is that how you'd like to carry out the rest of your miserable existence?"

"Of course not, Patrick. We want what you want. Freedom to do as we please without the restriction of society's moral obligations," Javier explained. "I think though, what Wesley's saying, is he doesn't know what more we can do. And frankly, neither do I."

"Well, for starters, Javier, I need you to apport Eshanti's latest works here to London immediately, and then, Wesley, you need to get here ASAP to see what you can glean from them using your abilities. I'm convinced there's something to her paintings, regardless of what she says. Even if most of them are landscapes, perhaps you'll be able to sense their location with your magic mirror. There may be a psychic waiting there for us."

Wesley's voice carried icily across the line. "It's not a magic mirror, Patrick. Scrying is no less respected in the psychic community than your clairvoyance, and I take offence to the contrary."

Before losing his temper once again, he reminded himself that he need only to put up with Wesley and the others for a short while longer until he could be rid of them for good.

"Duly noted," he acquiesced. "Now that it's been settled, we don't rest until we find Number Seven. There is no other option."

CHAPTER
17

ESHANTI

Saturday, September 10
Mumbai

Eshanti hated Patrick. Not quite as much as she'd hated her deceased husband, Aarush, but close. After hanging up from his demanding predawn phone call, she'd begun reviewing the mental inventory of reasons she had to despise him. She added his lack of patience to the list.

She continued taking stock of their strained relationship as she picked at her breakfast, a bowl of suji upma prepared just the way she liked it with roasted rava and sautéed vegetables. Usually she delighted in the simple pleasure of the morning meal, but today, she found her appetite was lacking.

She glanced at the clock on the wall of her Mumbai apartment, located in the penthouse of one of the city's newest high rises. Of course, she had Patrick to thank for her accommodations, fully-furnished with a rooftop terrace in South Mumbai, home to the city's wealthiest inhabitants. The apartment and everything in it was another source of frustration for Eshanti. There was nothing she loathed more than being indebted to a man, even if that man was also a part of the Sevens Prophecy. After Aarush's death she had promised herself she would never become dependent on another person again, and yet, here she was.

It was just after 7am and she felt the familiar urge to perform the morning rituals of her youth. The morning purifications, the sun worship, and the tilak and postures. She had given up these things after her husband's untimely passing, turning away from not only the Hindu rituals but the associated beliefs as well.

What good were gods if they couldn't protect her from the pain of existence?

Eshanti gave up on her breakfast, and after covering the bowl in cellophane, slipped the untouched suji upma into the Sub Zero refrigerator. She retreated to her studio, a room Patrick had insisted on setting up for her the day the apartment was procured. There were easels and canvases scattered throughout the window-lined space, along with every imaginable production medium – oils, crayon, chalks, pencils, acrylics. Eshanti wanted for nothing.

Nothing except the two babies Aarush had forced her to abort.

Impressions of her daughters' faces covered the walls of the studio, etched into the drywall with a blade in much the same manner a sculptor would carve into marble with a chisel. She assumed she'd been drawing the girls as they could have been. As they should have been, if they'd been allowed to grow into the playful, smiling children who adorned her walls. She crossed the room now and their eyes seemed to follow her, pleading 'Why Amma, why?'

The illustrations of her daughters and predictions of the prophecy were born of the same psychic power. Falling into a trancelike state, she'd first experienced automatic drawing at the age of seven, using a charcoal brick from the fire to create an image on the concrete floor of her family's shanty, scorching the skin on her palm in the process. She came to render the same likeness dozens of times in the years that followed, but wouldn't realize she was drawing

Patrick until he appeared at the entrance to her jail cell seventeen years later.

The day she traded one form of captivity for another.

She glided across the studio now in what had become her signature attire – a richly colored mekhela sador with the mekhela wrapped around her waist and the blouse and sador draped across her shoulders. As requested by Patrick, she gathered the most recent landscape drawings into a pile for Javier to apport to Wesley. Many of the mountains she'd drawn were tree covered. Some were barren. Others were topped with snow. She had absolutely no idea where they were located and doubted they bore any connection to the prophecy, but it was a waste of her time to argue against Patrick on the matter. Once his mind was made up, she knew it was better to acquiesce.

The same had been true of Aarush. Her marriage to him had been arranged, as were many Indian marriages. Although she'd drawn the middle-aged lines of his face for many months before their families reached an agreement, the first time she met him in person was the day before their nuptials at his parents' house for dinner. Even at the tender age of fifteen, she'd known immediately she could never love Aarush. His callous demeanor, the way he refused to look her in the eye, confirmed her suspicions he sought only to possess her. There had been no affection involved.

Which is probably why, years later, it had been so easy to push him in front of the oncoming bus.

CHAPTER

18

JOSE

Saturday, September 10
Phoenix

Andrea's recovery was nothing short of miraculous, and Jose delighted in watching her improve, allowing himself greater access to her than he had with any other patients in the past. It was widely known that the two had formed a friendship, so his presence was seen through the lens of familiarity. Within hours of his intervention, he had been there as the pain began to subside and the nurses stopped administering the narcotic medication. Now, five days later, he stood by her side as she took her first unassisted steps out of her room into the hallway.

"I would have never guessed you'd have been walking so quickly after seeing how severe your injuries were when you came in," her nurse remarked as they turned the corner toward the courtyard. "But here you are, walking on a hip being held together with titanium rods and pins like you're training for a marathon."

Andrea laughed, the first genuine laugh he'd ever heard from her. It was bubbly, effervescent even, and worked to ease his fears. Since the moment she'd agreed to their arrangement, he'd been waiting for her to go back on her word. To reach out to her boyfriend, Alejandro, in some way. But she hadn't.

"I'm bionic now," she told the nurse. "I'm practically unstoppable." And to prove as much, she began picking up the pace.

"I've seen some miraculous recoveries in my time here in the ICU, and I would put yours in the top five," the nurse continued, causing Jose's heart to race involuntarily. "You just never know who's going to pull out of something and who isn't. There have been a couple I was convinced we were going to lose and then blam! - they're better, seemingly overnight." She laughed as she raced alongside Andrea. "Miracles of modern medicine, right Jose?"

He caught Andrea's conspiratorial sideways glance as they rounded the final corner and prayed she wouldn't divulge his secret to the nurse.

"We live in amazing times," he agreed.

Once Andrea was safely ensconced in her room, the nurse scooted off, mumbling to herself about the growing list of patients in need of her care.

Andrea rolled her eyes. "I thought she would never leave."

"I could tell," Jose said. "I thought you were going to run that last stretch past the elevator bay. You gotta slow down or someone's going to get suspicious. I don't care how annoying she is."

She shrugged. "I was going as slow as I could. Do you have any idea how hard it is to pretend you're disabled?" She extended her arms above her head, stretching like a pampered housecat. "How much longer do you think I need to stay in here?"

He considered how the pieces of his plan had been falling into place, as if the universe wanted nothing more than for him to succeed in keeping Andrea safe. After recovering in hours instead of weeks, she realized Jose was telling the truth about his ability to heal, and although she informed him at the time it was still 'against her better judgement,' she relinquished not only her boyfriend Alejandro's name but also his address.

Jose immediately began working to procure sufficient evidence for the man's arrest. When he wasn't working his shifts at the ER or visiting with Andrea in the ICU, he cloistered himself at the public library, searching online for information about the Wedgewood Chicanos. As one of the city's oldest gangs, there was no shortage of arrest documentation from past and present members. He quickly discovered Alejandro had been arrested a total of three times but had never been convicted. And although two of the arrests were for armed robbery, the third was for assault. Based on his findings, he shared Alejandro's name and likeness with hospital security to prevent him from gaining access to her while she was admitted. So far, it had done the job, but now that it was almost time for him to go to the police with Andrea's statement, he knew hospital security would be no match for Alejandro and his fellow gang members once she pressed charges. One way or another, they would get to her if she remained in Arizona.

There was nothing more they could do but wait until sufficient time had passed as would be plausible for her to be recovered. Then she could board her flight to his aunt's safe house in Baltimore, and he could finally have Alejandro arrested.

"Based on the normal recoveries I've seen from the sort of injuries you sustained, you should be in here another ten to fourteen days. But I think another week or so will be long enough not to raise any red flags. You're gonna have to keep faking it."

Her eyes bulged out of her head in an exaggerated gesture meant to convey her extreme displeasure. "Another week? Are you kidding me? Do you have any idea how bad the food is in here?"

He could only imagine how difficult it was for her to be locked away like a canary in a cage, especially when she was already fully recovered, but her complaints smacked of an ungrateful brat. "You made a promise," he reminded her, "to play along and not blow my cover. And remember all the pain you were in? You could still be recovering. Or worse yet, you could be dead."

She pouted, her lower lip shoved forward as she blew her hair out of her face.

Despite feeling somewhat unappreciated, knowing how miserable she was, he felt his heart soften. "Tell you what, I'll bring you food when I come into work from here on out," he offered. "Where's your favorite spot?"

She raised an eyebrow. "Really?"

"Yes. Really. Now where's your favorite spot?"

He could tell she was mulling over her options as she chewed absentmindedly at her thumbnail.

"There's this Thai place on the corner of 5th and Thomas."

He thought for a moment. "By La Paloma?"

She nodded. "I love the number eleven – yellow curry."

"You got it. Yellow curry." He sat on the bed beside her and wondered why he was going through so much trouble for this woman he barely knew. Beyond the food and the hours spent researching her case, he'd purchased her plane ticket with his own money and involved his aunt, potentially putting her in danger. He had always been, at his core, a humanitarian, but going this far out on a limb was above and beyond, even for him.

It was as though he couldn't help himself.

"Did you call my Aunt Carla and talk to her about the arrangements?" he asked.

Her shoulders slumped. She clearly didn't want to discuss it. "Yes. I called her. She seems nice."

"She is nice. And she knows exactly what you're going through. She'll be a good mentor."

Andrea scowled. "Because what I need is another person in my life telling me what to do."

"Maybe you do. If that somebody can keep you alive." He could feel his blood pressure rising the way it always did when Andrea seemed incapable of listening to reason. He took a slow, deep breath and had begun counting backwards from ten when she placed her hand gently on his thigh.

"I'm sorry," she said. "I know I'm being a real pain, especially considering all you've done for me." There was no sarcasm in her voice. Only pain. "It's hard though, always depending on someone else. Knowing I clearly can't take care of myself."

He leaned into her. "You can totally take care of yourself. And Carla will teach you how. If you let her." He remembered what a great mother Carla had always been to his cousins. After being granted full custody of them in the divorce proceedings, she'd given them a solid upbringing in Baltimore, full of love and security. In fact, it was a point of contention between him and his own mother that all three of Carla's boys were in college – two of them on full-ride scholarships. They were a constant reminder that even though he graduated from high school with a 4.2 GPA, he'd chosen a technical school over academia. Regardless of his own situation, he had no doubt his Aunt Carla could reset Andrea's course in the right direction.

She picked at the Band-Aid protecting where her IV had been inserted just below her elbow earlier in the week. "She said she's already got a job at a temp agency waiting for me. And she wants me to go with her to this support group for abused women." Her voiced hitched on the word 'abused,' and it was almost as if she wanted to gnaw it away as she bit her bottom lip.

"Sounds like a good idea to me."

"Of course it does, to someone who's got it all figured out." She nudged into his shoulder with her own and grinned. "I'm starting to figure you out, Jose. Tell me though, what happens when the clock strikes midnight? Do you turn into a field mouse and do I go back to being Cinderella? Or an ugly stepsister? Or something worse?"

He draped an arm around her shoulder. "I promise you nothing bad is going to happen. It's all going to be okay."

19

LANYING

Saturday, September 10
Baltimore

Her mother's warning about being mindful of Americans who might not have her 'best interest at heart' gnawed at her as Lanying perched at the bar. The heels of her pumps, tucked behind the rung of the chair, were the only things keeping her from fleeing the scene.

That, and the overwhelming desire to find out what was about to happen next.

She hadn't been surprised to see Thomas playing the piano in the hotel lobby the day before. Physically, he was exactly as he had appeared to her for many months, in the waking dreams which plagued her existence. But in all that time she had only seen brief images of his life – his actual persona was much different than she had imagined. She was proud of herself for plucking up the courage to speak with him, and now, as she waited for him and his girlfriend, Mia, she wondered just exactly what she had gotten herself into. For although he had seemed mild-mannered, as her mother was always quick to point out, you could never really know for sure about another person's intentions.

Unfortunately, it wasn't just her mother who taught Lanying to be cautious – life had shown her most people were seldom worthy of trust. By the time the cause of her obesity was diagnosed as PCOS at sixteen, the emotional damage had already been done. She'd been scarred by what her classmates said about her. Traumatized by the way they gawked at her when they assumed she couldn't see them.

But she could see them.

She saw them whether she wanted to or not.

Such was her curse.

She'd been alone on the bus on the way home from secondary school when her consciousness was unexpectedly transported to her classmate Huilang's house. Vividly, Lanying saw and heard Huilang talking to her mother about who she wanted to invite to her upcoming New Year's party. There were invitations on the table and a handwritten list set before the girl. She mentioned Lanying as a possible guest, but the mother laughed, saying, "Certainly not! If we were to invite her, there would be no food left for the others to eat."

It wasn't the first time her visions had warned her of people's true natures. And as painful as it was to endure, she knew it certainly wouldn't be the last.

Lanying was still nursing her first mojito when Thomas appeared at the far end of the bar, a petite brunette by his side. Instinctively, old insecurities bubbled to the surface. Mia was stunning, in a girl-next-door sort of way, and Lanying chastised herself for agreeing to join them when she should have just ordered room service and spent the evening alone in her hotel room with a good book.

But it was too late for all of that. He spotted her and waved enthusiastically, side-stepping his way through the rows of chairs and patrons to cross the space between them. Within seconds, he and Mia were sidled up beside her at the bar and the introductions were being made.

"It's so nice to meet you!" Mia gushed in a way that somehow bolstered Lanying's confidence. "I can't believe you agreed to meet us," she continued, rolling her eyes. "I mean really, Thomas coming at you with that whole 'we have the same birthday' thing had to have been a little weird!"

"Definitely an interesting pick-up line," Lanying agreed, adjusting her position on the seat to make room for them to squeeze in beside her.

Thomas shook his head good-naturedly. "It wasn't a pick-up line! We all really do all have the same birthday!"

A look passed between the couple which could have been interpreted as seditious, but something compelled Lanying to trust them. "Thomas tells me finding people who share your birthday is something of a hobby for you."

"You're number four," Mia replied, motioning to the bartender for two drafts. "It's pretty strange meeting three people who share my birthday this year. Especially since before that I hadn't met any."

Lanying wondered if everyone from the US was so open and friendly. Her prior knowledge and personal assumptions regarding the country's cultural norms were based solely on characters from American movies. Thomas and Mia were the first Americans she'd ever actually interacted with on a personal level.

If people are so kind here, do overweight American children face the same bullying I endured?

She had so many questions but decided to keep them to herself, at least for the time being.

"Sharing a birthday is certainly coincidental," she said finally. "Although my grandfather always told me there are no coincidences in life."

The beers arrived and her words hung heavily in the space around them as Mia took her first sip. Obviously, she was missing something important about their meeting.

"It's funny you should say that," Thomas began, the cadence of his words carefully controlled so they rolled slowly off his lips. He glanced at Mia, and she gave him an almost imperceptible nod. "There's something we would like you to read, if you don't mind."

Lanying accepted the sheet of paper Thomas slid across the bar. The two obviously had an ulterior motive for meeting with her, but she found the realization didn't make her anxious. Only curious.

She began reading what was printed on the sheet of copy paper, collected from an 'Obscure Prophecies' website. She finished reading and then skimmed through it a second time.

An unexpected calm washed over her, and it was as if she was finally able to set down the millstone of questions she'd been carrying around her entire life.

Maybe there was a reason for her visions after all.

She glanced up. They were watching her expectantly.

"Is this for real?"

"We don't know for sure," Mia replied, biting nervously at the inside of her cheek, "but we've experienced some extraordinary events over the past few months, and we're growing more convinced every day."

Lanying considered the possibility there were other people in the world with abilities like hers. It wasn't a concept she'd ever really pondered, as she'd always been dismissive about her visions. Was it possible these strangers knew her secret? "Do you know any of the people this prophecy speaks about?" she asked them.

Thomas and Mia shared another knowing glance, and it was obvious they'd come to the bar having already established what they would and wouldn't share with her. "You're looking at two 'children of the light,'" he told her brightly. "Mia and I both possess abilities we consider gifts. And because you share our birthday, we were sort of hoping maybe you do too."

"Because, of course, that would be really amazing," Mia added. "And it would give credence to the prophecy itself."

Lanying set the paper on the bar and slid her drink to the side. She never imagined when she agreed to meet Thomas she would be confronted with something so utterly absurd — or strangely comforting. She'd been an outsider her entire life, never quite squeezing herself into the expectations of her culture. So to belong to something as important as this?

It was more than she could imagine.

It was more than she could have ever hoped for.

She heard her mother's voice, nagging somewhere in the far recesses of her mind, begging her to guard her secrets and walk away.

And then she stared into Thomas' eyes. The eyes which had been a part of her visions for more years than she could remember, and that's when she knew – there were no coincidences in life.

"I began having visions when I was four. At the time I didn't realize what they were or that other people didn't have them. I'd see people I knew grocery shopping or walking their dog, only I wasn't with them. I was at my house. Just sitting there, watching their lives from my bedroom floor. I didn't think it was strange to have these visions about what was happening to them, but when I had my first one about a person I didn't know – that's when I got scared. I remember calling to my mother from the kitchen where I was experiencing one while pouring myself a glass of juice. I asked her why anybody would whip a child with a belt."

She hesitated, taking a deep breath to compose herself. It had been a long time since she'd thought about that day. The day that stripped a layer of her childhood innocence, exposing her to the harsh reality of the world.

The first time she'd seen Thomas when he'd been just a boy.

Before she could continue, Mia placed a gentle hand on her wrist. "She didn't believe you when you told her, did she? About how you knew about such a thing?"

She cocked her head to the side and regarded Mia with the sort of compassion she herself had always hoped to elicit. They were kindred spirits in more ways than she'd imagined. Because it was clear she'd been doubted too.

"No. She didn't. In fact, she accused me of sneaking behind her back to watch television shows she didn't allow." She shook her head, tossing the memory aside. "Anyway, that was the last time I said anything to anyone besides by grandfather about what I see. Until you, here today."

"You never confided in anyone else? No friends?" Mia asked.

"There was no one to tell." She reflected on her immediate family – just her mother, father, maternal grandfather and paternal grandmother. With the exception of her grandfather, they were a conservative, serious assemblage whose minds were far too narrow to accept the possibility of her visions. And as for friends, there had never been anyone she trusted enough to share her confidence, especially after developing symptoms of PCOS. They hated her for being fat. She couldn't imagine what they would've done to her if they'd known she could hear what they were saying about her, even when she wasn't with them.

She saw tears pooling in the corner of Mia's eyes. "My mother actually left," Mia told her. "She didn't like that I was different. That I could see things she couldn't see. She was never able to accept me for who I was or forgive my father for embracing my gift. One day, she just never came home."

"That's awful."

She shrugged, hastily blotting her eyes with a paper napkin. "It's life."

"I'm still sorry for you, just the same. Everyone needs a mother."

They sat in silence for a long moment, each of them taking sips from their respective drinks. Lanying wondered if the others sensed the electricity pulsing between them.

"What is it that you can do?" she asked finally.

Mia brightened, the color returning to her face. "I see people's auras. Everyone is bathed in luminosity or shrouded in a dark cast. It shows me if their souls are good or evil."

It sounded crazy to Lanying, that Mia could look at someone and tell if they were good or bad. She supposed she knew now how her mother had felt all those years ago when she explained to her about the visions. Then she had another thought.

"And what do you see when you look at me?"

Mia smiled. "Radiant light."

She was surprised by the relief she felt from Mia's admission. Part of her had always wondered if her visions were more sinister than they appeared.

"And what about you?" she asked, turning her attention to Thomas.

He set down his beer and settled on the stool beside her. He seemed embarrassed by the question. "Well, unlike the two of you, I didn't consider myself gifted until Mia actually pointed it out when she started putting the pieces of this whole prophecy thing together earlier this year. I never thought my ability was anything more than run-of-the-mill intuition, but apparently, what I experience is anything but typical."

"He senses danger," Mia interrupted. "He can feel when bad things are about to happen."

"Do you see the bad thing happening?" Lanying asked. "Like my visions?"

"No," Thomas told her. "It's just this horrible sense of urgency. I can't ignore it. It causes actual physical pain if I try."

She saw Mia beaming at Thomas. It was obvious she cared deeply for him.

"There was this one night," Mia interjected again, "we were walking to the light rail after a ballgame at Camden Yards, and out of nowhere Thomas grabbed my hand and started dragging me in the opposite direction. He almost pulled my arm out of its socket!" She laughed, remembering the event. "I told him the station was the other way, but he refused to listen and told me to hurry up. He just kept saying 'We need to get out of here.' So anyway, we got about 50 feet from where we'd been standing when a knife fight breaks out between two fans over Lord knows what, but somehow Thomas knew it was about to happen. Their auras were both dimly lit, so even if I'd seen them, I probably wouldn't have given them a second thought." She nudged him now, playfully in the ribs with her elbow. "You kept us safe that night."

"I've kept you safe a lot of nights," he grinned.

Watching them together, Lanying felt the tiniest pang of jealousy, but more than that, she felt grateful. For the first time in her life, she was home.

CHAPTER

20

THOMAS

Sunday, September 11
Baltimore

Thomas couldn't sleep. He tossed and turned for the better part of two hours before finally giving in and getting up.

He wasn't typically an insomniac. Most nights he was asleep seconds after closing his eyes. But tonight all he could think about were Lanying's visions. More specifically, the visions she'd been having about him.

Listening to her recount the specific instances during which she'd observed him over the years was surreal. She was there when the audience gave him a standing ovation at his high school's talent show in eleventh grade. She'd been watching when he bussed his first table at Belinda's. She'd seen him mourning at his father's gravesite with Mildred on the day he was interred.

And she witnessed him riding in a police car alongside Kate on the way to rescue her sisters.

It disturbed him to think there was no way of knowing if he was actually by himself when he was alone. Recognizing now there was at least one person in the world who had the ability to see outside herself and into the lives of other people gave him pause. How many others were there?

It was little consolation that Lanying's intentions were pure because he couldn't be sure about anyone else's.

Thomas tiptoed past his mother's room, down the stairs into the homey kitchen, with its café curtains at the window and sprigs of basil and oregano growing out of empty soft drink cans on the sill. Dishes from last night's dinner were piled in the sink and he considered washing them, but then thought better of it, not wanting to wake Mildred. Instead, he fetched their shared laptop from where they stored it beneath the coffee table in the living room and booted it up at the kitchen table.

Lanying's confession about her visions was all the proof Mia needed to confirm the validity of the prophecy. And although he remained marginally skeptical, he also couldn't deny the strangeness of their situation.

Four people. Four psychic abilities.

Same birthday. Same city.

He sat staring at the Google landing page, not quite sure what search to attempt. He remained there, paralyzed, until his eyes became so unfocused the search engine's logo was merely a swath of colors on the white background of the screen.

Finally, he settled on the birthdate. It was really the only thing he had to go on.

As he scrolled through site after site of public records and genealogy reports, the graveness of their situation sat heavily upon his shoulders like an albatross he couldn't shake. It seemed as though somehow the prophecy was bringing the seven children of the light together. First Thomas and Mia. Then Kate. Now Lanying. If their paths were connecting, it only stood to reason the children of the dark were probably being pulled together too.

Thomas needed to find them before they found each other.

And then he needed to figure out a way to keep them apart.

Three hours later, as the first beam of morning sunlight crept slowly across the kitchen's floral papered walls, he pushed back from the table, bleary-eyed and exhausted. His preliminary search uncovered hundreds of people from all over the country, all born on his birthdate. Unfortunately, cross-referencing the people he discovered with the keyword "psychic abilities" hadn't yielded a single hit.

He was at a complete loss. If only the psychic community had a registry, he thought.

The digital clock on the microwave confirmed the need to temporarily abandon his search in order to make it to work at Belinda's. But instead of dragging himself into the shower, he called Mia.

"This is going to be impossible."

"What is?"

"Finding the bad psychics."

She chuckled. "You think?"

"You're better at this sort of thing than I am, with your job and all. I searched online for hours last night and found nada. I'm thinking you should probably take over."

"I might know a guy," she said.

"You always know a guy."

"No, really. When I was in seventh grade I reached out to this psychic guru guy – Les Joplin. I thought for sure he was gonna be a hoax because his name was all over the place. But it turned out he was legit. He helped me through a really rough patch, and we've stayed in contact all this time. He knows people. Lots of people. And I already sent him an email."

Thomas felt like an idiot, wasting an entire night spinning his wheels while Mia had already taken the driver's seat, as usual. Given the serious nature of their predicament however, he wasn't resentful. He was grateful.

"And?"

"And I haven't heard back yet. I just sent it yesterday morning. But I bet he'll have some leads for us."

"You're sure we can trust him?" He couldn't help thinking about scam artists like Madame Freakshow.

"I've never met him, so I've never seen his aura, but I've seen firsthand what he can do. And I can tell you I've only heard of him using his gift for good. So yeah, I trust him."

Thomas closed the laptop and made his way upstairs into the bathroom to get ready for the day. "What can he do?"

"Just like Haley Joel Osment in The Sixth Sense, he sees dead people." She paused, waiting for him to respond. "Thomas, I can hear you rolling your eyes."

"Seriously, Mia? Anything but that. Dead people? Lie to me if you have to." He turned on the shower, knowing it would take a few minutes for the water to warm up.

"I'm not gonna lie to you. I swear, he's the real deal. He's helped hundreds of people and works closely with the FBI, tracking down missing persons and helping them solve murders. He was offered one of those reality TV shows, and he turned it down. He's not a fame-monger. He's just trying to use his gift to make the world a better place."

Thomas knew he needed to squelch his skepticism. Clearly, their options were limited. They'd have to use any resource they could find.

"Okay," he said finally, "call me if you hear from him. And Mia?" He hesitated then, reaching his hand behind the shower curtain to test the temperature of the water streaming out of the showerhead. "One way or another, we're totally going to find them."

"That's my man," she said, and he could hear the smile in her voice. "Cautiously optimistic." And then she disconnected.

CHAPTER

21

PATRICK

Thursday, September 15
London

There was nothing Patrick hated more than waiting. Except maybe being let down by the people he relied on. On this day, he was dealing with both.

It had been several days since he and Wesley had discussed the pressing matter of interpreting Eshanti's landscapes, and despite repeated phone calls and emails, the slacker hadn't seen fit to drag himself away from his most recent harlot to respond. Now Patrick saw no other option but to fly directly to Wesley's French chateau to deliver the paintings himself.

He pressed the call button on his desk and his assistant appeared in the doorway of his office.

"Find out how quickly Desmond can have the chopper ready to take me to Cote d'Azur."

"Yes, sir. Right away."

"And reschedule any afternoon meetings until tomorrow, since it seems as though I'm going to be forced to spend today sitting over Wesley like a school proctor to assure he finishes what's required of him."

"Yes, sir. But what about your 2 o'clock phone call with the Forces Nouvelles leader. You've put him off twice already, and if you recall, he wasn't happy the last time."

She was right. His relationship with the diamond smuggler was shaky at best, making it all the more necessary to take the call. After the UN Security council banned all diamond exports from the Ivory Coast, it had become one of his most profitable trafficking operations. He couldn't afford to lose his shipping route to the international trading centers via the Forces Nouvelles controlled section of the country.

"Make sure Rawlings installs a secured satellite connection before takeoff. I'll take the call from the air."

"Right away," she agreed before ducking out of the office.

Patrick went to great lengths to secure his illicit deals and back-alley investment opportunities, and having established his vast empire on the backs of insignificant men, there was no way he was going to allow the light psychics to overthrow his destiny. He knew, without a shadow of a doubt, if they were allowed to congregate first, his wealth would immediately disappear. It was no wonder finding the seventh dark psychic was his primary mission.

However, despite the pressing nature of the prophecy, he also understood the necessity of keeping his poker in the proverbial flame. In addition to his extremely profitable human trafficking ring and diamond smuggling operation, he also blackmailed lobbyists and many of the world's most powerful leaders, controlled significant portions of the Middle Eastern oil fields, and had widespread influence among many of Central America's drug cartels. He was able to establish and maintain all of his relationships using his ability to view events and other people's thoughts and feelings via the astral plane.

To that end and in anticipation of his afternoon trip, he retreated now to his meditation room, a small alcove hidden behind a moveable bookcase just beyond the sightline of the door. He pressed the button under his desk which simultaneously locked the door to his office and slid the bookcase aside, revealing the meditation chamber within.

The room itself was small and far less ornate than his public spaces. The walls were painted a charcoal grey and were bare save for a single framed print which read: 'Don't let what other people think of you stop you from doing the things you love.' It was one of his favorites. A simple reminder about staying true to himself from one of the few men he deeply admired, Adolf Hitler. He read the text now and smiled unabashedly, knowing he would eventually achieve the sort of greatness his mentor was never able to attain. And he would do so by focusing on that which he loved the most.

Turning people against one another for his own profit.

As was his ritual, he settled himself into the upholstered armchair in the center of the room, resting his feet on the accompanying settee. For simple musings, he could access the astral plane on the fly, but for more complicated matters, he found it was best to find a more solitary location. He closed his eyes and allowed his mind to wander, separating his true self from his physical self. Once his consciousness was no longer tethered to the earth by his body, he was allowed to roam along the astral plane, searching for markers indicating the presence of disturbances he could exploit for his personal gain.

Today he was looking for markers which indicated specific points of unrest between the rebel Forces Nouvelles leaders in the north and the French Foreign Legion in the south. Before his afternoon phone conversation with his Forces Nouvelles liaison, Bourou Ouamarra, Patrick needed to find out if they had any inkling of his surreptitious relationship with the French, as he had been pitting them against one another for several months, acting as a double agent while safely smuggling his diamonds across the Ivory Coast's border.

Deep in meditation, he found Ouamarra easily, the man's confidence standing out against the fear and anger of those around him. He reached out, searching the man's mind for unfavorable opinions about him, but was pleased to discover only amicable thoughts. In fact, Ouamarra was actually nervous about speaking with him because of a possible breach in the supply route – a breach Patrick was already aware of.

Satisfied with his findings, he sought out one of his contacts from the French Foreign Legion and connected quickly with Lieutenant Taché. A no-nonsense patriot, he'd never doubted Patrick's contrived loyalty to their mission of Muslim suppression or suspected that Patrick's only allegiance was to himself. After passing himself off as a Christian sympathizer, he'd convinced the Lieutenant he could supply intel on the rebels' strategies, which he did to a certain extent. Now, as he searched the man's mind, he was satisfied with the state of their alliance.

Coming out of the meditative trance-like state, Patrick took several minutes to compose himself, adjusting his tie and straightening the laces on his Stefano Beyer camel calfskin shoes. Satisfied his affairs in the Ivory Coast were under control, he turned his attention back to the more pressing task at hand.

Finding Number Seven.

CHAPTER

22

WESLEY

Thursday, September 15
Cote d'Azur

Wesley was 30 minutes into a 60-minute four-hand hot stone massage when the doorbell rang. Earlier in the day he'd seen Patrick's arrival in his mirror but had been unable to deduce just when the man would be arriving.

"Of course," Wesley muttered under his breath, waving the masseuses away. "He couldn't have shown up just an hour later."

By the time Wesley showered and changed, Patrick's irritation was palpable as he greeted him in the front sitting room of his 12,000-square-foot estate.

"Your timing is impeccable as always," he said to Patrick as he shook the man's hand, taking the seat beside him. "I assume you're here about Eshanti's drawings."

Wesley had, of course, already looked at the landscapes. Days ago in fact. Had he gleaned any insight, he certainly would have contacted Patrick immediately, but as there was nothing of consequence in the images, he'd remained aloof, a sort of experiment to see just how long Patrick could last before showing up at his doorstep for answers.

He'd lasted longer than Wesley expected.

"I don't like having to take time out of my day to come hunt you down," Patrick scolded. "I wouldn't have sent them to you if I didn't think it was important. I need you to go look at them now."

Wesley loved toying with the man. He loved toying with everyone. Pushing people's buttons was what he did best and it gave him great satisfaction.

"Sure," he said, jovially. "Let's go look at them now."

He led Patrick through a maze of lavishly furnished rooms and corridors into his study. He certainly didn't mind that one of the perks of being part of 'Patrick's Prophecy' was that the billionaire supported the other dark psychics, providing an endless supply of funding to assure both their safety and their comfort. His life was now a far cry from the carnival circuit he'd been plucked from several years ago.

"Here they are," Wesley said, gesturing toward a stack of canvases leaning against a mirrored wall.

He watched as Patrick crouched down and began sorting through them, running his hands across the rough splays of dried paint as if he too had the power to harness their energies.

"This is all of them?" he asked at last.

Wesley nodded.

"They're all landscapes."

"Yeah. Eshanti said that from the beginning." He couldn't resist the urge to pick at Patrick's psyche. "You know, she's been wrong before. And not everything she creates has to do with the prophecy. You get that, right?"

"Don't be insolent," Patrick warned, returning to his feet. "The Amazonian landscape helped lead us to Akantha. There's no reason this won't do the same."

Wesley saw the desperation on Patrick's face and thought it comical. Although he too was looking forward to ushering in the age of darkness, he lacked Patrick's urgency. He was certain everything would all work out in the end. It always had for him.

Patrick pointed at the mirrored wall. "Go ahead then," he said.

Earlier in the day when he'd seen Patrick's impending arrival, Wesley decided he would put on a show for his associate, just like he'd enjoyed doing during his carnival days. As Patrick looked on, he made a great production of setting out the canvases in a tidy row against the wall. When he was satisfied with their placement, he took several steps back, centered himself in front of the mirror, and began staring into its depths, training his unfocused eyes somewhere beyond the confines of the room.

Wesley hadn't always been the brute of a man he eventually became. As a child, he was small. Elf-like even, with large pointed ears which earned him the nickname 'Bilby' after the small, nocturnal rodent frequently seen in the Australian desert. He'd grown up in Broken Hill, in the arid lands of far-western New South Wales. Originally established as a mining town, the Broken Hill of Wesley's youth consisted of mostly sheep herding families and pub owners, of which his family was the latter.

His father, Wesley Sr., ran the pub at the West Darling Hotel, and Wesley attended second grade at the Broken Hill Public School, a short walk down the street. With little interest in academics, he spent most of his days avoiding the heckling of his peers as well as the consternation of his teachers. Toward the end of the school year, he discovered a hole in the playground fence, just large enough to squeeze through if he crawled low on his belly, and he began ditching his afternoon classes in favor of hiding out in the alley behind his father's pub. There, he retreated into his imagination, setting up kingdoms of knights and serfs using beer cans and bottle caps he found lying around the dumpster. It was peaceful and no one made fun of him for his ears or being small or not knowing his subtraction facts.

That was until the day they found him, three of the worst offenders, after school on their way to O'Neil Park.

He'd heard them coming down the alley, their sneakers pounding on the packed gravel, leaving a trail of dust billowing in their wake, but they were upon him before he could skitter completely behind the closest dumpster.

They'd spotted him trying to hide.

"Hey, Bilby!" the biggest boy, Hudson, shouted as they approached. "You been hidin' out in the dumpster like a bilby in a burrow?"

They all laughed, not waiting for Wesley to reply.

The second bully, Luke, took a step closer and kicked at Wesley's shins with the toe of his sneaker. "Hide in a hole, little Bilby," he teased.

Out of the corner of his eye, Wesley spotted a long-neck bottle of Tooheys he'd been using as the monarch of his imaginary kingdom. There was something unusual moving behind the glass, however, and although he was certain it wasn't the case, there appeared to be a sort of milky liquid inside. It began to swirl around and an instant later an image appeared in the glass.

An image of Wesley lacerating Luke with the jagged edge of the very same bottle.

He blinked once. Twice. The rage building inside him as the boys' torments continued. The vision in the glass persisted, as if to encourage him into action.

Luke struck Wesley's shin with a powerful kick. "Why ya lookin' so scared, little Bilby? You gonna cry? Huh? Hey, Hudson, check it out. The little Bilby's gonna cry."

Luke turned toward the others for a split second, but it was long enough for Wesley to grab the bottle, smash the bottom against the side of the dumpster, and embed the serrated neck into the meaty flesh of the boy's thigh.

As Luke let loose an agonizing scream and the other two dispersed, Wesley felt the relief of a job well done wash over him. He picked up a broken fragment of the bottle from the ground beside him and saw someone smiling at him. It took him a moment to realize the image was merely a reflection of his own face, and he laughed at the absurdity of it all.

And then, as Luke's cries began to draw the attention of the pub's kitchen staff, Wesley slipped the piece of glass into his pocket and scurried around the corner like the good bilby he was, confident in the knowledge the boys would never bother him again.

"Please tell me you saw something I didn't," Patrick said as the image of the snow-covered mountain faded from the mirror.

Wesley shook his head. "Nada. Nothing but mountains and trees and more mountains. Not a single soul. Not a single indication of where the mountains are located. They could be anywhere."

"Well, that's something then," Patrick said. He was pacing now. "Since there were no people, we know the location is remote. We know whoever these renderings are leading us to is probably not in any of our databases."

"Maybe they're just paintings," Wesley offered. "Maybe they're not leading us to anybody."

Patrick narrowed his eyes and Wesley knew he'd gotten under his skin yet again. It was almost too easy.

"Are we done here?" Wesley asked casually as he gathered the paintings and restacked them in the corner of the room. "Or would you like to stay for dinner?"

Patrick huffed. "I have business to attend to this evening," he said condescendingly. "But don't let me trouble you further. I'll see myself out."

Wesley watched him disappear down the hallway and once he was out of sight, pulled the well-worn shard of glass from the bottle of Tooheys out of his pocket. He gazed into it, looking past his own reflection to an image of the future.

Another time.

Another bully.

Only this time Wesley wouldn't just harm the bully. This time he would kill him.

CHAPTER

23

LANYING

Saturday, September 17
Baltimore

Lanying stood at the edge of the harbor with the toes of her ballet flats hanging over the edge of the concrete. The water lapped the manmade seawall several feet below, and she watched as an empty Coke bottle bobbed on the surface. While she waited, the mouth of the bottle dipped below the surface and as the water began to flood inside, the rest of the bottle disappeared into the murky depths.

Two young girls with matching braids darted past, closely followed by their parents who called for them to 'slow down' and 'watch out for other people' as they nearly knocked over a couple holding hands in front of the aquarium. She scanned the Inner Harbor's crowded retail district for a third time, searching for Thomas and Mia. It was her last night in the city, and her flight back to China was scheduled to depart from BWI first thing in the morning. Over a crowd of spectators watching a juggling street performer, she spotted Thomas' sandy blond hair. Perpetually fearful of being stood up, relief washed over her as they drew closer, and she waved furiously in their direction until they saw her.

"The smell of those crabs is about to send me over the edge," Mia was telling Thomas as they approached. Then she turned her attention to Lanying and leaned in to give her a hug. "I'm so glad we're getting to see you again before you have to go home tomorrow," she said. "So tonight, we are gonna show you what living in Baltimore is all about."

By way of greeting, Thomas wrapped his arms around her as well. This caused her to feel somewhat uncomfortable, as she had never been touched by a man in such an intimate way before. It seemed perfectly normal to him though. "How was the conference?" he asked.

As they began strolling together toward Phillips Seafood, she filled them in on her week. "I learned so much and met a lot of nice people from all over the world. My favorite speaker was on Wednesday afternoon, Dr. Marlene Vance from Johns Hopkins. She had a lot of valuable insight into how I can help my clients establish reasonable, attainable goals for themselves. She also spoke a lot about the psychological side of obesity which we are just now starting to understand in China. It was absolutely fascinating."

"What exactly are you planning to do with your degree when you graduate?" Mia asked.

"It's my dream to be a counselor for overweight teens. There's a lot of defamation associated with being overweight in my country. It's quite difficult for young people to endure."

Thomas asked, "A lot of bullying?"

She nodded. "It's actually something that's encouraged in my culture. It's perfectly acceptable to shame someone for being overweight."

"That's awful," Mia said.

They arrived at the restaurant to find a mob of patrons milling about the entrance, waiting to be seated. Mia threaded her way through the crowd to where the hostess was standing with her tablet just outside the door to inquire about their reservation. A moment later she was calling for them to join her, and to Lanying's surprise, they were taken back to their table immediately.

"Being the police chief's daughter has its privileges," Mia whispered as they followed the hostess through the restaurant.

After ordering mini crab cakes and a round of drinks to start, Lanying settled into the evening, enjoying the playful banter between her new friends.

"There's no such thing as too much Old Bay," Mia was arguing with Thomas. "You can't ruin something by being too 'heavy handed.' It just isn't a thing."

"When I can't feel my lips after a meal, that's too much," he countered. "Remember the time your lips got all shriveled up when we had steamed crabs with your dad? I told you you should have washed some of that seasoning off."

Mia turned to face Lanying. "Don't listen to him. When those crab cakes come, you're gonna want to add extra Old Bay. Trust me on this. There's no other way to eat them."

As it turned out, Mia was right. The spicy heat of the seasoning was the perfect complement to the sweet, flakiness of the crab. There was very little conversation as the three devoured the appetizer.

In the lull before the main meal was brought out, Lanying decided to broach a discussion about the prophecy. During her free time at the conference, she'd spent time exploring more about it online. It was important for her to learn as much as she could about the topic before returning to China since the government censored much of what citizens were able to see over the World Wide Web. Certainly sites regarding psychic prophecies had the potential for being banned.

"I spent some time reading about the Sevens Prophecy this week," she began. "And I'd like to discuss its implications a bit more with you before I have to leave."

Thomas swallowed his last bite of crab cake. "Just because you're leaving doesn't mean we're never going to talk to you again. I think it's a fair assumption that you aren't getting rid of us that easily. Especially if we're bound by the prophecy."

"Yeah," Mia chimed in. "We have Skype and Facetime so I'm sure we're going to be seeing a lot of each other. But let's definitely chat about it now. What'd you want to know?"

Ever since she'd arrived in the states, and especially since meeting Thomas in the hotel lobby her first night, she couldn't shake the sense that she was right where she belonged. And when Mia and Thomas shared their insight about the prophecy and her probable link to its long-term effect on the world, the feeling only strengthened. This call to stay was counterintuitive to the reason for her visit in the first place, which was of course to learn how to better counsel her clientele back at home. It was ridiculous to imagine she could remain in the states while fulfilling her dream of becoming a certified obesity counselor in China.

"I must be honest with you both. When I think about leaving, about going back to China, I feel a pain in my heart. A physical ache. It's something I can't describe and something I have never felt before. Perhaps it's the power described in the prophecy which compels me to stay. And perhaps I should try to find a way, at least until the other four light psychics are called to meet us as well. I could apply for an education visa, at the very least. It might buy us some time."

Thomas took an uncomfortable sip of his Coke while Mia folded and refolded the paper napkin in her lap. "You wanna tell her or should I?" he said.

Mia lifted her chin and met his gaze, an unspoken gesture for him to go on.

"You're actually the fourth light psychic who's been drawn here to Baltimore."

"That's what you said the other night," Lanying interrupted, clapping her hands to her chest. "Do you think we could meet?"

"I'm afraid not," Mia explained, sadness pinching the lines of her face. "She passed away. Earlier this year. Before we really got a chance to know her."

She saw Thomas reach under the table, giving Mia's knee a gentle squeeze.

Mindful that there were moments in life when there was nothing appropriate to say, "I'm sorry," was all she managed.

Before either could respond, the waitress delivered their meals and the trio began picking at their food in uncomfortable silence. As she swallowed each bite of her Chesapeake fish and chips, she couldn't shake the feeling there was something she was missing. And then it hit her.

"If one of the seven of us is dead, the dark psychics will gather before us." She hesitated, following her thought through to its miserable conclusion. "We have no chance of saving the world."

Thomas set down his fork and wiped the sauce from his crab mac and cheese off the corners of his mouth. "We thought the same thing at first. But then we realized there's still hope."

"Hope for saving the world?"

Mia chimed in. "Hope for keeping the dark psychics from ushering in the age of the seven deadly sins."

"I don't understand."

He took another bite of macaroni. "Mia and I have already begun searching for the seven other psychics born on our birthday who are part of the dark side of the prophecy. We're hoping if we can find them before they find each other, maybe we stand a chance of keeping them apart, thereby negating the prophecy altogether."

Lanying brightened. "Who else have you found?"

"No one yet. We've only recently gotten our hands on a list of known psychics, and we've been slowly going through the list, searching for the ones who share our birthday."

"Can I help?"

Mia nodded enthusiastically. "That'd be fantastic. If you want I can email you part of the list and you can start going through it, assuming you'll have viable web access back in China."

"I don't know if I will, but I can certainly try."

"That's good enough for us," Thomas smiled.

The sun had set by the time they emerged from the restaurant into the pungent, warm city air. Twinkle lights illuminated the path around the harbor, leading in one direction toward Harborplace, the USS Constellation, and the Maryland Science Center, and in the other direction to Fells Point.

"You have karaoke in China?" Mia asked Lanying as they strolled along the promenade.

"Yes," she admitted, "but I've never done it before."

Schoolyard grins passed between Thomas and Mia. "I told Jack and Stella we'd meet them at Max's Taphouse between nine and ten." She checked her phone for the time, then turned to Lanying. "It's not that far a walk if you're up for it."

Gazing across the busy harbor with its dinner cruises and water taxis, she realized for the first time in her life she was about to enjoy a night out with people who genuinely liked her, despite her size or shape. Ostracized and avoided for so many years, the excitement of being included in an activity some would consider banal thrilled her to no end. A karaoke bar with friends? It was almost as if she'd been waiting her whole life for this one opportunity to arise, and there was no way she wasn't tagging along.

She crossed her purse strap over her chest and tucked a stray wisp of hair behind her ear. "You think they have Billy Joel?" she asked.

"*Piano Man*, here we come!" Mia replied, linking arms with her as they headed into the night.

CHAPTER

24

JOSE

Saturday, September 17 – Friday, September 23
Phoenix

Coercing Andrea into the line at the airport security check had been a bit like shoving an introvert onto the stage at Carnegie Hall. It had taken fifteen minutes of encouragement to remind her that escaping to Baltimore was not only necessary, but also in her best interest. He'd watched from his obstructed vantage point behind the partition as she lowered her hands from above her head in the x-ray scanner and began dragging her borrowed rolling carry-on into the terminal. He felt a pang of disappointment at their parting, but just before she was completely out of sight, she'd stopped abruptly and turned around, as if motioning one final goodbye to him was something of an afterthought. She seemed surprised to discover he was still standing there, watching her. She held up her free hand and touched her fingers to her lips, blowing him a chaste kiss before rounding the corner and disappearing from view.

Jose drove directly from the airport to the police station. Along the short route, he'd imagined Andrea's new life in Baltimore with Carla – how under his aunt's careful tutelage, she'd progress toward independence while building the confidence she'd need to sustain life on her own when it was safe for her to return home to Arizona. He'd turned the radio up a little louder and began singing along, pleased with himself for the work he'd done on her behalf.

His life wasn't full of worldly treasures, but it was certainly rewarding. All the academic degrees in the world couldn't buy the satisfaction which came from being someone's cure. He was certain, once he slipped the final cog into place by presenting the police with Andrea's statement and the dirt he'd dug up on Alejandro in the community, with any luck, an arrest, trial, and sentencing wouldn't be far behind.

Now, a week later, his phone buzzed in his pocket while he was mopping an examination bay floor at the end of a particularly harrowing overnight shift. The number on the screen was unfamiliar.

"This is Jose."

"Mr. Torres, this is Lieutenant Westin with the PPD. Is this a good time to talk? I have some information regarding your friend's case."

Jose peeked out from behind the drawn curtain to see if any other staff was around, and when he saw he was alone, darted into an adjacent room and closed the door.

"Uh, yeah. It's a good time." His heart fluttered nervously inside his chest. "Did you make an arrest?"

Westin sighed deeply, and Jose could feel the weight of his disappointment across the line before he ever spoke. "I'm afraid not."

"Do you need more information from me?" he interrupted.

The officer cleared his throat. "No. What you provided was more than enough for an arrest warrant. Now the problem is we simply can't find him to issue the arrest."

Jose couldn't imagine why the Lieutenant was taking time out of his day to let him know they couldn't find Alejandro. "But you're still looking, right?"

"Of course. Of course. But we've tracked just about every lead we had, so now I'm calling you."

Their conversation wasn't boosting Jose's confidence. "I already told you everything I know about the guy. I didn't leave anything out, I swear."

"Oh, yes, I understand. It's just that we were hoping perhaps we could speak with Ms. Morillo directly. Maybe she knows a place he might hide if he thought the police were after him."

A small bubble of anger rose to the surface. He knew he shouldn't be upset because, of course, the police were doing their best, but he couldn't help feeling as if he might have done a better job of finding Alejandro himself. "Why would he think you were after him? Did you spook him? Did you tell other gang members you were looking for him?"

"Mr. Torres, I'm not at liberty to discuss all the details of the case." The officer's sudden annoyance was palpable. "We do what we have to do to get the job done. What I need from you now is Ms. Morillo's contact information."

Jose considered how Andrea would react to being contacted by the police. He knew it was a lead they should follow, given the police department's lack of progress, but he thought perhaps she would be more willing to share what she knew with him, instead of the Lieutenant.

"I think it might be better if I spoke with her first," he explained. "I'll see what I can get out of her and call you if she gives me anything."

He could hear the officer drumming his pencil against a hard surface while he deliberated. "You think she'll tell you if she knows anything?"

"She'll tell me before she tells you," Jose countered.

The Lieutenant grunted. "Mr. Torres, let me remind you, we're on the same side here. This isn't a competition." He paused for a beat. "But if you feel like you can get something out of her, I'll let you try first. The only condition is I need you to speak with her right away. No time like the present. I expect to hear back from you in the next half hour. You have my direct number?"

Jose suddenly realized he would be the one who would have to admit to Andrea that Alejandro was still roaming the streets. A pinpoint of pain radiated behind his left temple.

"I have your number. I'll call you as soon as I speak to her."

"You have 30 minutes," the officer reminded Jose, his voice rife with authority.

Then the line disconnected.

Jose cautiously opened the door to the examination room where he'd been hiding to be sure it was still a safe place to talk. Gloria was wheeling a patient toward the elevator bay in the opposite direction, but otherwise, the hallway was deserted, so he ducked back into the room and shut the door.

Andrea answered, breathlessly, on the fourth ring.

"Hey," she puffed into the phone. "What's up?"

He was slightly taken aback by her uncharacteristically easygoing demeanor. Was it possible being in Baltimore was already having a positive effect?

"What are you doing?" he asked.

"I'm at a support group meeting with Carla. When I saw your number, I ran outside to take your call." She laughed. "And for the record, you have good timing. This girl Latoya's been running her mouth for the last 20 minutes about 'Terrell this and Terrell that.' Lord knows I could use a break." Her breathing had steadied. "So really, what's up?"

He wished he could report that her abuser was safely behind bars. But, of course, that would be a lie. He would have to tell her the truth, and he honestly didn't know whether she was going to be disappointed or relieved. He took a deep breath. There was only one way to find out.

"I just got a call from the officer in charge of your case, and they can't find Alejandro. They wanted me to call you to find out if you might know where he could be hiding out."

His account was met with silence. He didn't know what else to say.

"*Do* you know where he might be hiding out?" he continued, hoping to elicit a response.

"Jose?" Her voice was small, like a timid child speaking to a stranger.

"Yeah?"

"Promise you won't be mad at me."

Immediately his mind began to run wild, imagining the worst possible scenarios. What had she done? What did she know?

"I promise," he told her, although he knew it may be an impossible assurance to keep.

Andrea blew into the phone. "I called him," she said. "The first day I got here. Just to let him know it was really over. That I didn't want him looking for me because I didn't want to be found."

"You did what?" Jose exploded. He couldn't believe what he was hearing. "After all the precautions I took to keep you safe? That would be crazy stupid, you know that, right? Please tell me you're kidding!"

"I'm so sorry, Jose," she wept. "I thought I was being super careful. I used my cell phone, not a landline, so I assumed he wouldn't be able to use caller ID to figure out where I am."

Jose imagined Alejandro already halfway across the country. "Is there any chance he installed spyware on your cell?"

She hesitated. "I don't know what that is."

"Did he ever have access to your phone while you weren't around? If he installed a spyware program it could allow him to trace where your call originated from."

"Wait a minute. Are you some sort of hacker? How do you know this stuff?"

"Jesus, no. I'm not a hacker or anything like that. I just have this buddy who's into breaking codes, and I've heard him talk." His frustration with her was growing. "Stop changing the subject and be honest with me – do you think it's possible he put a tracker on your phone?"

"Maybe? You're making me really scared, Jose."

He considered the potential danger she and his aunt were now in. If her jealous, abusive boyfriend was on his way to Maryland, Jose needed to be on his way as well.

"Do you think he'd come looking for you there?"

"I don't know. If he was angry enough, I guess."

He was already moving toward the break room to collect his things and clock out early. And although he already knew what she would tell him, he ventured one final question.

"And just how angry was he when you told him it was over?"

A whimper, barely audible across the line, escaped Andrea's lips. "He told me it'd be better if I was dead than gone," she confessed in a whisper. "Oh, God, Jose. He's coming for me, isn't he?"

CHAPTER

25

LANYING

Sunday, September 18
Shanghai

Lanying's trip home to Shanghai had been uneventful, which was to say, all of her connections had gone smoothly, and she hadn't spoken to a single soul, save the ticketing agents and flight attendants who delivered her microwaved pasta and cranberry juice, no ice. At the arrivals exit, there were no friends or family members waiting curbside to pick her up, and although she hadn't expected to see anyone, it was still disappointing to take the metro and a taxi home alone instead.

It was close to 6pm by the time she stumbled through the door of her family's modest high rise apartment, located in the city's Minhang district. A sprawling suburbia with over two and a half million people clamoring about, she met only silence as she set her bag on the foyer's tile floor.

"Mother?" she called. "Father?"

"They're out for the night at some charity event." Her grandfather's voice was feeble, and she followed it down the hall. Light from his television seeped out from beneath his bedroom door, and she inched it opened to peer inside.

"How was your trip, Granddaughter?"

He patted the space beside him, an invitation to join him on the bed, and she could see the diminishing outline of his frame beneath the wool blanket. Even after moving in with her family the year before, her grandfather's health had steadily declined. As she gazed upon him now, the sunken hollows of his eyes suggested he would not be with them for much longer, and her heart ached.

"It was nice," she told him. "Lovely, in fact. I learned a lot at the conference."

He took her hand, holding it between his own. "And what of the United States? How did you find it?"

Knowing he would ask on her return, she'd taken many photographs of Baltimore to share with him, but given her newly discovered knowledge of the prophecy, she had no desire to bore him with details of the cityscape.

"I made some American friends," she told him conspiratorially, because this was always how she spoke with him. "Their names are Mia and Thomas."

"Part of your conference?"

She grinned and squeezed his hand. "No. He's a musical protégé, studying to become an instructor, and she's a police officer." She went on to tell him about their unusual meeting and then fished a folded sheet of paper from the pocket of her jeans. "They gave me this," she said, handing it to him. "I'd like you to tell me what you think."

He straightened himself against the wedge of pillows propped behind his back and plucked his glasses from the nightstand while Lanying switched on the overhead light. She watched as his eyes scanned the paper, darting from left to right and back again, and wondered what his reaction to the prophecy would be.

The moment Mia revealed it to her, she had known her grandfather would be the first, and only, person she would share it with. Their relationship was such that there had never been any secrets between them. During her childhood, when others called her names and crushed her spirit, her grandfather provided a safe haven. He was the person she confided in when no one else cared to listen, much less to understand.

In less time than it should have taken to read the prophecy in its entirety, he laid the paper on his lap and slid his glasses to the tip of his nose in order to see her properly. "The Sevens Prophecy," he said simply. "So now you know."

The look on his face did not betray him, as it was neither joyful nor angry nor amused, and this cryptic response confused her.

"The prophecy, yes. But Grandfather, did you know about the prophecy as well? Before reading the paper?"

The air felt heavy in her lungs, and she thought perhaps her grandfather felt it too, because it seemed as though it was taking a great effort for him to speak. Finally, he said, "This prophecy, printed here on this crisp white sheet by a modern laser printer, may seem as though it is fresh and new. And it is understandable that it feels that way to you. But I assure you, Lanying, the prediction you carry with you now has been carried for millennia – by word of mouth, on scraps of parchment, and in ancient texts. It has been cast aside by theologians. Revered by soothsayers. Discounted, abolished, canonized, and sanctified. Some say it is the will of a benevolent force. Others the work of Satan."

"And you?" she interrupted.

The tiniest hint of a smile played on his lips. "Does it matter?"

"Of course. I've only shown it to you in the hopes of garnering your opinion."

He took her hand between his, and she could feel the fragility of his skin against her own. "If you know yourself as I know you, you must admit now that regardless of what I say about this prophecy, your mind is already set."

It was a true and jarring admission, realizing the depth of his understanding as she recalled the sense of peace which accompanied her first reading of the text. If she'd already committed to belief, why *had* she sought his counsel?

Of course the answer was that she didn't want his opinion, she wanted his approval. Needed his approval. But for what exactly?

"What if I am one of the seven?"

His expression shifted and his dispassion was replaced by rapt curiosity. "What would make you believe that you are?"

"Mia and Thomas have psychic abilities as well, and what's even stranger is they share my birthday. They've come to believe they are part of the prophecy. They're hopeful I may be as well."

His hand tightened around hers and he studied her face, as if he was searching for something hidden within her features he'd never seen before. "Is it possible?" he said, more to himself than to her, tears welling in his eyes. "My own granddaughter's been part of the prophecy all along?"

Suddenly the weight of knowing, of understanding, collapsed upon her from atop the scaffolding she'd carefully constructed to hold the admission at bay. Because, of course, it was absurd. Ludicrous. Who in their right mind would believe a group of psychics living in the twenty-first century would stop an impending apocalypse? It was too ridiculous to consider, and yet, her grandfather, the person she admired most in the world, had not dismissed it. Instead, it seemed as though he was confirming her suspicions.

He chuckled softly and shook his head, obviously still reeling from Lanying's revelation. "I don't know how I didn't see it. Some keeper I turned out to be."

"Without knowledge of the common birthday, how were you to guess? The birthday was what tipped them off about both me and the other girl they found as well."

His eyes widened. "A fourth?"

"Yes. A fourth, but she recently passed away."

For the first time in the course of their bizarre conversation, her grandfather flinched. "And she's one of the seven light?"

"Yes. That is what they said. She died earlier this year."

He began twisting then, maneuvering himself from beneath the blankets until his feet appeared along the side of the bed. With great effort, he hoisted himself from the mattress into what almost passed as an upright position.

"Grandfather?" she asked, but he ignored her as he shuffled across the room to where his black lacquered trunk stood beneath the window. He crouched beside it, and the bronze hinges creaked as he wrestled open the lid. After several moments, he came up with the item he'd been searching for – an intricately carved wooden box with his name, Feng Manchu, etched in the top. He returned to the bed, collapsing under the weight of his activity and handed it to Lanying.

"I should have given this to you long ago. I've suspected for many years the time was drawing near for the prophecy to be fulfilled and with the strength of your abilities, it shouldn't surprise me that you, my granddaughter, are one of the seven. I hope and pray though that the others are wrong about the one who passed away. She must not be one of you. She cannot be. For if she is, then all may be lost."

CHAPTER
26

JOSE

Saturday, September 24
Baltimore

Without giving it a second thought, Jose emptied what little remained in the savings account he opened when he was eleven and bought a ticket for the first direct flight out of Phoenix into Baltimore. After assuring him she would destroy her phone, Andrea and his aunt booked a room at a nearby motel and went immediately to the police. They were still at the BPD headquarters on Fayette Street when Jose arrived later that afternoon.

He'd never been so happy to see two people before in his life.

"Hi," Andrea said meekly, rising to greet him as he rushed into the waiting room.

He gathered her into his arms, shuddering when he realized just how desperate he'd been to see her with his own eyes. Alive and well.

"Hi, Aunt Carla," he said, leaving Andrea's side to embrace the woman he hadn't seen in over a decade. "It's good to see you again."

"Good to see you," she replied, holding him at arm's length to give him a once over. "Look how you've grown. Into an honest to goodness man."

"Yes, Ma'am," he smiled. His eyes cut to Andrea and then back to his aunt. "Sorry I got you into all this mess."

She shook her head, resigned, and slouched back into the metal folding chair. "Ni modo, así es la vida. I just hope they find the bastard before he finds us."

He lowered himself into the empty seat beside Andrea to wait with them for the officers assigned to their case. "How long have you been here?"

Carla glanced at the clock on the opposite wall above the reception window. "About an hour. Apparently they already assigned officers to our case before we got here. The guys searching for Alejandro in Phoenix must have already gotten up with the people here. That's why they wouldn't let us just talk to the next available cops. We have to wait for the ones who've already been assigned to the case. At least that's what they told us."

"That makes sense." He turned to Andrea. "What about you? How're you holding up?"

She looked small. Smaller than she'd ever seemed before. There was no doubt she was genuinely fearful.

"I'm okay," she muttered, chin in her chest. "I feel like an idiot."

He wrapped an arm around her shoulders because it seemed like the right thing to do. He was relieved when instead of pulling away, her muscles relaxed and she sunk into him. "Don't beat yourself up. You're safe now. And according to the guys I've been talking to in Phoenix, when he turns up, they've got enough evidence against him to make sure he never has a chance to hurt you again."

"*If* he turns up," she said.

He didn't like thinking about the possibility that Alejandro would find Andrea before the cops found him. As he sat stewing about it, two officers, a man and a woman approached them from the interior of the station.

"Andrea Morillo?" the man asked.

"Yes?"

"I'm Officer Anderson and this is Officer Rosetti. We were contacted by the PPD and have been assigned to your case." He nodded toward the hallway which led further into the building. "Let's have a chat about what's been going on back in our office. Meanwhile, can I get you all some waters? Or a cup of coffee?"

Everyone agreed they were fine as they followed the officers through the snaking corridors of the precinct. Jose noted how much the chaos of the station reminded him of his emergency room – the woefully desperate interspersed between the manically harried.

Anderson and Rosetti's heads were bent together in quiet conversation as Jose and the others filed into their office behind them.

"Have a seat," Rosetti told them, settling herself behind one of the two small desks taking up a majority of the room. She shuffled through a stack of papers and came up with a spiral notebook. Smiling, she turned her attention to Andrea. "We're glad you came in," she said.

Andrea sighed. "I didn't have much of a choice."

The resignation in her voice disappointed Jose. After all she'd been through, the idea that she still felt remorse for speaking out against her abuser seemed absurd. But the intensity of her guilt was unmistakable. It was written all over her face.

The female officer leaned in then, close to Andrea. The space around them became intimate, effectively shutting the rest of them out. "There's not much worse than betraying someone you love. And I'm speaking as someone who's done just what we're asking you to do here today. But before you can help us, you've got to be willing to help yourself. You have to believe you are valuable. You are important. You are worthy of happiness that doesn't come with the cost of fear." She stopped then and fingered a small picture frame, hidden behind the laptop on the corner of her desk. Jose expected to see a photograph of someone smiling brightly or maybe the officer's child, but instead there was a memorial prayer card from a funeral pressed beneath the glass. She turned to Andrea and said, "You aren't the first woman who's been taken advantage of by a man. And you won't be the last. But as I sit here today, I promise you it's going to get better. All you have to do is put your faith in me and the people in this room who care about you. We're not leaving. No matter what."

The sincerity of Rosetti's words resonated with the obvious suffering she'd experienced in her own life. This realization wasn't lost on Andrea, who responded to the officer by throwing her arms around her neck in an unprecedented display of vulnerability. Carla reached for Jose's hand.

"I don't want to die," Andrea wept into the officer's shoulder.

"We're doing our best to find him," Anderson said, "but we're going to need you to tell us everything. From the beginning."

Andrea found her voice then, explaining to the officers how she'd met Alejandro at a party, a friend of a friend. How he'd taken her in when she needed a home. How he'd loved her and protected her. She explained how several months into the relationship, jealousy over presumed infidelity resulted in her being kept under lock and key, unable to leave without an escort, 'for her own safety.' She described the first time he'd hit her over the head with a dinner plate, and how he'd promised her he'd never hurt her again. She told them everything, tears streaming down her face, until Jose couldn't stand to listen to another word.

"How is rehashing the past helping you to find him now?" he demanded, cutting Andrea off mid-sentence.

The others stared at him, stunned by his disruption.

"Well?"

"We need to understand Alejandro's mindset. What motivates him. What makes him tick. Knowing more about him and the actions he's taken in the past will help us predict what he's going to do now," Anderson explained.

"We already know what he's going to do!" Jose exclaimed, exasperated. "He's already come to Baltimore to find her. And when he does, he's going to kill her."

The seriousness of his statement sliced through the air. Rosetti glanced toward her partner and then at him. "A moment outside, if you don't mind?"

He followed her out of the office where she shut the door behind them and began strolling down the hall.

"How do you two know each other?" Her tone wasn't accusatory; she was asking out of curiosity.

"I work at the hospital where she's been treated a bunch of times." He concentrated on placing his shoes directly inside the linoleum tiles, careful not to step on any cracks. It was an old habit from his youth, something he did to occupy his mind when he was afraid of thinking too much. "I only wish I'd tried to help her sooner. I should have notified someone the first time she came in. I just knew something was wrong."

"Been there," Rosetti told him. She worked her hands into her pants pockets. "The girl on the memorial card back in my office died because of a decision I made. Because I thought she was safe when she wasn't." She stopped then to look at him, and he could see the pain in her eyes. "I know about regrets, but let me assure you, you've done everything right when it comes to this case."

With Alejandro still at large, he wasn't ready to pat himself on the back just yet. Still, it was nice hearing he hadn't botched the entire operation. "You think so?" he asked.

"Yeah," she agreed, and began walking again. "So, do you love her?"

Jose lost track of his footfalls and misstepped onto a crack. "Andrea?"

She grinned. "Yes. Of course, Andrea. You seem pretty vested in her."

For months he'd convinced himself it was simply his nature to feel compassion toward others. That what he felt for Andrea was platonic and benign, just one person caring for the well-being of another. However, in light of the officer's observations, he considered the true depth of his emotions. And in that moment he couldn't deny the truth, as obvious to the officer as it should have been to him.

"Yeah. I guess I do. And I don't know why. I don't know much about her really, except that she has supremely crappy taste in men and horrible self-esteem. There's just something about her I like. Something that makes me want to be around her." He looked up at Rosetti, feeling like a wuss. "Should I turn in my man card to you or Officer Anderson when we get back?"

She laughed and patted him on the back. "You don't have to turn it in. Your secret's safe with me. I actually had a point in asking though."

"Which is?"

Rosetti abruptly did an about face, doubling back to return to her office. Jose followed suit.

"Which is I think you need to be as careful as Andrea and Carla when it comes to Alejandro. If he finds out you've been helping her or thinks you're involved with her romantically, even if you're not, he might come after you too." She chewed at the corner of her thumbnail. "Actually, he might come after you first."

He hadn't even considered the potential danger associated with helping Andrea. It hadn't even crossed his mind. His sole focus was on her, and now that it was brought to his attention, it did nothing to deter him. He wasn't afraid of Alejandro finding him. In fact, he almost welcomed it.

He stopped in the middle of the hallway but stepped aside to let several officers pass through. He leaned against the wall. "So what if he did?"

She turned to face him, hands on her hips. "I already know what you're thinking and the answer is no. We'll get to him some other way."

"We could use me as bait. Put me in front of the news media. I'll give some speech about how she's missing, and I'm looking for her. He won't be able to resist."

"No."

The more he thought about it, the more he liked the idea. "Please, Officer Rosetti. I want to help. I trust you all to keep me safe."

He saw something akin to excitement flicker across her face, but a second later, it was gone. "The thing is, we don't typically involve unauthorized personnel in this sort of thing. We have protocols to adhere to and using civilians as bait just isn't something we do."

"Just because you don't *typically* do something doesn't mean you never have."

She narrowed her eyes at him.

"I know I'm right. I watch *Law and Order* reruns just like everybody else."

She took a deep breath, which she held for a beat, before slowly releasing it through clenched teeth.

"TV is not real life," she explained calmly. "We follow procedures. Real procedures that aren't mandated by the need to tie up loose ends in a beautiful bow at the end of an hour. And besides, this case is in its infancy. We've got lots of leads to follow before we start doing stuff like that."

"Stuff like using the Mexican boyfriend/not boyfriend to lure in the fugitive gang-banger?"

She rolled her eyes but beckoned him to follow her to into the office.

"Just consider the possibility," he called from behind. "I don't want them to get hurt."

Rosetti thrust her chin over her shoulder but didn't slow. "Neither do I," she said. "Neither do I."

CHAPTER
27

PATRICK

Sunday, September 25
London

"I don't understand why we all had to race here to London," Wesley groaned from his seat beside Lillian at Patrick's mahogany dining room table. He was picking at his lobster tail, sulking, the way a small child would when he was told to finish his homework or turn off the TV. "We have lives, you know."

Patrick was at his wits end. After the hassle he'd gone through to deliver Eshanti's landscape drawings to France, only to have Wesley fail miserably in his attempts to glean anything from them, bringing them all together was the only move that felt like progress.

"From here on out, until the prophecy is fulfilled, we must all stay together in one place. No exceptions."

"Why now?" Javier asked, taking a bite of asparagus. "What's changed?"

Patrick hadn't told anyone about his latest premonition, not even Javier. That the light psychics were gaining strength so quickly while they remained stalled frustrated him to no end. He didn't like having to admit they were losing ground.

"I've called you all here because the fifth light psychic joined the others yesterday. I wanted to alert each of you when I felt the shift but thought it more prudent to bring you all here today instead. With their numbers growing in such rapid succession, we need to remain vigilant, which means remaining together, all in one place."

"Here in London?" Eshanti asked.

"Or here in your house?" Lillian grinned, taking a suggestive swallow of wine.

Early in their relationship, he and Lillian spent many nights, and mornings, together. He chalked up his initial attraction to her as weakness of the flesh, and had subsequently fallen into her web of alluring propositions. But as tempting as it was to allow himself to fall back into their old affair, he knew better now than to distract himself with matters outside the prophecy. There would be plenty of time for frivolity after the seventh psychic was found.

To that end, he ignored Lillian's remark and addressed the others. "You are welcome to stay here at my Compton Avenue estate, or I'm happy to put you up at one of my other properties for the duration. As you know, Akantha is staying here, locked safely away in the east wing under my watchful eye. I certainly would never expect to place all of you under the same level of restriction, but I would ask that you not leave the city for any reason, business or otherwise, until Number Seven is found. The worst case scenario would be for any of you to be out of reach when the discovery is made, allowing the light psychics a window of opportunity to gain the upper hand. I simply won't allow it."

Eshanti set her fork down beside her plate and removed her linen napkin from her lap. "And what exactly are we to do here while we're being kept under lock and key?" she asked, visibly offended by Patrick's request. "You don't control us, Patrick. We are free to do as we please."

He hadn't anticipated the Indian woman's defiance. How could she be so short sighted in light of their current situation?

"What I expect is for all of you to use the abilities you've been given to locate the seventh dark psychic."

She scoffed. "What abilities? Javier can move objects with his mind. Akantha can set things on fire. Lillian can be in two places at once. But just how are *they* supposed to track down Number Seven?" She looked around the table to each of her fellow psychics, finally settling on Patrick. "The truth is Wesley and I are the only ones who can actually provide the insight you seek, but my gift cannot be forced. It requires patience. Serenity. The more you force me to concentrate solely on the prophecy, the less focused my art becomes. So to require me to stay here with you would be counterproductive, and I cannot allow it."

"But what if Number Seven appears on his or her own here in London? The only prudent thing is for us to stay together, especially given the rapid speed with which the light seems to be gathering," Patrick reiterated.

The others eyed him skeptically from around the table. They had all stopped eating and it was as if he was suddenly the one on trial for a crime he did not commit.

"She speaks the truth, Patrick," Wesley said. "I've looked into the future for you hundreds of times, searching the horizon for signs of the world to come. But as you know, the future is a fluid, changing entity. We've followed dozens of leads based on images I've seen but none have ever panned out. I am powerful, yes, but I can only do what I can do. Perhaps instead of cramming this down our throats, what we all need now is a break. Some time away to recharge and concentrate on something else for a while. By your own admission, you've only felt five connections, so there are still two more to be made. Certainly we have a little bit of time."

He couldn't believe what he was hearing, that in the face of losing everything they had worked for, his fellow dark psychics were choosing to be passive rather than press on, guns drawn, to the finish.

Lillian batted her eyelashes and although he couldn't feel it, he saw her hand making its way up his thigh. "I think you should listen to them, Patrick, darling," she said, eyes sparkling. "You're not infallible yourself and you know it. Because the truth is, if you were as strong as you claim to be, you'd have reached out across the plane and found Number Seven yourself months ago. You wouldn't need any of us." She looked at him then as if he was a wounded animal, with pity and disappointment, before continuing. "But here we are. Maybe it's time to admit you need a break as well."

Her words sliced through him, severing the tightrope of confidence upon which he was balanced. His gut reaction was to lash out, deny her declaration, but before he could form a cohesive argument in defense of his contributions, Eshanti stood.

"While you may have amassed a great empire using your ability to sense the unspoken emotional shifts in the world around you, your power has proven ineffective in the search for the remaining dark psychics. You've sensed only the light psychic's assemblage, nothing more. Why haven't you been able to sense more about who they are or what they're doing? Why haven't you been able to use this spectacular ability of yours to bring an end to the prophecy, once and for all? Perhaps it's because you want it too badly. Because you're too close to the prophecy to see the bigger picture, and it's forced you into a box." She slid her chair beneath the table, scraping the feet noisily against the polished floor. "I won't allow myself to be imprisoned alongside you."

She glided out of the room, a wash of ornamental fabric, while the others gawked speechlessly after her. Patrick's face reddened in both embarrassment and anger, a combination of emotions to which he was unaccustomed.

"The rest of you feel the same, that I am worthless to the cause?"

He watched as they fumbled with their napkins in their laps and stared at their hands, unable to meet his gaze.

"Perhaps a week, maybe two, wouldn't be too much to ask," Javier ventured. "We've been at this for a very long time. It could be a short holiday is just what we all need. Even you, Patrick."

The others nodded in agreement, murmuring to one another.

He couldn't stand the thought of losing everything. Even now it was all he could do to keep his mind from reaching out into the astral plane in search of something. Anything. He was grabbing at straws.

"What of Akantha? Certainly you don't expect me to leave her here, unattended? What if she were to escape? To unleash her on the world at this point would be suicide. The authorities would kill her and that would be the end for us. Is that what you want?"

"I'll take her to Butron," Javier offered. "Put her in the castle's dungeon. She'll be safe there until it's time to regroup."

"She won't go willingly."

"We'll slip her something. A horse tranquilizer if necessary. And I'll see to her safe transport myself." He paused, wiping the corners of his mouth with his linen napkin. "I believe our minds are set, Patrick. The rest of us need a break."

He couldn't believe what he was hearing. They weren't making any sense. Fury rose within him and he pushed back from the table, knocking his chair to the floor.

"If the light gather while we rest," he spat, "it will be you who is to blame."

CHAPTER

28

MIA

Monday, September 26
Baltimore

Jack tumbled into their office, a disheveled mess of paperwork, drive-thru breakfast, and day-old stubble.

"Good Lord, Jack. What the hell happened?" Mia asked as he deposited his armload haphazardly onto his desk.

"It's Stella. And the baby. We spent the night at the hospital, thinking it was time, but it was sort of a false alarm. She wasn't in labor, so after running a few tests to confirm everything was fine, they sent us home."

"And you're here now because..."

He rolled his eyes, defeated. "You know Stella. The minute the doctor told her there was nothing to worry about, she sent me on my way. Insisted the citizenry needed me more than she did. That woman's gonna be the death of me because frankly, it would have been nicer to have stayed home with her to catch a few zzzz's."

"Well you look like crap, and we've got a full calendar. You sure you don't just wanna call in sick and go home? I don't mind grabbing Mike or somebody to head out with."

He took a bite of his egg and sausage burrito and a swig of coffee. "You kidding me? Truth is, there's no way I can blow days with the baby coming. I gotta save up. So I'm yours, all day. Just lemme hit the locker room and grab a shower."

Twenty minutes later, Mia met him at their patrol car parked in the secure lot on the back side of the building. Freshly shaven and still nursing his extra-large black coffee, he slid into the driver's seat beside her and yawned.

"Heading into MS-13 territory to see if anybody's heard anything about Alejandro coming into town?"

Mia pulled up coordinates on the GPS. "That was my plan. If he's a Wedgewood Chicano, there are only a couple gangs I can think of he might have connections to here in the city. MS-13's the biggest, so I figured we might as well start with them."

"Makes sense," he agreed, easing into traffic. "You think Trece might talk?"

"Or Sisco, if we can find him."

They were both quiet as they cruised up Route 40 East, out of the city. Then, breaking the amiable silence, Jack spoke up.

"How am I gonna keep this baby safe, Mia? She's not gonna have your ability to look at some guy and tell whether he's a creep or not." He white knuckled the steering wheel as he concentrated on the traffic ahead. "I might just hire you as her personal assistant full-time once she turns sixteen."

"Better make it fourteen," Mia quipped, not missing a beat. "Kids grow up fast these days."

His eyes cut to her. "That's not funny."

"Are you kidding me? Your daughter is *not* gonna get involved with some creep."

"This poor kid Andrea got involved with some creep, and now he's trying to kill her."

"Correction. He already tried to kill her. Now he's hunting her down to finish the job."

He glanced away from road to scowl at her. "You're not helping."

They were having these sorts of conversations more and more frequently, as his daughter's birth became eminent. "We've been through this before. With you for a dad and Stella as a mom, bad guys aren't gonna stand a chance. Andrea didn't have the two of you. She was on her own. That's how the trouble happens."

It was easy for her to extol wisdom when she wasn't the one staring down the barrel of impending parenthood. But she wasn't worried for Jack's daughter-to-be. As long as she was a part of the child's life, Mia would watch out for her.

Jack parked the cruiser curbside along a side street in one of the known MS-13 neighborhoods. MS-13 was short for Mara Slavatrucha, a prominent and violent gang with a longstanding foothold in the Washington DC suburbs. And although she wished it wasn't the case, over the past few years, the gang's activity had begun to spread throughout the Baltimore region as well. With ties to other Hispanic gangs around the world, there was a good chance Alejandro would look to them if he needed back-up or just a place to crash.

"This is where Paul said Trece and Sisco have been seen?"

"Yeah. Just a couple days ago."

"You think they'll talk if they know anything?" he asked, holstering his sidearm before getting out of the car.

After some digging, Mia had discovered a recent report of someone with Sisco's description selling drugs to a minor near Collington Square Elementary School. It wasn't confirmed, but she thought it might be enough to snag his attention. She also knew Sisco was a snitch. On two separate occasions she'd witnessed him throwing fellow gang members under the bus to save his own skin, and he wasn't above making deals with the district attorney's office. With a little finesse, she hoped the dirt she had on him would translate into information about Alejandro.

"He was the one who squealed on those Bloods last year for holding up the CVS on Wolfe Street, remember?"

"Vaguely. But telling the cops about a rival gang is a lot different than giving up your own people."

She tucked her hair into her hat and cracked open the door. "Please. We've got so much stuff on this guy..." She winked at him. "He's gonna be afraid not to talk."

Mia shielded her eyes from the morning sun. The rays barely crested the tops of the row houses as she left the air conditioned comfort of the car and was embraced by the warmth of the day. Mindful of the traffic, she crossed the street to the other side where a group of surly-looking men were loitering at the corner. Her confidence was bolstered knowing Jack trailed close behind.

"Good morning, Gentlemen. Beautiful day, isn't it?"

All six of the men pretended not to have heard her, shuffling their feet and staring at the ground.

"The lady asked you if you're enjoying the day," Jack added, hands on his hips. "I would suggest you answer her."

A layer of sooty engine grease covered the man closest to Mia. His hands. His clothes. His face. He was squat, only a few inches taller than she was, and she saw the remains of a deep laceration which tore across his cheek, from just below his eye to his upper lip. This was clearly a man who knew about trouble.

He spat at her feet.

Mia turned to Jack, her eyes bulging from their sockets, feigning shock and horror. "Did that just happen?"

"I think it just did."

"It'd be a real shame to have to haul him into the station for harassment, don't you think Officer Anderson?"

"I agree. That would be awful, Officer Rosetti." He pulled his cuffs off his clip. They clanged noisily as he dangled them by his side.

Eyeing the cuffs, the greaser finally spoke. "You got nothin' on me."

Mia shrugged. "I might."

He cursed under his breath in Spanish.

"You know, I might be willing to just walk away if you can tell me where to find Sisco."

The men's eyes darted to one another, each of them attempting to communicate without speaking, none of them knowing how much Spanish Mia spoke. There was more shuffling. More absentminded smoking.

"Okey dokey then, I guess we can take you down to the station, and you can spend some time in lock up thinking about why you shouldn't harass an officer by spitting on her shoes."

"I didn't spit on your shoes!"

"Your word against mine. And, uh, Officer Anderson, did you see some of his saliva make it onto my footwear?"

"That I did."

"Then it's settled," Mia said, snatching the cuffs from her partner's hand.

"Ay! Last time I saw him he was at La Roca. Earlier this morning."

Mia couldn't keep from grinning. The seedy underbelly of society was nothing if not predictable. "The liquor store off Pulaski Highway?"

"Si. That's the one."

"Muchas gracias, gentlemen," Mia called over her shoulder, tossing the cuffs back to Jack.

It was only about a two-minute drive to La Roca, where another unsavory group of men were milling about the entrance of the store. A few were engrossed in a raucous conversation Mia could only partially understand, and three others, barely out of their teens, were leaning against the side alley wall smoking Faros. She identified Sisco immediately.

"He's here," she murmured to Jack as they jogged across the busy intersection. "The tall one with the belt buckle the size of Texas."

She wanted to add that his aura was so dark it was if a magnetic field caused the smoke from his entire pack of cigarettes to collect around him.

Sisco, aka Victor Suarez, recognized Mia before she made it to the curb, and began to back away down the alley. She called after him. "We only wanna talk, Sisco. I swear. Unless you're gonna run, and then we can detain you for reasonable suspicion."

He froze and turned around slowly to face her. "I ain't got nothin' to say to you."

The first time Mia met Sisco she'd been only seventeen years old, observing a lineup with her father from behind the one-way glass. He'd been identified as the culprit on that occasion, as well as the two subsequent lineups she'd seen, also leading to his arrest. That he was still out on the streets was a testament to his 'negotiating abilities.'

That he was still alive was a testament to the power of 'street cred.'

"I think you might, my friend. Cuz we've got an eyewitness who saw you selling weed to a bunch of kids at Collington." His eyes flickered, and she knew she had him. "Now we don't wanna have to drag you down to the station for that because I hate paperwork as much as the next girl. So we can make sure your little indiscretion gets buried, but my partner and I are gonna need a little info from you." She took a few steps closer to where he'd stopped in the middle of the alley and lowered her voice to just above a whisper. "Consider it a simple negotiation between friends."

Without a word, Sisco motioned at the two other men, still holed up against the wall of the liquor store, to go away. They slinked around the corner and out of sight before he said quietly, "What the hell do you want, Rosetti?"

"I wanna know what you know about a guy named Alejandro. He's a Wedgewood Chicano outta Phoenix. He's just come into town."

Sisco held out his hands. "I don't know nothing about some new guy."

Mia got the sense he was lying but she wasn't ready to push him just yet. She reached into her breast pocket for a copy of the photograph Andrea provided to the department for identification purposes and handed it to Sisco.

"This is the guy we're looking for. You see him, you send someone to let us know. Otherwise, we'll be in touch about your proximity to the elementary school." She stared him down until he became so uncomfortable, he was forced to avert his gaze. "Do we understand each other?"

"I heard what you just said," he growled.

"You've got 'til tomorrow afternoon. Five o'clock. Then we'll be back."

CHAPTER
29

THOMAS

Monday, September 26
Baltimore

Thomas enjoyed being a student again. There was something peaceful and reassuring about returning to the classroom, a place which had always served as a refuge for him, and it brought him joy to take his seat among the other college freshmen in his Intro to Music in the US class.

They were discussing colonial folk music with its African and native influences. It was fascinating to Thomas, listening with his eyes shut as the professor played a piece written by one of the country's earliest composers, Supply Belcher. He had never taken a proper musical history or theory class, and he was parched for knowledge, drinking every drop of information his professors had to offer.

As a commuting day student, he kept mostly to himself. Older than much of the student body living on campus full-time, he was something of an outsider, but it didn't bother him in the slightest. He didn't mind sitting alone at lunch, eating under a sprawling oak he'd discovered in the quad just outside one of the larger student apartment buildings. In fact, he actually relished the time with just his thoughts and his peanut butter sandwich packed from home.

On Mondays however, he had a large break between his early morning and late afternoon classes, so while the weather was still nice, he walked the five blocks to Belinda's Café to have lunch with Belinda and put in a couple hours of work. He hadn't yet made it off campus when his phone began chirping in his pocket. He could tell by the ringtone it was Mia.

"What's up?"

"So much. It's been a crazy morning. What's up with you?"

"Heading to Belinda's for lunch and work. She promised to make banana muffins to bring home to you, so you're welcome."

"I can taste them already," she said. "Tell her thanks. That woman's a goddess when it comes to baked goods." She paused and Thomas could hear her shuffling about, excusing herself to someone as she moved. "Sorry. I had to walk outside so I could talk. It's like a full moon around here today. Lunatics everywhere, and I'd like to keep our conversation private."

"Oh! So it's gonna be *that* type of phone call," he teased. "I'm wearing jeans and a t-shirt, if you must know. Pink Floyd. The Wall. Seriously sexy."

She laughed into the receiver, infectiously, and he couldn't keep from laughing back. He loved being able to make her smile, especially knowing there was often little to smile about during her workdays.

"Well, I'm wearing a blue police uniform. Holster, sidearm, cuffs, baton."

"Mini skirt?"

"Polyester pants."

"Hmmm. Still sexier than my outfit, even without the skirt."

She laughed again. "Believe it or not, I wasn't calling to describe my outfit to you," she said. "I actually wanted to let you know I got an email back from that psychic guru I was telling you about. He gave me a list of names."

"Sweet. That's great news. But isn't giving us the names of other psychics breaking some sort of confidentiality agreement."

"He's a psychic, Thomas. Not a physician or a priest. There's no laws against sharing information if you're clairvoyant."

"That makes sense, I guess. So how many are on the list?"

"A couple thousand, I'd say."

They were both quiet for a beat.

"That's a lot of names," Thomas said finally.

"At least it gives us someplace to start."

"Any chance he keeps records of everyone's birthdates?"

"If he does, he didn't share them with me. And he knows we're looking because of the prophecy, so I think he would have given us more than just names and addresses if he had them."

He stopped at the street corner, pressed the button to make the light turn red, and waited for the walk sign to indicate it was safe to cross. "So how do you think we should go through the list? Alphabetically? By state? Intuition?"

Mia sighed deeply into the phone. "I don't know. There are people on there from all over the world, not just the US, and part of me feels like we should start with the foreigners. I mean, it would be pretty insular to think the only people capable of saving the world are living here in the states."

The walk sign illuminated, and he hurried across the street toward Belinda's. It occurred to him that Mia was still focused on looking for the light psychics – a dead end as far as he was concerned. "I agree that we should definitely look to other countries, especially since we know two of the fourteen are from here in the US. But Mia, you do realize we're not looking for the good guys? It won't do us any good. We gotta set our sights on the people who are going to usher in the apocalypse. You get that, right?"

"Yeah, I know. I get it. We're looking for the bad guys. I just wonder…" She paused and he could feel her tension pulling through the line. "What the hell are we gonna do if we find them?"

CHAPTER

30

JOSE

Tuesday, September 27
Baltimore

"I don't know if I can do this anymore," Andrea complained to Jose as they sat beside one another, their heads resting against the faux wood headboard, watching reruns of People's Court on the motel room TV.

The weekly motel they'd checked into in the wake of Alejandro's disappearance was straight out of a B-rated film from the 80's. Mauve and teal floral spreads adorned both mattresses, which sagged uncomfortably on each side, leaving noticeable lumps in the center of the beds. The matching teal wall-to-wall carpet was heavily worn, with distinct paths leading from the door to the bathroom and the bathroom to the beds. So far Jose hadn't noticed any bugs, but he continued to keep a watchful eye. Regardless of the outdated décor, the motel felt safe, and Jose knew, even collectively, they couldn't afford any better accommodations.

"We said we were gonna give it two weeks and then reassess. It's only been a couple days. We gotta give the cops a chance to do their jobs, and it may take a little time. Until then, we just gotta sit tight and try to make the best of a bad situation."

After assessing the state of affairs upon his arrival in Baltimore, he'd called into work and requested to take time off. Since he had never used any of his accrued annual leave, the head nurse was more than willing to remove him from the schedule until the middle of October. When she wished him safe travels on his 'well deserved vacation,' he hadn't corrected her about the nature of his trip. Things were less messy when he held his cards close.

Andrea picked up the remote and began surfing channels. "I was trapped when I was with him, and I'm trapped now that we're apart. Outta the frying pan, into the fire. At least before I ran off he wasn't hunting me down, trying to kill me."

Jose raised an eyebrow.

"Okay. Maybe he was trying to kill me. But it was only because I threatened to leave. I shoulda just kept my mouth shut."

Being holed up together, 24 hours a day, he was beginning to lose patience. And yet, he knew he couldn't be just another guy intent on controlling her every move. In her short adult life, she'd been oppressed by a parade of dictators, and although it didn't make their confinement any easier, he knew her current attitude was purely reactionary.

"Are you even listening to yourself right now?" he said, rolling himself up off the bed. "The next week will be much nicer for the both of us if you'd just try to focus on the positive."

She scowled, although she was clearly trying to ignore him by focusing instead on a reunion episode of Teen Mom. Jose took two steps and manually clicked off the television.

"I'm done," he announced.

And Andrea burst into tears.

Adrenaline surged and his emergency room training instinctively kicked in as he approached her cautiously from the far side of the bed.

"Let's go to a meeting."

"I don't want to go to a meeting," she sniffed, barely audible from where she'd buried herself beneath her arms.

"You need to talk this through with other people. You need to share your feelings. I'll call a police escort to come take us. I'm sure that nice girl cop, Officer Rosetti wouldn't mind helping out."

"Carla doesn't need a police escort to leave."

"Carla isn't being hunted down by a maniac."

She came out from under her arms then, her mascara streaked around her eyes. "Why do you care?" she asked. Her voice was calm. As calm as he had ever heard it.

"Why do I care what?"

"About me and if I get hunted down by some maniac. You gave me some BS answer about everyone being special back at the hospital in Phoenix, but I still don't buy it."

Could he explain being drawn to her in a way he'd never been drawn to anyone else? Would she believe, despite what others told her, that she was worthy of his love?

Would she dismiss him as just another guy looking to control her?

Did it matter even if she did?

"I love you," he said simply.

"What if I don't wanna be loved?"

"It's too late."

He watched her rolling his declaration over in her mind, deciding what to do with it.

"In our meetings we've been talking about the ten keys to a healthy relationship. The last time I went we were learning about patience." She looked up at him then and when their eyes connected, the sarcasm and anger melted away. "You've shown me what patience is all about. You've never yelled at me. Even when I probably deserved it. You've held it together so I didn't have to. I know you have it in you to keep being patient. At least I hope you do."

He sat down on the bed beside her and the space between them, less than a foot, buzzed with what could only be described as a tangible current. He wanted to touch her. Not to heal but simply to comfort.

"You tell me what you want me to do. And I'll do it," he said.

She looked away then, unable to hold his gaze.

"When monsoon storms would blow across the desert at night when I was little, my big sister Claire would let me crawl in bed beside her because I was afraid of the lightning and thunder. I never had to ask if it was okay, and I never had to explain why I was scared. She just opened her arms and let me nestle beside her until the last rumbles were so far in the distance you had to strain to hear them. I remember counting together 'one Mississippi, two Mississippi.' Most times, if I was still awake when the storm was over, I'd crawl back into my own bed on the other side of the room. But if I happened to fall asleep, she'd let me stay, and I'd wake up beside her in the morning."

"Where's Claire now?" he asked.

"She died of a drug overdose when I was twelve." Her voice was steady. Almost too steady.

Andrea had lost her safe place when she was a child and had been searching for a suitable replacement ever since. Immediately, her life story shifted into focus.

"I'll be your Claire," he said at last. "And if you decide at the end of the storm that you're ready to be on your own, you can go. Back to your bed on the other side of the room. And if you decide you'd rather stay…" He trailed off, wondering how many other men had suggested the same arrangement, only to retract the offer when the time came for her to go.

She shook her head. "I'm supposed to 'heal on my own' before 'allowing someone new into my life,'" she explained, making air quotes with her hands. "That's what they tell us in support group anyway."

"So heal on your own," he told her. "I'll just stand here beside you to catch you if you fall. No strings attached."

"You'd wait for me?"

"For as long as you need."

She exhaled then, as if she'd been holding her breath for days and relaxed into the crook of his arm. The last time he'd felt the heat of her body was at the hospital, healing her with his gift. At that moment she'd allowed him to touch her because she had no other choice. It was probably no different for her now. She was out of options, once again.

Or perhaps this time is different, he thought hopefully. *Perhaps this time she's choosing me because she wants to, not because she has to.*

CHAPTER

31

MIA

Tuesday, September 27
Baltimore

"You think Sisco's gonna be back at the liquor store?" Jack asked, clipping his handheld transceiver around his shoulder onto his lapel.

"If he knows what's good for him he will be," Mia replied. "And he better have something for us. I feel bad having to tell Jose we have nothing to report every time he calls, which, I swear to you, is like six times a day. I feel bad for the guy. I think he'd do anything to keep Andrea safe."

"Too bad she didn't meet him before she met Alejandro, huh?"

She shrugged. "I get the feeling she wouldn't have given him the time of day outside her current situation. Some girls are just drawn to the men who are the worst for them."

"Like Stella," Jack smiled.

"Oh, yeah. Like Stella." She tossed him the keys to the cruiser. "She picked a real bad boy when she picked you. And by bad, I mean like your singing at karaoke the other night."

The neighborhoods surrounding the station encompassed a wide range of diversity, but Highlandtown, just east of Patterson Park, accounted for one of the city's fastest growing Hispanic populations. Along with positive cultural experiences like LatinoFest, an annual celebration of Latino food, music, and dance, the inclusion of yet another ethnicity into an already diverse area often led to unrest. Mia and Jack were no strangers to the area.

"There he is, right where we left him," she said as Jack pulled the cruiser to a stop along the curb across the street.

"You got him or you want me to deal with him this time?"

She waved him off. "Nah. I've got him. Sisco and I have history, remember?"

"Mia, you started hanging out at the station when you were in elementary school. Who don't you have a history with?"

She laughed and followed him to where Sisco and his crew were lurking in the alley beside the store.

"You're looking well, Gentlemen," she called to them as they approached. "Glad to see you're making the world a better place today."

In the interest of privacy, Sisco sent the others away before responding, just as he'd done before.

"I heard something about your guy," he admitted.

"That's good news for you."

He lit a cigarette and took a long drag before going on. "Some people have seen him with a couple guys from Hyattsville over in Joseph Lee, at the billiards place."

"We don't care if he can play pool," Jack said. "We care about the reason he's in town."

Sisco eyed them evasively, taking another pull on his cigarette. "He's looking for the girl, just like you said. Talking about having somebody else take her out when he finds her."

"But he doesn't know where she is now?"

He shrugged.

"You don't know or you're not telling? Cuz I can always take you back to the station and you can tell us what you know there."

"All I know is he thought he'd find her in Essex, but she wasn't where he thought she'd be. Now he's got people searching the area for her."

"I see. And is that really all you know?"

Sisco flicked his cigarette butt to the ground and crushed it under the heel of his boot. All the while he continued sneering at her, his lips pressed together in a tight line. "That's all I have to tell you."

Mia was careful to avoid making any eye contact with Jack as they headed back to the cruiser. She didn't want to give Sisco any inkling as to whether they knew where Andrea was.

"You think it's safe she's holed up at Duke's Motel?" Jack asked as he fastened his seatbelt. "I know it's in Rosedale, not Essex, but it's only about five miles away from Carla's apartment."

Mia had the same thought about Sisco's disclosure. "Jose and Andrea suspected he'd tracked her here to Baltimore, but didn't have any way of knowing how close a trace he got. Based on what we know now, I think it might be smart for them to move further out."

"Should we swing by there now?"

She looked over her shoulder through the car's back window at where Sisco was still leaning against the side of the building. "It's probably better if we head back to the station, just in case he has someone following us. There's a good chance he's working both sides of this game, and we can't chance giving him even a direction to take back to Alejandro." She fished her phone out of her pocket. "We should probably call Jose though."

Jack circled around the block back in the direction of the station while Mia called Jose and Andrea to let them know what they'd discovered. She put the phone on speaker.

"I can't stand the thought of him being so close," Andrea told her in response to the news. "But do you really think we need to find somewhere else to go?"

"I do," she replied. "It's for your own safety."

Jose piped up, "What about my Aunt Carla? She doesn't have a car and needs to stay close to her work. We can't afford to split up though."

Mia hated that finances often took precedence over everything else, but for many people, herself included, it was often the case. "I can't force you to find another place. I can only share what I know, and unfortunately we now have confirmation he's traced you to Essex. If he and his cronies are prowling around, it's more important than ever for you to put some distance between you and then sit tight until we find him."

Andrea suggested, "What if I just went back home to Phoenix?"

"We don't think that would necessarily be safe either. You know as soon as he hears you're back in town – and he will hear – he'll waste no time coming after you there." Mia could hear Andrea's disappointment across the line. She knew what it was like to be trapped inside a dangerous situation, both literally and figuratively. "We really think the best thing to do now would be for all three of you to find another place to stay in a different part of town."

"Carla too?" Jose asked.

Jack spoke up. "Listen guys, if he traced Andrea's call to Essex, there's a good chance he was able to pinpoint her location down to the apartment complex, if not the precise unit. None of you should go back there."

The line hummed as all four of them were silent, and Mia contemplated their next move. Her instincts were telling her it was only a matter of time before Alejandro discovered them at the motel. And if there was one thing she'd learned over the past year it was to trust her intuition. "How about if Jack and I head over to Carla's apartment to find out if anyone's been inquiring about your whereabouts.

If someone's been asking around, it might give us some insight into Alejandro's next move. Until you hear back from us, you might want to get online to start searching for another place to hide out."

After everyone said goodbye and they disconnected, Mia turned to Jack.

"You think anyone's been following us?"

He glanced in the rearview mirror. "I've been watching and haven't seen anything. Wanna head over to Mansfield Woods?"

They took a circuitous route to Carla's apartment complex in Essex, stopping by a taco truck near Middle River where they both ordered fish tacos to go. They sat in an adjacent parking lot, balancing their tacos on the electronics console between them as they discussed their recent night out together at the karaoke bar.

"So Lanying was nice," Jack was saying. "Too bad she had to go back home so soon."

Mia picked a chunk of pico off the napkin on her lap and tossed it into her mouth. "Yeah. She's really sweet."

"Funny though, how Thomas picked her up in a bar."

She saw him smirking out of the corner of her eye and was loathe to take the bait. But after finishing her second taco, she couldn't hold back any longer.

"For the last time, he didn't pick her up at a bar. They met in the hotel lobby where he plays on Friday nights. He called me as soon as he got off work to tell me about her and said she seemed lonely and that we should get together because we all might hit it off. He was being kind. There's nothing more to it than that."

Jack tossed his wrapper nonchalantly into the paper bag on the floor. "It's not my business what the two of you are into these days."

Mia knew he didn't actually believe there was anything inappropriate going on between the three of them, but she also knew his teasing stemmed from his desire for her to come clean about the true nature of the unusual friendship.

Of course, it was weird for Thomas to have latched onto a random stranger in town for a conference, so she could understand his curiosity. They'd been partners long enough that he could tell when she wasn't being completely honest, but she wasn't ready to talk to him about the prophecy. At least not yet.

Instead of giving him the satisfaction of a response, she took their trash bag across the parking lot to a dumpster and tossed it in. Upon returning to the cruiser, she immediately changed the subject.

"You think we should say anything to the apartment management about Alejandro or just go straight to the neighbors?"

He put the car into gear and eased out of the parking lot onto Eastern Boulevard. "I can't see them walking into the office to inquire about the whereabouts of a new tenant, can you?"

"No," she agreed. "So let's just knock on a few neighbors' doors and ask if they've seen or heard anything."

No one was home at the first four apartments they visited. At the fifth, a teenage boy wearing a Cheetos stained t-shirt and gym shorts cracked the door briefly before immediately slamming it shut in their faces.

Mia knocked again, more forcefully this time.

"We're not truancy," she called. "We just have a few questions about your upstairs neighbor. You're not in any trouble. I promise."

After several seconds, the door creaked open and the boy peered out. "I had a fever this morning," he croaked.

"I'm sure you did," Mia replied, noting his light aura. "Now about your upstairs neighbor, Ms. Garcia. Have you seen her around recently?

"Is she the older lady with the long, frizzy, grey hair?" he asked, using his hands to demonstrate the fullness of her tresses.

"That's her," Jack said.

The boy furrowed his brow. "I haven't seen her in days. Actually, I haven't heard her either. Usually she's up early on Sunday mornings. I hear her cuz her room's right above mine. I guess she goes to church or whatever, but this past Sunday I didn't hear her. Slept in 'til noon. It was awesome."

"Okay. So you haven't seen or heard her in a while," Mia remarked, taking rudimentary notes in a small steno. She found people took her more seriously when she at least pretended to write down what they said. "And what about anybody else? Have you seen or heard anyone unusual around the building? Someone you didn't recognize or don't typically see?"

"No. Not that I can think of," he replied. He glanced over his shoulder at the television where she could see Call of Duty was paused on the screen.

"What about this guy?" Jack held out a photo of Alejandro for the boy to examine.

"No. I haven't seen him, and I definitely would have remembered him if I had."

"Fair enough," Mia said, handing him her card before backing off the doorstep. "Don't hesitate to call me if you see or hear anything unusual, okay?"

The boy nodded and without saying goodbye, shut the door.

As they climbed the stairs, Mia said, "His aura was light. I'm pretty sure he's telling the truth."

"Like about that fever he had this morning?"

"He only said that because he didn't want to get in trouble. But he has no reason to lie to us about the other stuff."

They knocked on the door of Carla's next door neighbor and heard someone padding toward the door. A moment later, a squat Greek woman wearing a housecoat appeared before them, a dishtowel in her hands.

"Yes?"

Mia introduced herself and explained the reason for their visit.

"Why don't you two come on inside," she said, ushering them through the doorway. "I was just making a pot of tea and I don't want my kettle boiling over. My name's Phyllis, by the way."

It was customary for them to accept invitations, especially from the elderly, so without so much as a nod between them, Mia found herself in a cluttered yet homey living area decorated with doilies and flea market tchotchkes, the product of a lifetime of accumulation.

As Phyllis rounded the corner into the galley kitchen, the top of her head was barely visible above the opening of the pass through. "Have a seat on the sofa," she called into the living room.

They were still getting situated when moments later, Phyllis appeared again with a tea service tray, complete with shortbread cookies. "I don't get visitors very often," she explained, settling herself in the rocker beside them.

Politely, she and Jack helped themselves to cups of tea. As Mia stirred in a teaspoon of sugar, she explained, "We're here because we're looking for some information about Ms. Garcia from next door."

"She isn't in any trouble, is she?"

"Oh no, not at all."

"Well, I wouldn't expect so," Phyllis nodded. "She's always been so kind to me. Brings up my mail from time to time so I don't have to climb the steps. Drops off leftovers. That sort of thing."

"Has she been by recently?"

"As a matter of fact, no. I haven't seen or heard her in a few days." Her eyes widened in alarm as she began piecing together her own conclusions. "Oh, my goodness. Is she missing?"

"No, Ma'am, she's not," Jack consoled her. "She's fine. But someone other than the police are interested in her whereabouts. Has anyone unfamiliar stopped by?"

She was thoughtful, stirring her teaspoon absentmindedly around her cup. "No. No one's been here to see me. But two nights ago, or maybe three, I was putting lotion on my feet… You have to do that when you get older with bunions and all." She paused, unashamed, and returned her cup to the tray. "I heard men's voices just outside my door. I couldn't hear every word, but I could tell they were angry and they were looking for something." Understanding crossed her face. "Were they looking for Carla?"

Affirmation laced with disappointment seized Mia. "That's what we're trying to find out," she explained. "Can you remember anything else about what you heard?"

Phyllis shook her head. "When I heard them clomping back down the stairs, I thought about going over to the window to see if I knew who they were, but like I said, I had lotion on my feet, and I didn't want to smear it all over the carpet. I usually sit through two of my programs to make sure it's completely absorbed before I walk around."

With no further information to glean from Phyllis, Jack and Mia wasted no time in finishing their tea. After thanking their hostess for her time as well as the cookies, they returned to the hallway.

"We're 0 for 2," Jack said glumly.

"Let's try one more door. Maybe the third time will be the charm," she said, already halfway to the apartment across the hall.

When the tenant appeared in the doorway, Mia strained her neck to meet his gaze. Pushing seven feet tall and sporting a mane of unruly dreadlocks, he appeared to have recently washed ashore from a shipwreck.

"What can I do for you today, Officers?" he asked warmly in a thick Caribbean accent.

Mia held out her badge and introduced herself. "We're wondering if you've seen or heard anything unusual going on around the building in the past few days?"

"Are you asking 'bout what's going on with Miss Carla and that young girl stayin' with her?"

Mia and Jack exchanged a glance. "What exactly do you know about their situation?" he asked.

The man leaned against the doorframe and crossed his arms in front of his chest, in an easy-going sort of way. "She told me they had to go away for a little while but there was nothin' wrong. Is that the truth?"

"Yes and no," Mia assured him. "We're actually here on their behalf."

He nodded now, chewing on a toothpick as he considered his words carefully. "What I know is that Miss Carla stopped by a few days ago, asked me to collect up her mail and water her geraniums. She said she didn't know when she was gonna be able to come back but hoped it wouldn't be too long. I asked her, but she wouldn't tell me where she was goin'. Told me it wasn't safe for me to know."

"And since she left, have you noticed anyone unusual around?"

"Oh, yeah, I have. Two nights ago, 'round 10 o'clock, I heard some voices out in the stairs. And I hear them a lot on account of these walls are so thin, but that night, I paid attention, because the voices stopped right outside a my door. So I came a little close to take a listen, and I hear them talkin' 'bout Miss Carla's girl, Andrea. About how she was supposed to be there. And oh, they was so angry about them not bein' there."

"Did they go inside?"

"Ya! They went inside. Saw 'em with my own eyes, pickin' the lock and walkin' right in."

Jack's brows stitched together disapprovingly. "And you didn't think to call the police about someone breaking into your neighbor's place?"

The man scoffed. "By the time the police arrive, those men are gone, and who do you think the police are gonna suspect then, huh?" He thrust his own thumbs into his chest. "The reefer black guy from across the hall, that's who. Naw, man, I stay outta stuff like that. It's none a my business."

As much as she didn't want to admit it, she knew the guy was right. Sometimes the easy suspect turned out to be the only suspect. Unless of course she was on the case and could vouch for the state of someone's soul.

"Okay," she told him, "since you didn't call in the intrusion, at least tell me you got a good look at the guys."

"Oh yeah," he said. "I can tell you what they looked like. Mean lookin' SOBs. All teeth and tats."

She had to laugh at his description considering his own demeanor was equally domineering. Jack handed him Alejandro's photo.

"Now that's it. That's one a the dudes right there. Seen his face plain as day." He handed the photo back as if it pained him to hold it. "Told ya he was nasty lookin'."

Now that Alejandro had been positively identified at Carla's apartment, Mia was overcome by a sense of urgency. It was imperative for them to track him down before he discovered where Andrea was hiding, and as they plodded down three flights of stairs to the ground floor of the building, she recalled Jose's request.

"Hey, Jack," she said as they slid into the car beside one another, "I feel like going fishing, and I'm thinking it might be time to chum the waters with some bait."

32

Tuesday, September 27
Baltimore

"I can't believe you printed all these out," Mia laughed as she thumbed through the considerable stack of papers atop Mildred's kitchen table.

Thomas pulled his tablet out of his messenger bag and powered it up. "I don't know how people operate straight from digital files. I need to be able to see and feel what I'm working on."

"You just like using a Sharpie to cross off names," she said, eyeing up the pile of markers in the center of the table.

"There's something spectacularly satisfying about crossing something off a list," he told her without a drop of sarcasm in his voice.

She pulled a chair up beside him, closer than it needed to be, and their legs brushed into one another. He loved sharing space with her, and since she'd dropped plans with Chelsea to spend the evening alone together, he knew she still felt the same way about him.

Overwhelmed by the sheer number of psychics in the file from Les Joplin, Mia's psychic guru, he'd called her that afternoon from the university's copy center, as he watched sheet after sheet of the printed file stacking up like pancakes at an IHOP. Les hadn't pared down the list, at Mia's request, in case they needed to contact someone who wasn't necessarily part of the prophecy. She didn't want to rule out using another psychic's power to assist them in their search.

Mia booted up her work issued laptop, and as she logged in through numerous firewalls, commented, "With access to the police database, we should be able to find out the birthdays for all the Americans on the list. The foreigners are going to be a little trickier, but I'm sure we'll figure something out."

They began the laborious process of inputting name after name into the system, searching for a birthday match. After about an hour they began recognizing patterns with names and locales.

"Here's an Edith. Skip her?" Thomas asked.

"Yeah. There aren't any 25-year-old Ediths living in Tampa."

"How about Horace Flannigan from Boston?"

"Skip him," Mia said.

They'd found six psychics born in their birth year, but none on their exact date. Felicia, Max, Tanner, Ashley, Kayla, and Desiree.

"What do you think someone with retrocognition can do?" he asked, reading the notation beside the name Helen Greenly.

"It's sort of the opposite of your precognition." She looked up from her computer to look at him, the soft light of the screen illuminating her face. "But instead of getting a feeling about what's about to happen, like you do, they get a feeling or an understanding about something that's already happened."

"Like the people who work with the police to help solve crimes by seeing what took place in the past."

"Yes. Exactly."

It was with a sense of awe that he listened to Mia sharing her knowledge of psychic abilities. He had a lot to learn from her when it came to knowing not only the names for what other people could do but how their abilities shaped them fundamentally.

"How about this one – Chase Watkins. Says his abilities lie in psychometry. What's that?"

Mia continued to type. "Psychometry is the ability to touch an object or a person and learn something about it through that connection. So, for example, if someone with the gift of psychometry came across the shirt I was wearing when I was held captive in the warehouse, they might be able to see the basement or sense how I was feeling when I wore it." She glanced up at him then. "It's all very personal. And Sarah Burke is a no."

He crossed Sarah's name off the list with his red Sharpie. "So you think that's the name for what I can do? Precognition?"

"As you describe it and as I've witnessed it, it's really the only known ability that fits. The fact that you can only sense when something bad is going to happen, as opposed to good things or random neutral things, makes it a little unique. But yeah, I think precognition describes what you do pretty well. Except for the weird shielding thing you can do. I have no idea what that's about."

He considered the label 'precognition' and decided it might take some time for it to settle into his definition of self. He'd been labeled many things during his life – unworthy, unstable, vagrant, loser. Precognitive didn't seem like such a bad addition to the list.

Thomas flipped to the next sheet of paper, having eliminated another column of possible prophecy members and handed it to Mia. "How much do you know about precognition?"

She shrugged. "Only what I've read. I've never actually met one." She paused, reconsidering. "Well, besides you," she added.

"And most can sense all sorts of events, not just bad ones?"

"I think that's typically the case."

185

He drummed two markers against the table as a new understanding dawned on him. "So what if I'm not unique? What if I'm just untrained?"

Her fingers froze over the keys, and she turned to face him. "Untrained how?"

The idea was just solidifying in his own mind, and he found it difficult to put what he was thinking into words. "It's just that, my entire life I was surrounded by bad stuff. Stuff I needed to avoid. Like my abusive foster parents and kids who bullied me. So maybe the focus of my ability grew into what it's become as a result of my personal experiences, like you said. Maybe I can sense when good things are about to happen, but I just haven't trained myself to notice. Because really, what good does it do to know if you're about to have the good fortune of catching the last blue line bus for the night? It's a lot more important to know if there's a thief waiting in the back to pick your pocket. Right?"

She stared at him, unblinking.

"Right?" he repeated.

Instead of responding, she slid off her chair and into his lap in one swift motion, her legs wrapping around his torso so their noses touched. And then she kissed him. Tenderly at first, and for a moment, he was caught off-guard, wondering what he'd said to elicit such an amorous response. But as she began kissing him more forcefully, running her fingers through his hair, he forgot to care. For several moments he was able to ignore the fact that he and Mia were making out in his mother's kitchen while she watched television in the adjacent room. But when he felt the coolness of her hands underneath his shirt against the heat of his chest, he forced himself to pull away.

"We really need to get our own place," he whispered into her ear, her hair draped across his face.

"Someday," she whispered back, returning to her seat at the table but not to the keyboard. "You think it's possible? That you might have the ability to sense more than just trouble?"

"I don't see why not. I think I might just need to start focusing more on the positive and see what happens."

She looked at him then, deeply, in a way which made him feel valuable and worthy of her love. "Because what I was thinking is that maybe we could figure out a way to use your gift to help us find the other members of the prophecy."

It hadn't occurred to him until that moment that his abilities could be tapped for any other purpose than his own personal well-being. That others could benefit from his intuition felt almost like a spiritual revelation.

"But how?"

She shook her head. "I don't know yet. We're gonna have to work on it. Together, if you'll let me help."

She turned back to her computer then, and he could tell she was still thinking about harnessing the power of his precognition. He flipped through the stack of remaining names, noting how many other psychics were listed as having precognition when Mia gasped.

"Holy crap, Thomas. I think I may have found one."

33

LANYING

Thursday, September 29
Shanghai

Lanying stared blankly at the textbook in her lap. She blinked in an attempt to refocus the words on the page, but it was no use. She was far too preoccupied with the unexpected turn her life had recently taken to concentrate on her studies, so instead of forcing the issue, she turned off the bedside lamp and settled in beneath the crisp cotton sheets.

A moment later she switched on the light again and leaned over the edge of her bed to fish for the wooden box hidden beneath the mattress. In the days since her grandfather had given it to her, trusting her with what he described as his most cherished possession, she'd been over the contents a dozen times, reading and rereading each scrap of information. There were fading Polaroids of inscriptions carved into ancient ruins in Tibet. There were charcoal rubbings of symbols from temple walls in Central America, written in a language she couldn't begin to comprehend. There was a leather-bound journal, worn from overuse, filled with notes about the many civilizations throughout history with knowledge of the Sevens Prophecy.

As she flipped idly through the journal, she was struck by the juxtaposition between contemporary knowledge of the prophecy as compared to its obvious pervasiveness throughout history. For truly, until Mia and Thomas shared what they knew, she'd been completely unaware. Yet it was clear from the stack of artifacts within the box, for thousands of years, devout believers from every continent stood in watchful anticipation of the ancient prediction. Had it simply been forgotten over time or had it been systematically eliminated from the world's collective consciousness?

The corner of a yellowing sheet of newsprint at the bottom of the box caught her attention, and she slipped it out from beneath the other artifacts. She began unfolding, taking special care not to cause any tears, and once it was completely unfurled a single line of text was revealed, written in a strange symbolic script. Underneath was a translation in Chinese characters – "Seven light to save the earth. Seven dark to destroy it." Below that was the word 'Bantu' written in her grandfather's familiar handwriting.

Upon reading these words, Lanying felt the familiar pull of what her grandfather called her 'distant visions.' In an instant, she was no longer in her bedroom, safely in Shanghai. Instead, her mind was spirited away to some unknown, remote location, and before her sat a man on a grass mat at the edge of a primitive hut. Spread around him were photographs of hundreds of men and women, all African, and all without hands. It was unclear as to whether they were born without hands or if they'd been removed later on for some reason, but either way, the images were horrifying. She watched as he held one picture after another, closing his eyes as if surrendering to their unseen power. He remained motionless during most of what appeared to be some sort of ritual, twitching only slightly from time to time, a scowl crossing his brow.

His skin was smooth, the darkest brown she'd ever seen, and she wished in that moment she had the power to reach out and touch his cheek. She was certain it would feel like satin if she could. His hair was clipped short, almost to the scalp, and in contrast to the native looking sarong draped around his hips, a pair of thick, horn-rimmed glasses adorned his face.

Coming out of his trance-like state, he blinked repeatedly and then bowed his head, as if to recover from something. After a moment, he pulled a tablet out from beneath the woven mat and powered it on. His fingers flew across the screen, searching, and then finally he began to type. Lanying strained to see the words on the screen but the text was blurry and unreadable. She watched him from within the vision for several more minutes until slowly, the image started to retreat.

The following afternoon, as she sat in her Advanced Bariatrics seminar, she was yanked away, without warning, back to the African jungle. Initially concerned about missing important information from the day's lecture, she quickly reconsidered when she realized the importance of the scene she'd been called to witness.

The man from the first vision was there, dressed now in a filthy t-shirt with a logo for World Vision emblazoned across the back. He sat among a circle of women and infants, as well as boys and other men, most of whom looked to be between the ages of 12 to 40, and on the ground in the center of their group was a large scale model of what she assumed was the surrounding area. There was a highly forested section and beside that numerous fields displayed with different crops. By the way he slid the sections around and moved them in and out of the display, it was clear he was explaining crop rotation. She glanced away from the group and saw that just beyond the small clustering of thatched roof huts, there was a makeshift granary, where teenage girls worked to load baskets of maize onto a World Vision delivery truck.

As abruptly as she'd been pulled into the vision, she was dismayed to discover being returned to her class with the same degree of haste. Thrown slightly off-kilter, she blinked several times to reorient herself to her surroundings, from the blazing African sun into the dim classroom. Her professor was pontificating about the pros and cons of LAP band surgery, and Lanying immediately tuned out. The last thing she wanted to think about was people who had access to so much food they needed operations to keep themselves from eating, especially having just witnessed people living in a place known for extreme bouts of famine. Without the slightest hesitation, she gathered her belongings and slipped unnoticed out the back of the lecture hall.

Most of the visions she'd experienced during her life had been benign. Of people driving to work, grocery shopping, watching television. And the truth was, she hadn't been particularly inclined to think very much about the meaningless visions peppering her existence. She'd mollified herself about remaining at a distance, uninvolved, because what went on in other people's lives simply wasn't her business. However, after meeting Thomas in real life, outside the visions she'd observed him through for so long, she now realized she could no longer ignore the truth.

She was part of the Sevens Prophecy.

She was chosen to save the world.

And therefore, it stood to reason that the visions she was having of the man in Africa were important. She was sure of it.

She headed to the closest Wi-Fi area on campus and booted up her laptop, Googling World Vision from her phone. Within moments she learned they were an agency dedicated to 'working with children, families, and their communities worldwide to reach their full potential by tackling the causes of poverty and injustice.' She began skimming their website, searching through hundreds of active development projects across dozens of countries in Africa when she spotted a photograph of the man from her vision.

His name was Salomon Maunb, and he was a junior agricultural specialist from the Democratic Republic of the Congo.

Immediately, she searched for information about the country, having little knowledge of its location on the map, much less its history or current status, and the first image on the screen turned her stomach. Dozens and dozens of men, women, and children frowning into the camera, all without any hands, exactly like the photographs she'd witnessed Salomon inspecting in her first vision. *What had Salomon been doing with the pictures?* she thought. *And what in the world happened to the Congolese?*

Discovering the truth behind the mutilated natives was the easier of the two inquiries. Two clicks later, the answer was revealed by an online encyclopedia page describing the atrocities committed by King Leopold II of Belgium against the Congolese during his reign at the turn of the nineteenth century. After claiming much of the land in the Congo for himself, Leopold used mercenaries to exploit forced labor from the native population, harvesting and processing rubber. The king went on to amass a great fortune at the expense of nearly ten million Congolese lives. Sadly, if the Congolese were unable to meet their daily rubber quota, the punishment was death; although many Congolese children and wives whose fathers and husbands did not meet their quotas also paid a severe penalty by having their hands removed.

Upon reading all of this, Lanying was appalled and overwhelmed by the brutality Salomon's ancestors endured and immediately wondered to what degree Salomon was motivated by this information. Did it make him angry? Sad? Emboldened? It also bothered her that she'd lived her entire life without knowing anything about this narrative of world history, causing her to speculate about other gaps in her knowledge base. Her curiosity sparked, she dove deeper into her search, reading more about Leopold's reign of terror and the current state of the Democratic Republic of Congo. And then, an hour into her search, she stumbled across *Heart of Darkness,* Joseph Conrad's seminal call-to-arms against the Dutch occupation and downloaded it immediately.

She was three-quarters of the way through the novella, still sitting in the same Wi-Fi station in the university's library when her phone buzzed in her pocket. She pulled it out and saw that Thomas was attempting to Skype. Mindful of the library's strict no calls policy, she dashed into the nearest restroom, leaving her backpack and laptop behind.

As soon as the restroom door closed safely behind her, she answered the call. "Hello!" she said, waving enthusiastically at the screen with her free hand.

"Hi," he grinned back. "It's good to see you."

"You too." She was surprised by the sense of relief she felt at seeing his face. Since leaving the United States she'd been plagued by the feeling that her trip there had been a dream and that Mia and Thomas didn't actually exist outside her own mind. There'd been several text messages sent between them, but visual confirmation of his existence sparked renewed confidence in her path.

"Listen," he began, "I don't want to keep you long because I'm sure you're busy and it's really late here in Baltimore, but I wanted to let you know Mia and I may have found another psychic from the prophecy."

"That's terrific news!"

"I know. We're still researching specifics about her, but her birthday is a match and she's part of this psychic registry we've been working from. We have no idea whether she's light or dark, but we're working on finding out." He paused. "Any news from your end?"

She thought of the hours she'd wasted reading about the Congo and *Heart of Darkness* and felt a pang of regret, until she remembered her grandfather's warnings about the prophecy. "Something quite strange, actually," she told him. "As it turns out, my grandfather, who I thought was simply an archivist at the Second Historical Archives of China in Nanjing, worked secretly as a historical theologian prior to his retirement. Thomas, he knows about the prophecy. He believes in the prophecy. And the weirdest part is, he suspected for many years I was part of it."

He was silent for a moment and she saw the awed expression on his face. "What does he know?"

"A lot. He gave me a box of old relics and notes from his research. I've been trying to go through it..." She stopped then, the guilt of her misdirected attention weighing heavily, until she suddenly remembered her first vision of Salomon occurred as she was going through the box. *Was it possible?* she thought.

"Thomas, I think I may have found another psychic as well."

His eyes widened in disbelief. "You're kidding."

She was piecing it all together quickly in her own mind – the scrap of paper written in Bantu and Salomon's trance-like appearance while holding the photographs of the handless Congolese. It wasn't impossible for him to be one of them. He even appeared to be about the right age. And if the reason her ability had shown her Thomas was because he was part of the prophecy, perhaps that's why it was showing her Salomon as well.

"Remember when I told you I had visions of you long before actually meeting you in real life?"

"Yes, of course."

"Well, I believe it might be happening again. Now that I've made an actual, physical connection with you, I believe my focus may have now shifted to another member of the prophecy. Since returning from the United States, I've had several visions of an African man named Salomon working in the Democratic Republic of Congo. I didn't know all of that at first, of course, but it didn't take long to uncover with a little online research."

"And what makes you think he might be psychic?"

She called to mind the way Salomon held the photos in his hands. The way he sat motionless, as if in prayer or meditation. As she described what she'd seen to Thomas, she became even more convinced there was something inherently supernatural about it.

"It could be psychometry," Thomas said, without missing a beat, clearly unfazed by the ridiculousness of what she was suggesting.

"Which is what?" she asked.

"Mia described it to me as the ability to use an object to understand more about the events surrounding it. He might have been using the pictures to see back in time to the point at which they were taken. What were the pictures of?"

Her stomach churned at the thought. "Mutilated native Congolese. They were enslaved and tortured by the Dutch monarchy in the late 1800's. I've just been reading up on it. Such a tragedy."

Thomas looked away from the screen, and she could tell he was thinking. "Do you have a gut feeling about him? About whether he's light or dark? Because maybe he's interested in their persecution because he's looking forward to its return."

Another woman entered the restroom and eyed Lanying suspiciously as she slipped into a stall.

"I had the same thought initially, but the more I think about it, the more I'm inclined to think that's not the case." She spoke more quietly now that she was no longer alone in the room. "He works for World Vision, an organization which partners with communities to address immediate food needs and to grow sustainable food for the future. When I saw him, he appeared to be teaching a village about crop rotation. He was hands on, Thomas. He was helping those people. And I think he might actually be Congolese himself."

They were both silent as the other woman appeared from her stall, washed her hands, and returned to the library without attempting to make small talk or even eye contact. Lanying's muscles relaxed as the door clicked shut, and she realized just how nervous it made her to think someone else might discover her secret.

"So you think, assuming he's one of us, that he's light?"

"Yes. My gut tells me he is."

He frowned. "So really, we're no better off than we were before, right? Because finding good guys doesn't do us any good if it's the bad guys we need to keep apart."

She hadn't considered this, however, she felt compelled to trust her gift. It had to be showing her Salomon for a reason, and not just to prove there were other good psychics in the world. She already knew that. Her visions had a purpose, she just had to figure out what it was.

"I'm going to reach out to him, Thomas. There was an email contact on World Vision's website for him. I don't know quite what I'll say, but we need to at least find out if his birthdate matches ours. Beyond that, perhaps bringing him into our circle won't stop the dark psychics, but it can't hurt to have another person on our side, can it?"

He smiled into his phone, and she saw herself smiling back in the tiny image on the bottom corner of her screen. "I like your thinking," he said. "And it's not a bad idea. Although to be honest, he might not even respond. He might think you're crazy."

She returned his smile, surprised by how their conversation emboldened her. For the first time in her life, she felt truly purposeful, a valuable member of a team. Crucial even. And it felt wonderful. "I can handle it," she said.

CHAPTER

34

MIA

Friday, September 30
Baltimore

The phone on Mia's desk rang. It never rang. She looked at it for several seconds before registering that she should pick up the receiver.

"Hello?" she said cautiously.

"Is this Rosetti?"

She recognized the voice immediately. Sisco.

"What do you want?"

"I got something for you on the guy you been lookin' for."

Criminals didn't typically call her out of the blue, offering unsolicited information. It was clear he needed something from her. "What do you want?" she repeated again.

Jack looked up from his laptop, curious now about who was on the other end of her conversation.

"Mi amigo, Trece."

"What about him."

"He got picked up by your department this morning."

This was the first she was hearing about his arrest, but it wasn't a surprise. The question was whether the arresting officer would be willing to make a deal to get her the information she needed about Alejandro.

"And?" she said. She was going to make him ask. It felt good to make him say the words aloud.

"And I'm willing to give you what I got if they let him go."

"And if they don't?"

"Then I ain't got nothin' to say to you." And with that, the line went dead.

She set the receiver back on its cradle and had to laugh at Jack's expectant expression.

"That phone never rings," he said.

"I know. And you won't believe who it was." She gave him the CliffsNotes version of the conversation and he followed her out of their office to the detaining facilities. "I hope they haven't already shipped him off to central booking."

She needn't have worried because as they reached the holding cells she spotted one of the senior officers escorting him into a room for questioning.

She nodded at Trece. "Is this guy your perp, and if he is, can I get a minute with you, Zelnick?" she called.

"He's not mine. Just dropping him off. If you need somethin' you're gonna have to talk to Fields. Last time I saw him he was with the Chief."

Her heart sank. Fields was about the last officer she would have chosen to deal with, given their past history and current situation. Jack shot her a knowing glance as she called to mind the last run in they'd had with him just after Commissioner Dalton's arrest. A 'by the book' hardliner, he was a stickler for both details and justice. Which meant he hated that Mia went after Dalton on a hunch and carried out her plan for his arrest outside standard operating procedures. The fact that he'd defended Dalton on principle ensured the two officers would never get along, much less see eye to eye with regard to Sisco's negotiations.

"You wanna go talk to him, or do you want me to?" Jack asked.

"Let's just go together," she said. "Maybe my dad will run interference."

Fields was standing in the doorway of her father's office as she and Jack approached. She stood in the hall, just inside his line of sight, until they finished their conversation.

"You need me?" her father asked as Fields began to walk away without so much as acknowledging her presence.

"Actually, no," she said to both men. "I was looking for you, Fields."

He turned on his heel, making a slow production of her imposition. "Can it wait? I've got a guy detained in questioning for me." He checked his watch. "I'm late already."

"That's actually what we wanted to talk to you about," Jack said, taking the lead. "We've got an opportunity to get some intel on a case we've been pursuing if we can work a deal to get your guy sprung."

Fields laughed and continued down the hall. "Fat chance," he called over his shoulder. "I've had this punk in my crosshairs for months. Like hell I'm gonna let him off now."

He rounded the corner and was out of sight before Mia's father broke the tension. "What's going on?"

She rolled her eyes. "You know the case we've been working about the woman whose boyfriend followed her from Phoenix to kill her?"

"Yes."

"Well, Fields has this guy Trece down in holding. I have no idea what he picked him up for, but his buddy Sisco called me a little while ago to make a deal – Trece's freedom for intel on Alejandro, the guy who's out to kill his girlfriend."

She could see her father weighing their options. He walked a fine line between being the chief of police and being her dad. 99 times out of 100, he erred on the side of the department, but she still held out hope.

"You think your informant is credible?" he asked.

"As credible as any criminal can be," she answered honestly.

"And you trust him to keep his end of the bargain?"

"He knows I've got stuff to bring him in on if he doesn't."

Her father glared at her over the top of his glasses. "I'm gonna pretend I didn't hear that, Officer. But let me talk to Fields about it."

Mia couldn't keep from smiling. It was good to have friends, or family as the case was, in high places.

"Wipe that grin off your face, Mia. I'm not making any promises. If he's got this Trece kid in here for something legit, I might have to let it ride."

"It's a girl's life on the line, Dad." She didn't love playing this card with him, but sadly, it was all she had.

He shooed her off with both hands, ushering her back down the hall in the direction she'd come. "I said no promises."

An hour later, she and Jack were sharing a foot-long turkey melt and a bag of chips when her father appeared in the doorway. His expression spoke volumes.

"So it's a no," she offered before giving him a chance to speak.

"I'm sorry, Mia. Fields has him on felony charges. If it had been a misdemeanor, maybe I could have pulled some strings. But I can't let this go. I'm sorry, but you're just going to need to find this guy another way." When she and Jack didn't respond, he apologized again and walked away.

A moment later, without a word to Jack, she picked up her cell to place a call.

"Hey, Jose," she said. "This is Officer Rosetti. You ready for your 15 minutes of fame?"

CHAPTER

35

JOSE

Monday, October 3
Baltimore

The makeup artist from WJZ's crew would not leave him alone. Just when he thought she was finished with the powder and the hair gel, she returned, her fingernails manicured into severely lacquered points. He hoped she wouldn't somehow lacerate him with them, and was relieved when the show's producer, Frank, appeared to escort him to the sound stage.

"How's it going this morning?" he asked.

"I'm a little nervous," he replied honestly.

"First time on TV, huh? It gets to the best of us," Frank said, draping an unwelcome arm across Jose's shoulders. "Just do your best out there, and Denise will do the rest. She's the best."

He had no doubt the seasoned anchorwoman would paint him in the very best light, commanding the screen with all the talent he lacked, however, he didn't need her to win an Emmy. He just needed her to put the word out that he was looking for Andrea. And then he needed Alejandro to take the bait.

As the weather segment ended and the crew took a commercial break, he was whisked into an upholstered armchair toward the edge of the stage. A moment later, Denise arrived, looking much fresher than she should have for the early hour of the day. She greeted him warmly and within seconds the lights came up as the crew counted down to the on-air cue.

"This morning I have Jose Torres here with me with an appeal to the people of Baltimore. He's looking for his friend, Andrea Morillo, who disappeared unexpectedly from her home in Phoenix earlier this month, and now his search has led him here. Good morning, Jose."

"Good morning," he replied, as if they hadn't just greeted one another seconds before.

"What can you tell us about Andrea's disappearance?"

A recent photograph of Andrea, taken from her own phone, flashed across the screen behind them, and Jose attempted to slow his breathing as he recalled the words he and Mia had rehearsed the day before. "Andrea and I are good friends," he began, reassured by how steady his voice sounded despite the queasiness in his gut. "We had plans together and when she didn't show up, I went to her house, in Phoenix. Her keys were there, her purse… everything. I kept calling her cell, hoping she would pick up, you know? But she never answered." He tried to look convincingly distraught as he recounted the fabricated events. "Finally, last week, I got a strange call from a number with a 410 area code. Nobody said anything. There was just breathing and crying."

The anchorwoman nodded sympathetically. "Can you share with us why it's important for the people of Baltimore to be on the lookout for her?"

Mia had stressed the importance of not mentioning Alejandro in the interview. The last thing they wanted was to spook him. "She's been known to self-mutilate, inflicting pain to punish herself. She's been suicidal. In fact, she recently ran her car into another car, on purpose, in what I think was an attempt to kill herself. If she's here in Baltimore and she's still alive, I need to find her."

"Do you know why she'd come to Baltimore? Does she have friends or family here she might reach out to?"

He shook his head. "Not that I know of. The only other clue that brought me here, besides the phone call, was a paper she'd printed off the internet I found at her place back in Phoenix. It was for Absolute Tattoo in Dundalk. I already went there and she hasn't been by yet, but I'm not giving up hope. I've been looking around that area for her."

The stage assistant gave the signal that it was time to wrap up the piece and Denise immediately cut in, turning away from him to speak directly into the camera. "Let's take one more look at this picture of Andrea Morillo. Again, if you see or hear anything regarding her whereabouts or well-being, you're encouraged to call our tip line here at the station. The number at the bottom of your screen is 888-555-TIPS." She turned back to him, extending her hand in a gesture of consolation. "Hopefully we'll find her," she said sincerely.

The WJZ theme song began and Denise stood, unclipping her microphone from her lapel. "You did so well, Jose," she said. "Much better than my first time on air." She turned then to Mia, who'd appeared unnoticed off-stage during the interview and was looking expectantly, hands on her hips. "You think that'll do the trick?" Denise asked her.

Mia shrugged, acknowledging Jose with a small wave. "It's really the best we can do. We've given him a place to look for her. Now we just have to hope he sees the interview and decides to check it out for himself." She paused then, looking to him. "We have an unmarked unit posted there already. If he shows up, we'll get him."

He and Mia thanked the WJZ crew and walked to the parking lot together. It struck him then, as Mia clicked her key fob to unlock a Honda Civic halfway down the lot that she was alone, without her partner, and also wasn't dressed in her uniform. "Are you on duty?" he asked.

"I worked overnight," she said. "Got off at six and came straight here."

It seemed strange to him, that someone would go so far above and beyond what was considered reasonable to assist Andrea in her situation. Most people, he found, did only what was required. Nothing more. And yet here was this cop, who could have easily brushed their case aside as a lost cause, sending them on their way back to Phoenix to fend for themselves, but hadn't. She'd already done more than he'd ever expected the police to do for them, and now here she was, taking her off-duty time to check in on his interview.

"How're you getting back to the motel?" she asked.

"I Ubered," he explained, pulling out his phone.

"You want a ride back? It's not too far out of my way, and I'd actually like to talk to Andrea about a few things."

Sliding his phone back into his pocket, he couldn't help but feel as if there was something important he was missing about her. Something he should have known but didn't. He figured it wouldn't hurt to spend a few more minutes getting to know her, so he accepted her offer, saying, "Sounds good. As long as you're sure it's not out of the way."

"Not at all," she replied, smiling. "I'd do the same for a friend."

36

Monday, October 3
Democratic Republic of Congo

Salomon took the bandana out of his back pocket, wiped the sweat from his brow, and looked up from his trenching to survey his fellow field workers. Their backs bore the brunt of the late afternoon sun, hunched over their various tasks for the day. While many worked, as he did, to plant rows of cassava and maize, others strung twine in straight rows further down the field to help assure proper placement of the seeds.

In a region where drought was rare and land was prevalent, it seemed counterintuitive that such a large percentage of Congolese died from starvation each year, but it was most certainly the case for his fellow countrymen. However, thanks to his university training and partnership with the World Vision organization, he'd begun teaching farmers in his home village of Buganga to replace their common practice of scattering seeds randomly with the simple act of planting in well-spaced rows. Unbelievably, in less than two years, the families working under his tutelage had seen a 750% increase in their crop production, and had gone from being unable to sustain their own nutritional needs to producing enough surplus to share with others.

Now his village was getting ready to partner with yet another surplus producing group as part of a farming collective. Together, they would be able to pool resources for storage facilities and have greater bargaining power with seed and equipment suppliers. They would also get better prices for their surplus by selling directly with one another in nearby towns like Minova and even Goma, only a couple of hours' drive on a bumpy road that twisted and turned around Lake Kivu. Looking at his friends and family now, working not just to survive, but to thrive, gave him great joy.

And yet, he still couldn't help but doubt the longevity of his accomplishments, especially given the country's history of political and military unrest. Born in the final years of Mobutu Sese Soko's presidency, he grew up in the aftermath of the archetypal African dictator's reign - a world of great famine, tenuous alliances between warring factions, and death. Along with the other members of his village, he had never known peace.

As a small boy, he'd been fascinated by the elders' stories of the Belgian rule, occurring long before his grandparents' birth. They'd spoken of great atrocities. Of how their numbers had been reduced by several million over the course of King Leopold's reign, a man some of the tribe's wisest leaders felt certain was part of a great prophecy predicting the end of days. So strong were the stories' impressions on him, that when government scouts selected him for studies at the University of Kamina in Katanga, the genocide and the prophecy were the first things he researched at his arrival.

The moment he held the photographs procured from the university library of the disfigured Congolese in his hands, he'd been able to see his actual ancestors as if they were standing before him. He could hear their anguish. Feel their desperation. As horrifying as it was, he wasn't surprised to encounter visions similar to the one he'd experienced upon finding an inscription in a cave as a small boy. Touching those engravings had shown him images of ancient tribesmen fearful of the world to come.

Transferring knowledge from an object's history simply by touching it was a gift he could neither understand nor explain.

All he knew was that he saw what he saw.

The images of his mutilated, handless ancestors haunted him even still, but unfortunately he'd discovered very little at the university about the prophecy of which the elders spoke.

"Salomon!" his sister Manu called to him from the village edge beyond the wide expanse of dirt. "Come quickly. Marceau is here to see you."

On his way across the field, he offered water from his canteen to several of his fellow laborers, and as he drew closer to the collection of huts, he could smell prepared cassava roasting on the fire. Manu stood beside a bed of hot coals, tending to her pots.

"Are we meeting all together as a village or will it just be the two of you tonight?" she asked him as he approached, her pride in him unmistakable.

"I expect he's here to help negotiate our agreement with the village in Minova, so he might just meet with me this time."

"We're so blessed to have you, brother," she said, leaving her post at the cooker to walk with him to where the familiar World Vision truck awaited. "Without your influence in Katanga, Marceau would have never come to our village."

"It was pure luck I was chosen for university. Nothing more. Remember that." He looked at her sternly. "There's nothing special about me. It could have just as easily been Niyonkuru or Rochi or even Bamboula who was selected."

"It wasn't though," she said, wrapping her arms around his rib cage, "it was you."

"Well, maybe next time the university comes looking for students, they'll choose you."

"They won't take a woman," she scoffed.

"You never know, right, Marceau?" he said to the World Vision volunteer who was rummaging through the bed of his 4x4.

"Mais oui," he replied, slipping a laptop and a manila envelope under his arm. "In fact, some of what I have to discuss with all of you today pertains to women's rights."

"How so?" Manu asked.

"Well, like this, for example," he said, producing a sheet from his folder depicting a cumbersome looking piece of machinery.

"What is it?"

"It's a cassava slicer. It can slice up to fifteen tons an hour."

"Can you imagine, no more slicing with a knife?" she said, still staring at the paper. "It would free up so much time to do other things."

"Exactly," Marceau said as he walked with them to the largest of the village's communal huts. "Perhaps you'd be interested in using some of that free time to take a few classes on community leadership."

She bowed her head. "Those classes are not for me."

"Of course they are." He smiled. "Women are valuable assets, and it's time you start garnering the respect you deserve."

Salomon had already tried convincing his sister to enroll in the Women for Women International Program after she was held at gun point and forcibly raped while he was away at the university. That he wasn't there to protect all of his sisters from the daily threat of violence weighed heavily on his conscience, and that he hadn't made it home in time to prevent Manu's assault still caused him many sleepless nights. Nonetheless, he'd witnessed the success of the program, visible in the women who thrived in the city of Katanga - earning increased wages, influencing decisions at home and in their communities, and making their health and well-being a priority. It was no surprise he had chosen his own wife, Keicha, from among the program's graduates, but unfortunately, Manu still struggled to see her own value.

He laid a gentle hand on her shoulder now, a gesture of encouragement. "Perhaps it's time to reconsider."

She shook her head. "What about the babies?"

"Keicha and I can look after your children."

Of his five sisters, Manu was his favorite, partially because they were the closest of the siblings in age, born only eleven months apart, but mostly because she'd saved his life when they were children. Delirious with fever, the result of an infected laceration on his leg, he could still remember six-year-old Manu sitting by his bedside for several weeks, forcing drops of water down his throat and working tirelessly to refresh the wet sarong she draped across his chest. While the rest of his family worked in the fields and beside the coals to ensure their survival, Manu had tended to Salomon. And miraculously, he had recovered.

It was just after his brush with death that he'd experienced his first hallucination at the cave. When he placed his hands on the ancient inscription carved into the rock wall, he'd immediately seen the faces of those who had carved it, felt the truth of the prediction in which they believed. However, having experienced similar visions with the fever, he dismissed the images, convinced death was coming for him once again.

When the visions continued even as his health improved, he was forced to acknowledge something unusual was happening. In the years since, he'd discovered his visions only came when he touched objects of importance, and they usually correlated with significant historical events. Sometimes the event would pertain specifically to himself or his family, but more often than not, they connected him to the world outside Buganga.

"Just take what we discuss tonight with the other female villagers into consideration," Marceau encouraged her as they ducked into the hut. "It's never too late to make a change."

As twilight fell across the community, dozens of men and women trudged out of the fields, wilted from the day's labor, their faces and hands caked in the dark volcanic soil. They were joined by the other villagers for the evening meal, and as they ate, Marceau shared news from the city about their inclusion in the co-op. He also encouraged the women to consider signing up for the year-long workforce training, and as he spoke, Manu refused to make eye contact with Salomon.

Frustrated by her willfulness, he wandered from the group to the hut he shared with fifteen of his closest family members on the far side of the village. It was abandoned, as his wife, Keicha, and the rest of his extended family remained with the others to clean up from supper and prepare the fires for the following morning. Alone for the first time in days, he took the opportunity to log onto his university account with his tablet, using the Wi-Fi transmitted by the satellite server in Marceau's truck. Typically, he received only work related messages to his email account, so he was taken aback when at the top of his inbox was a personal communication.

All the way from China.

37

MIA

Wednesday, October 5
Baltimore

It had been two days since Jose's television interview and even though she hadn't expected for Alejandro to show his face, she was disappointed that even his associates hadn't made an appearance. The longer they went without a lead, the more her frustration grew.

"He's onto us," she told Jack on the way to their weekly staff meeting.

"I doubt that," he said. "Let's not jump to the worst conclusion. Maybe he just didn't see the clip."

They slipped through the door, and she took her seat in the back corner of the conference room just as things were getting started. "Someone saw the clip," she whispered. "He has to know."

One of the senior detectives, Bob Stoecker, began the meeting by reminding everyone about a mandatory weapons refresher class the city was requiring every officer to attend the following week. He shared the mugshot of a perp who they believed was running heroin into Prince George's county, gave an update on a kidnapping the unit was following, and passed out overnight assignments which needed to be filled. Just before the meeting was adjourned, he opened the floor to the others. Mia sprang out of her chair.

"Has anybody heard any talk about a guy named Alejandro from Phoenix being here in Baltimore? He's a Chicano so Jack and I've hit all the known MS-13 guys, but we're still coming up empty. Have any of you heard anything on your beats?"

Darnell Carson, one of her classmates from the academy spoke up immediately. "I mighta heard something about your guy the other day," he said, turning to his partner. "Remember the car theft on Highland last week, and the dude we talked to in the service station across the street who said he saw some locals with a new guy nosin' around the car the night before it went missing."

"Yeah. I remember," his partner said. Then he turned to Mia. "This store attendant seemed pretty intuitive, like one of those guys who knows what's going on around his shop." He pulled out a notepad from his shirt pocket. "His name is Lavelle Washington. We haven't been able to find the car or a suspect, but if this Lavelle guy noticed someone new, it might be worth checking out. In fact, if your perp's involved with the car, we might kill two birds with this one."

Mia glanced at Jack and then back to Carson. "Then we should swing by with Alejandro's picture. We're thankful for any lead we can get, and we'll keep you posted if we get any information on the car."

Half an hour later, Jack pulled the cruiser into the parking lot of the Royal Farms convenience store on the corner of Fayette and Highland. An elderly-looking black man greeted them from behind the counter as they entered.

"Morning, Officers," he said.

"Morning," Jack replied. "We're looking for Lavelle Washington."

"Well, you've come to the right place," he smiled. "What can I do for you today?"

Jack quickly explained the situation while Mia slid a photograph of Alejandro across the counter.

"Well now, it was getting on twilight when I noticed them," Lavelle explained, "but the one I didn't recognize did have longish hair like the man in this picture. Big across the shoulders like this guy too. He was with a few other Latino men I seen around from time to time, and they caught my attention on account a they was just standin' there doing nothin' but looking at that car. Almost called you all about it myself, but I try not to get involved if I don't have to, you know what I'm sayin? Anyway, wish I woulda now that all this is going on."

"If you see something, say something," Jack said, parroting the Homeland Securities slogan. "Don't ever hesitate. You never know when something might be important to pass along."

"I'll do that from now on," the man promised, and Mia could feel his embarrassment. She felt compelled to let him off the hook.

"You know, there's something more you can do for us now," she told him as she scrolled through the precinct's website on her phone searching for a mugshot of Sisco. "Any chance this was one of the local men you spotted that night."

Recognition crossed the man's weathered face the instant before he spoke. "Now that man there, he's stolen from me more times than I care to count. Mostly 40s outta the case over there when I'm with other customers. He thinks I'm not gonna do nothin' about it, and he's right cuz I don't want his boys in here starting trouble. Just get in and get out. But yeah, he was out there with the fellow in your photograph that night. They were together. Along with a couple a others."

This was all the confirmation Mia needed to hear. If Sisco and Alejandro were together, there was no doubt Alejandro knew they were looking for him. The only thing keeping Andrea safe was that he didn't know where she was. At least for now.

They thanked Lavelle and walked side by side in silent familiarity back to the car. They buckled up, but Jack didn't turn over the engine.

"They're running a stolen car operation," he said.

"Sisco and Trece."

"Yeah. Call your dad. I bet the felony charge Fields picked Trece up on was grand theft auto. He must have caught him with another car, and they haven't connected that theft back to this one yet."

A quick call to her father confirmed Jack's hunch. "Let Carson know to get up with Fields. I think these two cases are connected," she told him before disconnecting.

They continued to sit in the parking lot, paralyzed by indecision.

"Where do we go from here?" she asked Jack.

He puffed his cheeks and blew the air out slowly. "I have no idea. Sisco and Trece are stealing cars and now we know Alejandro is caught up with them somehow, even though he's probably just tagging along. Trece got caught by Fields, but we don't know for sure whether he was part of this heist."

"You think they're selling them off outta state or scrapping them for parts?"

"Who the hell knows."

Jack's dejection was contagious, and Mia felt herself growing more discouraged the longer they sat. That their morning's investigation had the potential to land Sisco in prison was little consolation, because despite all the time she'd spent searching on her own, he was still her only connection to Alejandro's whereabouts. There was really only one more lead to follow.

"Let's head over to the tattoo place," she said decisively. She'd been wary of going there herself for fear of tipping Alejandro off on their involvement, but if he was working alongside Sisco, there was no doubt he was already well-versed in her connection to the case.

"No one's been there," Jack said.

"Someone's been there," she countered. "Just maybe no one's talking."

Although Mia prided herself on keeping an open mind with regard to judging people by their outward appearance, she couldn't help but venture a sideways glance at Jack as they entered the tattoo parlor. Sitting just inside the vestibule behind the front counter was a formidable looking man. With most of his visible skin obscured by dozens of random tattoos and a bushy beard that would make even Paul Bunyan envious, the shopkeeper epitomized the subculture. Mia hoped he was more bark than bite.

"What can I do for you, Officers?" he asked them, his voice gruff but not antagonistic.

At the beginning of their investigation, they'd left the shop's employees in the dark about their operation because Mia felt there was too great a risk of the employees accidentally giving away their involvement. Instead, they opted to leave an unmarked car on duty to observe patrons entering and exiting the store. Now that their cover was blown, however, the need for answers trumped discretion, and it was time to fill them in.

"Any chance you saw the news segment on WJZ mentioning your shop by name a few days back?" Jack asked.

The man's jaw clenched. He clearly wasn't someone who enjoyed being put on the spot. And it seemed as though he was no stranger to confrontation. "Our books are clean. Been audited twice in the last three years and everything checked. I run an honest establishment."

"I have no doubt," Jack countered. "I'm not here about your operations though. I'm here about a missing girl. A friend of hers was on TV telling about how he thought she might be coming to your shop."

"Don't know nothin' about any missing girl. Only girls been in here are ones I know."

Jack nodded, scratching at the stubble on the back of his neck. "Understood. We're actually more interested in anybody else who might have come in here looking for her."

"You're talking about somebody come in here asking about some missing girl?"

"Exactly."

The man shook his head, but then held out a finger, an invitation to wait, as he called loudly into the back of the shop. "Hey, Slick, you had anybody in here the last couple a days asking about a missing girl?"

"Nah."

"How 'bout you, Ducky?"

Instead of answering directly, a squirrelly-looking boy, barely out of his teens, peered around the wall of his station. "Who's askin'?"

"The cops," he said, waving Ducky to the front of the store.

Skinny and pockmarked, Ducky strolled to the counter as if he had nothing but time on his hands. "Yeah, I talked to a guy in here the other day asking about a girl."

Mia's heart raced. If the stake-out officers hadn't spotted Alejandro, he had to have sent someone they didn't recognize. "What day was this?"

He shrugged. "Yesterday. Or maybe Monday. I don't remember exactly. The days all run together."

"And you told him you hadn't seen her?"

"Yeah. Cuz I hadn't."

"What else did you tell him?"

"He started asking if anybody else had been in to ask about her, just like you."

"And you told him no?"

"Yeah. Cuz nobody had."

"It was just one guy or more than one?"

"Just one guy."

"Can you describe him?"

Ducky ran his fingers through his hair which was thick and dark and tangled at the ends. Mia imagined the greasy film it probably left on his hands. It was all she could do to focus on his response.

"He was a Hispanic guy. Mexican maybe. About 5'10" or 5'11". Seemed smart, you know. But sheltered. Like he'd never spent a day of his life on the street."

Looking at Jack, she was sure his look of confusion mirrored her own. The man Ducky described didn't sound like any of the thugs Alejandro had access to.

He sounded like Jose.

CHAPTER

38

LANYING

Wednesday, October 5
Shanghai

It had been several days since Lanying had composed her email to Salomon. Since pressing send, she'd checked for a response no less than 37 times, but who was counting.

She placated herself by focusing on the time difference between China and the Congo, shortage of internet access, and sheer lack of time. All of this was to keep her from dwelling on the idea that he might never respond at all.

After a morning of classes and a quick chat with Mia and Thomas in the afternoon, she prepared a simple supper of dumpling soup which she shared with her grandfather off a tray table in his room. He'd begun refusing more and more of his meals and between that and his weakening faculties, she feared he wouldn't be with her for very much longer.

"Any news from the boy in Africa?" he asked her.

She shook her head, rolling her noodles around her chopsticks and into her mouth. "Not yet," she said after swallowing.

"You seem discouraged."

"I've had three more visions of him – working in the fields, laughing with his family, studying. I haven't seen him in that trancelike position again." What she didn't say was that she was starting to doubt she'd ever seen it to begin with.

"Give it time, child." He took the smallest bite of noodles. "Trust in your abilities."

Her grandfather's confidence gave her strength. Strength to follow her heart, which she knew ultimately would eventually lead her out of Shanghai and back to the US on a permanent basis. However, she was hesitant to discuss the call she was feeling because although she knew he would be supportive, she also knew being without her would break his heart. So instead of saying anything about it, she quickly changed the subject.

"Tell me more about the origin of the prophecy in Africa. And your trip."

He chuckled to himself, setting his barely eaten noodles aside before pulling his blanket over his hips. "I remember it now as if it were another man from another time, because of course, it practically was. It was the year before I met your grandmother, and I was a university student myself, just about your same age. One of my history professors, Dr. Yeung Wei, planned a trip to west Africa and needed a research assistant. Of course, I said yes when he asked. How could I refuse?" He took a sip of his hot tea and continued. "Now I thought we were going to Angola to archive antiquities housed at their Natural Museum of Anthropology in Luanda, and I suppose according to the university's bank account records we were. But I didn't know until we arrived that Dr. Yeung's main focus was the prophecy.

"According to what we discovered there, the Bantu people brought the prophecy with them as they migrated from the Middle East as early as 500 BC. It spread throughout the tribes for thousands of years and was eventually carried to the New World via slave ships in the 1700's."

"And the scrap of paper from inside your box?"

"I copied it off an ancient rock face where it was carved onto cliffs of a dried riverbed. Dr. Yeung believed the inscription was over 2500 years old." He closed his eyes, as if he was remembering the spot. "That trip to Africa sparked my fascination with the prophecy I've been exploring ever since."

Lanying tried to imagine what it would have been like to have been there, face to face with concrete evidence of the prophecy revealed by the ancients. A prophecy of which she was now a part.

"You know, based on a lifetime of extensive research, Dr. Yeung theorized that the culmination of the prophecy would occur in his lifetime. He was wrong, of course, because he passed away almost 25 years ago, but he was close, in the whole scheme of things. Very, very close." He struggled to catch his breath and Lanying heard a faint rattling in his chest. She was about to mention it when he continued. "There's something I need to tell you about the prophecy and my part in it. You see, as it turned out, Dr. Yeung was more than just a researcher. He was what those of us inside the inner circle call a 'keeper.' Someone who is tasked with using what he or she knows of the prophetic signs to watch for the coming of the psychics who will usher in an age of darkness or of light. They protect the secret of the prophecy, hoping to keep its prediction from the evil psychics.

"Just as there are seven light and seven dark, there have always been seven keepers. When one dies, he or she passes the mantle on to another who takes their place as a sentinel. Watching. Preparing. Waiting. When Dr. Yeung passed away a quarter century ago, he passed that task on to me, along with the contents of the trunk containing his lifetime of research and all the research that came before. I added my own findings, of course, but now, well, I suppose there's no purpose in passing my duties on to you. It seems, my child, you hold a much greater purpose in the development of what is to come."

They sat in silence for several moments, and she was overcome by the weight of what it meant to be called to the light. It seemed silly she should continue on with her paltry day-to-day existence, as if nothing more was happening in the world than life itself. But so much more was happening, under the surface. The fate of the world was being decided.

"I think I'm about ready to turn in for the night," her grandfather said finally. "Why don't you go check and see if you have any messages from that Congolese boy." He winked at her then, in a very uncharacteristic way, which she imagined gave her a glimpse into who he may have been as a younger man, in the days he roamed the African countryside.

Instead of heeding her grandfather's advice, she dawdled, afraid of being disappointed. She washed the dinner dishes and set plates of food aside for her parents to reheat when they got home. She straightened the books on her shelf and read two chapters of her counseling textbook. Finally, after brushing her teeth and changing into her pajamas, she logged onto her email to check for messages.

To her surprise and delight, there was a reply.

Until the moment she saw Salomon's name as the contact, she hadn't realized how nervous she'd been about their eventual connection, or lack thereof. Now, she found herself paralyzed again, unable to force herself to open the message for fear of what she may find inside. Finally, she closed her eyes and clicked the mouse.

> Dear Lanying,
>
> Your email greatly surprised me. I have never gotten a message from someone so far away before. Also, I was surprised by the unusual nature of your words, talking about visions you've been having of me from your home in China. I think to myself, how can this be, that a woman in China is seeing what I am doing in my village in the Congo? But the descriptions you shared with me are true,

so I must believe that you can do what you have confessed to me.

Now I must also confess to you about what I can do, because you were right in assuming visions are part of my life as well, although I see things much differently than you. When you saw me looking at the photographs, I was using my ability to channel information from them. I am able to learn more about many objects just by touching them. I've been able to do it since I was a boy. Sometimes I use what I see to learn about the past, sometimes the present, and sometimes, although rarely, the future.

I look forward to getting another message from you again soon. I would like to know more about your visions and the other people you can see. Until we talk again…

Very truly yours,
Salomon

After years of being judged and belittled by her peers, to have this man, a virtual stranger, validate her abilities, was surreal. After blinking back tears, she reread the email, confirming she hadn't misunderstood his intention to continue their communication.

She immediately composed an email in return.

Dear Salomon,

Thank you for your response to my correspondence and for trusting me with your secret. It must seem quite strange for me to reach out to you about our shared abilities, seemingly out of nowhere, but there is something more I need to confess to you regarding the gifts we've been given.

You asked specifically about the other people I can see in my visions, and one of them is a man named Thomas who lives in the United States. On a recent trip there for an educational conference, a curious thing occurred. I actually met this man from my visions. To say it was a coincidence would be an understatement. But the coincidences didn't stop there.

Through the course of our conversation, we discovered we share the same birthday – a birthday we also share with his girlfriend, Mia, and another woman, Kate, with whom they were also acquainted.

And, as if sharing a birthday wasn't strange enough, we also all have psychic abilities.

So now, I hope you don't mind, but I must ask if you are also 25 years old, born on February 17th?

Warmest regards,

Lanying

After composing the email and sending it off, she couldn't fall asleep. She tossed and turned, organizing what she knew about the prophecy in her mind in an attempt to make sense of the illogical. At 2am, she noticed her phone screen was illuminated, a notification of some sort. She powered it on to discover a new email from Salomon had just arrived. Upon opening it she discovered the correspondence contained only three words. Three words she should have been prepared for, but evidently wasn't, from the way her heartbeat quickened in response.

"You are correct," was all it said.

Thursday, October 6
Democratic Republic of Congo

Salomon loved manual labor. The dull ache in his shoulder muscles and small of his back at the end of a long day in the fields. The satisfaction that came with knowing he'd made productive use of his time, toiling not just for the sake of surviving another day, but in an effort to improve the lives of everyone around him. The best part, however, was how quickly he fell asleep each night, the exhaustion of his body always overpowering any lingering concerns from the day.

Tonight, though, it was different. After volleying a series of emails back and forth to the Chinese woman, Lanying, his mind would not be still. Since Marceau and his satellite communication would not return to the village for several days, he would be unable to correspond with her again until later in the week. He didn't know if he could wait.

He was pondering the prophecy now as he lay in bed beside his sleeping wife. His restlessness was bothering her, and she stirred as he struggled to find a comfortable position in the hopes of falling asleep. It seemed, though, to be a lesson in futility.

In her final email, Lanying had described a prophecy to him, the way she fit into the ancient prediction for the world, and how she believed he did as well. After reading the message several times, he'd been unable to respond to her. Unable to put into words just how unbelievable it all seemed.

And yet, he couldn't help remembering the strange etching he'd come across in a rock alcove as a child. Engrossed in the persistence of day to day life, he'd all but forgotten the message and the strange visions he'd experienced when he placed his hands upon the symbols. Now, thinking back to the inscription painstakingly rendered against the smoothest section of rock, he realized the possible significance of his decade-old discovery. And the truth behind the visions he'd experienced there.

Careful not to disturb Keicha, he rolled off the thatched mattress onto the floor, put on his glasses, and tied his shoes onto his feet. The moon was full and bright, and it guided his path as he easily slipped unnoticed past the sleeping members of his family into the steamy night air. Outside, he prepared a torch from the closest fire pit and set out into the forest. Surprisingly, after so many years, he remembered the way, although parts had become overgrown and the closest stream now cut through a small section in the valley. The forest exploded in a symphony of chirps and calls and croaks from the wildlife that soared in the canopy and skittered across the muddy earth. Mindful that he was more prey than predator at night in the jungle, he used the torchlight to deter snakes and spiders from his path. He was grateful for the distraction and had all but forgotten about the purpose of his excursion, when he spotted the familiar alcove of his youth carved out of the cliff side.

He stopped dead, reconsidering his decision. If he remembered the inscription in the cave and his visions correctly, what would it mean? Would it change who he was or force him to reevaluate his purpose?

"I believe you may be part of the prophecy as well, chosen to put an end to the evils of the world."

The last line of Lanying's message returned to him, and he closed his eyes, a spring of anger welling up. He already knew who he was. He already had a purpose. He didn't need eleven words in a cave to expose some new facet of reality.

And yet…

He ran through the last twenty feet of underbrush toward the cave at a sprint and stopped just short of its entrance. He held the torch out at arm's length, using it to burn away the cobwebs and illuminate the rocky interior. The inscription was still there, as he had known it would be, and with new insight he read the words aloud, his human voice a stark contrast to the primal echoes which filled the air.

"Seven light to save the earth. Seven dark to destroy it."

Without warning, his legs gave out beneath him and he crumpled to the ground. Had he been drawn to this cave all those years ago for a reason? Should he have been more intuitive, knowing the words were meant for him to find?

With a trembling hand, he reached out to finger the weathered inscription, terrified of the authenticating vision it might produce.

Almost immediately the ancients were there beside him, primitive and earth-worn, huddled inside the cave debating the validity of the prophecy. One of them, the youngest, was diligently etching into the wall with a sharp piece of quartz while the others deliberated about how and when the fate of the world would be decided by seven gifted souls.

"Seven light to save the earth. Seven dark to destroy it."

Was it possible the end of the world had finally arrived and that it was his responsibility to assure the evil was kept at bay?

Salomon didn't have long to ponder the possibilities because just as the moss of the spongy forest floor began to mold itself around him, he heard a shriek. The sound tore him from the vision, and he knew instinctively it wasn't the call of a monkey, a chimp, or even a gorilla. It was wholly human. And it was coming from the direction of the village.

Prophecy forgotten, he struggled to his feet and headed off in the direction of the cry. Moments later a second call rang out. And then a third. His feet careened through thickets and vines, as he veered off the well-worn path, opting for the straightest route back to the village. The closer he got, the more manmade chaos he could make out over the now relative serenity of the jungle – men's angry voices, vehicle engines, and deafening wails of women and children.

There was no question as to the bedlam's cause – an armed gang of Rwandan rebels.

Seven years before, a group of Rwandan men had been responsible for his sister's brutal rape. Now images of Manu's battered body drove him through the brush without regard for his personal safety. His face and arms were torn and bloody as he approached the village.

He did not stop when he saw the pile of rubble where the granary once stood.

He did not stop when he heard the staccato of machine gun fire ripping across the night.

He did not stop when he saw the inferno engulfing the homes of his neighbors.

He did not stop until he reached his own family's hut.

But by then, it was too late.

Behind him, he could hear the rebels loading into their trucks, taking what they wanted from his village before destroying the rest. He knew he should go after them, but he was paralyzed by the sight of his family - the bodies of his wife and sisters, brothers, nieces and nephews scattered across the floor as if they'd been blown there by the wind. For the second time that night, he fell to his knees, unable to scream, unable to breathe.

He remained there for a moment, consumed by the smoke and ash of the nearby huts, struggling to make sense of the horror surrounding him. And then, with sudden clarity he understood.

Darkness has arrived, he thought. *So now I must be the light.*

CHAPTER

40

THOMAS

Thursday, October 6
Baltimore

After he and Mia discovered the possible prophecy psychic off the guru's list, Thomas sent three emails and left twice as many voicemail messages on what he assumed was the woman's phone. Over a week later, he still hadn't heard back from her and was beginning to lose hope. Worse yet was that while Mia worked tirelessly on what she described as a 'hellish workload' at the station, he hadn't discovered any other potential matches from the stack of papers still piled atop his mother's kitchen counter beside the toaster and the recycling bag.

"You were up late again last night," Mildred commented as she stirred the milk into her breakfast coffee before sliding the half-gallon of 1% in his direction. "Been working on lots of schoolwork?"

He poured a splash of the milk in his own mug and took a steamy sip. "Something like that."

She looked at him expectantly, as if waiting for a legitimate explanation, and he averted his gaze out the window, feigning concern for their neighbor wrestling her garbage can to the street. In the interest of keeping things between them simple, he hadn't divulged any information about the prophecy or even his own abilities. He knew how she felt about 'the supernatural' and 'the occult,' so until he'd wrapped his head around the situation on his own, he hadn't felt comfortable bringing her into the fold.

The way she looked at him now, it was as if she already knew.

"Couldn't help but notice that pile of papers you've been poring over, like the answers to the universe are locked inside. And I don't snoop, because it's not my place, but if there's something you want to talk about, I'm always here to listen."

He turned to face her. Saw the kindness in her eyes. The same kindness that brought him out of the darkness of the foster care system and into the light of a loving home. He knew in that moment he should have confided in her months ago, because perhaps if he had, he wouldn't feel so helpless now.

The story of his abilities and the prophecy and the search for the other prophetic psychics spilled out of him, and the room was awash with all the things he'd been too scared to say and some he hadn't even allowed himself to think. When he finished, she stared at him, unblinking.

"Do you hate me?" he asked.

"How could I?" she replied.

"Because all of this stuff... all of these abilities and prophecies and good and evil and end of the world..." He trailed off, unable to say what he was really thinking about how all of those things were so out of line with Mildred's beliefs.

"'Beloved, do not believe every spirit, but test the spirits to see whether they are from God, for many false prophets have gone out into the world.' John 4:1."

He was aware his mouth was gaping open and he snapped it shut.

"'Do not despise prophecies, but test everything; hold fast what is good.' 1 Thessalonians 5:20-21."

They stared at one another for several seconds until the weight of expectation became too great to bear. "What does that mean? Do you think the prophecy is good? Or bad?" he asked finally.

"It doesn't matter what I think, Thomas. It only matters what you believe. In your heart."

He considered this. How the prophecy made him feel in his heart. But before he could respond to her, she continued.

"The Lord works in mysterious ways."

This particular line was a favorite of hers, a way of making sense of the incomprehensible. Perhaps it was time for him to begin subscribing to the belief as well.

"So then you think it could be true? You think I should keep searching for the others?"

She took a sip of her coffee, which he imagined was now completely cold, and reached her hand across the table, placing it on top of his. "I don't know anything about this prophecy outside of what you've told me. But it sounds to me as if the simplistic language of the prediction is not out of line with the truths I've come to believe. In fact, I've always found the best thing to do when I'm unsure about something is to compare what is said with what the Word of God says. If it contradicts the teachings, throw it out. If it agrees with the Bible, pray for wisdom and discernment for how to apply the message."

"And what about my ability? Do you think it's…"

"Unholy?" she finished for him.

He scrunched his nose at the distinct negative connotation of the word. "I was going to say bad, but yeah, unholy."

"Do *you* think it's a bad thing?"

He shrugged.

She squeezed his hand lightly with her arthritic fingers. "Thomas, God gives everyone gifts. Abilities to get through this life. Your music, for example."

He scoffed. His ability to play a sonata certainly wasn't going to usher in the apocalypse.

"Some people can paint. Others can sing or write or build bridges that don't fall down. So if I believe God gave people those sorts of gifts, who am I to say whether He has the power to give you the ability to sense danger?"

It made sense, what she was saying, and he felt better. Not only that he was no longer keeping such a large part of his life from her, but also that maybe things weren't as bad as they seemed.

Later that afternoon, in the middle of his Music, Technology, and Culture class, his phone began vibrating in his pocket. He initially ignored it, knowing everyone he cared to talk to knew he was in class, but then reconsidered, thinking perhaps Lanying was calling with news about Salomon. Under the desk, he checked the incoming number and immediately recognized the area code as the same one he'd been calling in an attempt to reach the psychic from the list. He leapt from his desk, knocking it over in the process, and raced into the hallway to answer before the call went to voicemail.

"Hello?" he said breathlessly.

"Is this Thomas Pritchett?" The woman's voice was deep. Older. With a thick, southern drawl. Not what he was expecting.

"Yes, Ma'am, it is," he replied. "Is this Lillian Hall?"

"No. As a matter of fact, it's not. This is her mother. But before you go gettin' all excited, I'm only calling to tell you, you better quit calling here, do you understand?"

His heart was beating out of his chest in anticipation of a possible connection with Lillian. "Yes, Ma'am. I understand. But I was really hoping to speak with Lillian herself. Do you know how I might get in touch with her directly?"

She made a noise which sounded like a cackle. "Oh no, dear," she said, her voice venomous. "That ship sailed long ago. If you want to contact my daughter, you'll need more luck than I've had. That girl disappeared six years ago without the courtesy of a phone call or a kiss goodbye. Only way I know she's alive is when I see her pop up on the news from time to time."

"The news?"

"Oh, yes. With that friend of hers, doing all that hocus pocus stuff she does. Smoke and mirrors, I promise you that. Lillian is a liar. She's always been a liar. She'll always be a liar. I'd advise you to stay away from her. That girl's nothing but trouble." Her voice had reached a fevered pitch, but she paused then, as if to compose herself. "Anyway, I need you to stop callin' here, or next time I'll be callin' the police."

"Sorry to have bothered you, Ma'am," he said, but before he finished, the line had gone dead.

CHAPTER

41

SALOMON

Friday, October 7 – Monday, October 10
Democratic Republic of Congo

Salomon wiped the sweat from his forehead with the same bandana he kept with him in the fields. Only today he wasn't working in the fields, burying tiny seeds in rows beneath the soil. No. Today he was burying his family.

He had lain with them, among the smoldering rubble of his village, until the sun rose and the activity of fellow survivors beckoned him from his waking nightmare. He was aware of someone standing over him, but he didn't move until they kicked at his back with their toes.

"Salomon?" came a small voice. "Are you alive?"

It was Petia, a neighbor girl, not more than ten years old. He rolled over on his side to get a better look at her face and saw it was charred and tear stained.

"I ran into the forest," she told him, by way of explanation. "So did Merveille. But we're the only two."

He didn't have to ask to know the rest of her family was dead, just like his own family, who were now lying in coagulated pools of their own blood. And so as much as he wanted to remain face down on the earth, until the ground itself consumed him, he forced himself to rise, gathering Petia into his arms.

"It's okay," he told her. "We're going to make everything alright."

Now he found himself along the edge of the jungle with the handful of other survivors, digging graves for those they lost. Each shovelful of dirt strengthening his muscles as well as his resolve. Educated in the ways of science, history, and law, he knew for every step forward his countrymen made toward a peaceful existence, there had always been someone waiting just around the corner to drive them two steps back. It was the way it always had been. It was the way it always would be.

Unless someone finally took a stand.

As he dragged his family's remains to the shallow grave, Lanying's words repeated like a mantra inside his head. "I believe you and I were born into this destiny for a reason. To fulfill the ancient prophecy and usher in a world without fear or pain or oppression."

If he was ever in need of a world without pain, it was in this moment.

He kneeled now, inside the pit, beside Manu and Keicha, unable to perform the proper burial rituals of his people due to the sheer volume of dead requiring his attention. There would be no wailing or dancing or ceremonial washing. Instead, he merely kissed each of their faces, a final 'love touch' bestowed upon them, ushering them into the life beyond.

When Marceau arrived, right on schedule in three days' time, each of the bodies had already been interred and the few remaining survivors waited for him with Salomon beneath a makeshift lean-to of his construction. He watched the horror wash across Marceau's face as he took in the scene – the circular rings of scorched earth where the villager's huts once stood, the primitive noises of the jungle now overtaking any human conversation, and the devastation in Salomon's eyes.

235

Salomon rose as he approached. They exchanged only embraces, as they were both clearly at a loss for words.

Finally, Marceau said, "Rebels?"

Salomon nodded.

Marceau gestured toward the others. "These are all who remain?"

He nodded again, biting his bottom lip in an attempt to hold his tears at bay.

"And the rest?"

He pointed toward the clearing at the edge of the forest. "I've already taken care of them."

The silence between the men spoke volumes as they walked together across what had once been the village center. Marceau knelt before the mass grave, the earth still unsettled and lumpy, and bowed his head in prayer. After making the sign of the cross, he rose again and turned to Salomon.

"What now?"

Salomon shook his head. "I've been giving it a lot of thought. There aren't enough of them to start again. They can't sustain themselves. They won't survive. The only good option is for them to find homes within another village. Maybe one of the others from the co-op."

Marceau's brow creased severely between his eyes. "They won't survive? What about you, my friend?"

"I'm not staying."

"Here in Katanga?"

"No," Salomon replied. "Here in Africa."

That afternoon, as Marceau made phone calls to other World Vision team leaders in an attempt to secure homes for the survivors within other co-op communities, Salomon logged on to his email account using the truck's satellite Wi-Fi.

There were three new messages from Lanying, each of them with further explanation of the prophecy and his part in it. At the end of the third message was a phone number.

He checked the time, and although it was almost 11pm in Shanghai, placed the call from Marceau's phone.

A small, weary voice answered the phone. "Hello?"

"Lanying?"

"Yes? Salomon? Is that you?"

"It is." He had to concentrate on his English. "It's nice to hear your voice," he told her.

She laughed good-naturedly. "It's nice to hear yours too. How are things?"

The casual nature of the question caught him off guard. It was clearly meant as a conversation starter. A way to break the ice. But he could hardly pretend everything was fine.

"Actually, Lanying, things are not well. Not well at all."

She fell silent, and for a moment he thought she'd disconnected. "I'm afraid to ask," she said at last, "but has there been a fire?"

"Yes."

"I saw it," she said. "But since I couldn't make out any faces or the surroundings, I didn't know exactly what I was seeing. Is everyone okay?"

He closed his eyes to compose himself. He needed to keep it together. Before he lost his nerve, he told her all of it, from the very beginning. By the time he finished, he could hear her sniffling.

"I'm so sorry, Salomon," she said. "What a terrible tragedy."

They were silent for a moment and after taking several cleansing breaths, he felt comfortable enough to broach the subject which was ultimately the reason for his call.

"I'm leaving Africa. Forever. There's nothing more for me here. No life. No family. No friends. I don't know where exactly I need to go, but I know I'd like to go to Baltimore to meet the others. And I'd like to meet you too. But I don't know how to do that. I don't have the money to buy a ticket and it's a long way to the airport. I'm afraid I'm going to need some help."

CHAPTER
42

THOMAS

Monday, October 10
Baltimore

During his lunch break, between classes, Thomas found himself beneath his favorite oak. The leaves had already changed from the dark green of summer to the bold crimson and gold of fall. An acorn fell heavily onto the ground beside him, leaving a divot in the mossy ground below, and he tilted back his head to gaze into the branches, reevaluating the presumed safety of his preferred location. The branches were teeming with tiny, bullet-shaped projectiles. *One knock on the head with one of those*, he thought. Before taking another bite of his peanut butter sandwich, he began searching his mind for any nagging inclination of an impending 'acorn-sustained injury,' but he felt no compulsion to leave. He readjusted himself more comfortably against the trunk for the duration of his meal.

Since he and Mia had begun their search for the other prophetic psychics, he'd taken her suggestion about honing his own abilities to heart. Instead of just passively waiting for a feeling to overtake him, he'd been mindfully probing his own psyche for clues about what was to come. He chuckled to himself, that he had taken the time to consider the acorns, but he figured he had to start somewhere.

As he finished his sandwich, his mind turned to Mia, where it always seemed to drift if he allowed it. They'd been up late the night before, she searching for other psychics and he researching the illusive Lillian Hall. It hadn't taken him long to discover several YouTube videos demonstrating her ability to be in two places at one time. Many of the comments below the clip of her appearing and disappearing beside herself in a crowded subway terminal accused her of forgery.

"Crappy digital software will produce the same effect," one stated. Another considered a less technological possibility. "Not hard to do if you have an identical twin."

Although for most of his life he would have been inclined to share their sentiments, he now recognized the images were probably legitimate, and it made him sad for this Lillian, whoever she was. It was no wonder, Mia, Lanying, and so many others like them, chose to keep their abilities hidden from the narrowmindedness of the world.

Thinking of her again, he felt an urge to hear her voice.

"Hey, you," she said when she answered.

"Hey yourself," he replied. "Guess what? I've been practicing my abilities, just like you told me."

"Oh, yeah?"

"Yeah, and my powers are telling me we should have Thai tonight for dinner."

"Really? They're sending messages about meal planning?"

"No. Not really. I totally made that up. But I know it's your favorite, and I was just thinking to myself 'Hey, Thomas, what can you make with ten cent ramen that you haven't already prepared this week?'"

She laughed. "You are a wizard with ramen."

"Maybe I'll add it to my list of known powers," he said. He finished his banana and stuffed the peel into his lunch bag. "Anyway, I don't want to keep you from work, but I was wondering if you'd had a chance to run the facial recognition software on that Lillian woman to see if any other info came up for her?"

"As a matter of fact, I did, and you are totally gonna love me when I tell you what I found."

"I totally already do," he said, mimicking her voice. "So tell me."

"It's an arrest mugshot from Interpol. From about four years ago."

His head snapped back. "Arrest."

"Yep."

"And I assume it wasn't because she was stealing to give to orphans."

"Larceny. High end art."

He couldn't keep the excitement out of his voice. "So then I guess we can assume…"

"Yes," she interrupted, and he could imagine she was shaking her head and rolling her eyes at his childlike enthusiasm. "If she's one of us, she's probably dark. If she's one of us," she repeated again with the emphasis on the if.

At that moment, his phone chimed, alerting him to an incoming Skype call. He checked the screen and knew he should take it. "Hey, Mia. Lanying's trying to Skype. Can I call you back?"

She paused and then hurried to finish their conversation. "It's pretty late there. You better take it. Hope something isn't wrong. And you don't have to call me back. I'll just see you tonight for Thai. Oh, and tell her I say hi."

He told her he loved her and disconnected before accepting Lanying's request.

"Thomas?" she said. There were heavy bags under her eyes, and he could tell she'd been crying.

"Yeah. Hey, Lanying. What's up? Is everything okay?"

Her eyes were wild, searching. "Yes. I'm fine. But, Thomas, the man Salomon I've been telling you about…"

"The one you think is another light psychic from Africa."

She nodded. "Something terrible has happened, Thomas. His family, as well as most of the other people in his village, were slaughtered in their sleep by a group of militants. I saw the fire and destruction in a vision. It was horrific. He's lost now. He has nowhere to go." She hesitated then, and he could hear, by the way her voice caught in her throat, how deeply she was affected by the tragedy. "He wants to come to Baltimore to meet you and Mia."

He brought the screen closer to his face so she could see him without the glare of the noonday sun. "He honestly believes he's part of the prophecy as well?"

She nodded, biting chapped skin off the corner of her lip. "He told me something about an inscription in a cave he believes is about the prophecy. He's certain finding the cave as a boy was his destiny and that to fulfill what's been written, he must come to Baltimore to gather with the other light psychics."

He imagined the man's excitement, believing it was still possible to save the world. Salomon must not have been made aware their goal was no longer to usher in the light, but to merely prevent the darkness from taking over. "Have you told him about Kate?"

"How could I? He's dealing with enough bad news as it is," she replied and when Thomas didn't speak again, continued, "He has nowhere else to go. He needs this, Thomas. He's one of us."

It was a lot to consider. He assumed Salomon had no money for transportation, so somehow they would have to obtain funding for his flight. It would be even more difficult to secure a travel visa into the States. "It might prove to be nearly impossible," he explained to Lanying. "And even if we could get him here, it seems like an awful lot of trouble to go through for nothing. We should be spending our time and energy on keeping the seven dark psychics apart."

"He wants to help," she insisted.

Thomas shrugged. "Then let him help from there, the way you are from China. We don't need to be together."

She was visibly frustrated with him now, raking her hands through her hair. "He lives in rural Africa. There's no means by which to help us from there. And besides, we don't need his IT skills. We need his psychic abilities." She was pleading with him, as if her life depended on it, and then it occurred to him that perhaps it wasn't her life she was trying to protect.

"He's that bad off?" he asked.

"Yes, Thomas."

As much as it went against his pragmatic nature, his heart wouldn't allow him to turn them away. "Lemme talk to Mia," he relented. "We'll see what we can do."

Tuesday, October 11
Baltimore

Mia, Jack, Carson, and his partner Harris were huddled around one of the small conference room tables with photos of almost a dozen stolen cars spread between them. They'd been working closely together since their separate cases appeared to be somehow connected.

"So here's the car Fields brought Trece in on," Mia said, pointing to a late model Lexus. She slid three other cars under the first. "And when you two checked out his place, you found these in an empty lot across the street."

"Right," Carson acknowledged.

Jack continued. "So then the rest of these cars were reported stolen and recovered over the past two months around the same area. The Civic and the Ford F150 in Sparrows Point. The three Accords in Dundalk. That Chevy pickup in Middle River. And the two Camrys in Essex. We gotta believe they're all being run outta the same operation."

"And if these are the ones we've found, imagine how many are still out there we haven't found," Harris agreed, rocking back in his chair. "Seems like it gets worse twice a year – when people leave the keys in the ignition to warm them up in the winter and when they forget and leave the windows open in the summer. It's easy pickins'."

"Totally easy," Mia agreed. "And since we still haven't tracked down the Altima Mr. Washington saw Trece and Sisco casing, I think that would be a good place to start."

Jack and the others nodded in agreement. "You have a printout of the current missing vehicle report?" he asked Carson.

He produced it from a folder stashed under his chair and tossed it on top of the stack of photographs. "Almost 300 of them right now."

Jack whistled between his teeth.

"We get reports of up to 4,000 a year," Carson explained. "This is actually a pretty light load."

"So what's the plan?" Mia asked.

Carson set both hands on the table in front of him and leaned in toward the others. "Lots of the cases we see are kids just being stupid. If this is a full-blown ring, they aren't just stealing to joyride. They're either shipping them outta state or scrapping them for parts. Either way, I'm betting they're moving them out down at the dockyard. They're probably storing them close by or somewhere in their own neighborhood they think is safe."

Jack summarized. "So you think we hit MS-13 territory and around the shipyard."

"Exactly," Carson agreed.

"And you don't think we bring Sisco in to see if he talks?" asked Jack.

"You think he'll tell us where he's stashing cars?" The others unanimously agreed he wouldn't. "Me neither," Carson continued, "which is why I think it's better that we keep the rest of the gang in the dark. All they know is that we picked up Trece on that one count. They have no idea we're aware of the bigger operation. Let's keep it that way."

"But how do we know which cars to look for?" Mia asked, scowling at the extensive spreadsheet. "We can't memorize all these. There are just too many."

"Let's assume most of the cars reported over three weeks ago are already out of the area, one way or another. Meaning we should concentrate on memorizing the most recent thefts. I printed out pictures and VIN numbers of the last 20 reports," he explained, passing out folders to each of the others. "And here's hoping if we find the cars, we find the men. Including your guy from Phoenix."

"Here's hoping," Jack agreed, flipping through the photographs.

Half an hour later, Mia and Jack were making their second pass through the MS-13 neighborhoods. The streets were relatively empty which suited Mia just fine, because as they canvassed the area, she was having trouble remembering the make and models of the stolen cars. Instead, she couldn't stop thinking about how trivial stolen cars were when compared to the atrocities Thomas described to her the night before. Her thoughts kept returning to Salomon; losing his entire family to Rwandan rebels, gunned down while they slept in their beds. It only made her feel that much worse, knowing Salomon's tragedy was but a preview of the life to come for the rest of the world if the other psychics ushered in the days of darkness.

No one should have to live in fear for their own safety, she thought to herself, remembering her time in the warehouse basement, alone with the trafficked women. *Not now. Not ever.*

"You're ridiculously quiet," Jack commented nonchalantly as they waited in traffic for the light to turn green. When she didn't acknowledge him, he continued. "We're gonna find Alejandro."

She loved that he thought he knew her so well, and in a lot of ways he did. But on this occasion he had it wrong, for although she wanted nothing more than to protect Andrea from Alejandro, her heart was heavy with other concerns.

"The world is a very bad place," she said at last.

He raised an eyebrow at her. "You don't really believe that, deep down."

She shrugged. "I'm beginning to think I do."

He laid a sympathetic hand on her shoulder, the way a great coach would after a particularly brutal loss. "Everything's going to be okay."

She pulled away from him, twisting her shoulders out of his reach and crossing her arms heavily across her chest. What did he know about everything being all right? He was blissfully unaware of just how un-okay things were about to get. About how after the destruction of Salomon's village, she was now tasked with getting the Congolese man to Baltimore without resources or funding in the hopes of somehow salvaging the prophecy. It suddenly pissed her off that his greatest concerns were for his pregnant wife, some stolen cars, and the life of one abused woman, while she was expected to carry the burden of protecting the fate of the entire world.

"That's the biggest pile of crap I've ever heard," she spat at him.

"What the hell, Mia?" he replied, gunning the patrol car through the intersection as the light changed. "You've been preoccupied with something for weeks, and I've kept my mouth shut, because I figured if you wanted me to know what was going on, you'd tell me. But screw it. Enough's enough. You're driving me crazy."

She narrowed her eyes at him, glaring across the distance between them which suddenly seemed greater than it ever had before. She didn't like it. In fact, she hated it.

Jack was her partner. Her confidant. Her best friend.

"The world, as we know it, is about to end. And I don't know if there's anything I can do to make it better. So yeah, forgive me if I've seemed sorta 'preoccupied.' I've been a little busy trying to figure out how to save the world. And it's not going very well at all, thanks for asking."

After nearly rear-ending the car in front of them, Jack pulled into the closest lot and parked.

"So is this an alien thing or a zombie thing or what?" he asked. "Do I need to start stockpiling ammunition and Tuna Helper?"

She wanted to punch him but was smiling before she could stop herself. She could never stay mad, but the fact remained that her part in the prophecy wasn't easy to explain, which was part of the reason she hadn't shared it with him already. The bigger reason was she feared he may have reached his limit when it came to accepting her weirdness. But he was staring at her with a look which implied that whatever it was, he could handle it.

She took a deep breath and dove in.

He stopped her about halfway through.

"So what you're telling me is there's a prophecy I've never heard of, foretelling two sets of psychics, one good and one bad, and whichever group finds all their members first wins?"

She gave him a weak thumbs up. "That's essentially it."

"And you and Thomas just happen to be two of the good guys and you think you've found two more."

"Three more," she corrected.

"You didn't say anything about a third."

"It's because we think it was Kate."

"Ohhhhhhhh." She watched the understanding taking over. "So how are you supposed to get all seven of the good guys together now?"

She appreciated that he was being a good sport. Making a genuine effort to buy into the whole shebang instead of just playing along.

"I don't think we can," she told him. "Thomas and I have been working to find the seven dark ones so maybe we can try to keep them apart, but…" She trailed off, unwilling to acknowledge their failure aloud.

"So you think because you're getting close to finding all seven, they probably are as well, and that's what's got you upset?"

She tucked her chin to her chest, unable to face him. The slaughter of Salomon's family had her considering another possibility. "That's what I've been thinking all along. That we would have to find a way to stop them. But now I'm starting to wonder if they might have already found him first."

Tuesday, October 11
Baltimore

"I think you should go back again," Andrea told him, tossing the remote control across the bed.

Her frustration was palpable, and Jose couldn't blame her for wanting to see their confinement come to an end. He was as disappointed with their situation as she was, and at a loss for what was taking the police so long to find Alejandro. But unfortunately, until they had confirmation of his apprehension, it wasn't safe for her to return to the world.

"The guy at the tattoo place told me no one's been in there asking about you. And the cops have been watching from the street just outside the building since the interview aired. We might have to accept the fact that he doesn't watch the news. Or if he does, that he's not buying what we're selling."

"We've got to do *something*," she moaned. "We need some other plan."

He looked at her now, unshowered, dressed in the same sweatpants and t-shirt she'd been wearing for a week. And although he knew he could be upset at her for her miserable attitude, he forced the anger aside. Lashing out wasn't going to help the situation. And neither was walking away. Because despite the fact that at any moment he could have hopped the next flight back to Phoenix, something compelled him to stay. He chalked it up to obligation, because he knew in his heart if he hadn't physically saved her life in the hospital the first time, he wouldn't need to be saving it emotionally now.

"I can go back on TV again. I'll do another interview on another station. Maybe at a different time."

She lowered her head, sulking. "No. It's hopeless. Just bring me the tablet so I can finish filling out that application. Maybe someday, if I ever get to leave this room, I'll be able to go to some of those classes."

In the days they'd spent hunkered down together, they'd devised a plan for her future, which included culinary school and a job working in the kitchen at his parents' restaurant. They'd spent hours talking about what it might be like for her to earn her own money in a career she loved, so she would never again be forced to rely on anyone else to support her financially.

As he crossed the room to retrieve the tablet from atop the small table, which served as both their kitchen and their office, his phone vibrated in his pocket. He pulled it out, but hesitated to answer because the number was blocked.

"Is it the cops?" Andrea asked expectantly.

"Dunno."

"Well, answer it," she said when he remained motionless.

He pressed accept and held the phone to his ear. "Hello."

"Is this Jose Torres?" The voice was aggressive and heavily accented.

"Who's asking?"

"I'm a friend of Alejandro's. He just wanted me to let you know he has something for you."

Jose tried to take in air, but it was as if someone was standing on his chest. His mind raced. The call didn't make sense. Someone had to be playing a prank. "How'd you get this number?" he asked, trying to call the man's bluff.

"A little bird told us," he laughed. "And she's right here with me."

Jose heard what sounded like struggling in the background, along with muffled cries. What the hell was going on? "Who's there?" he asked. "Who's with you?"

"Well, Jose, we've got your Aunt Carla here with us. And she isn't muy bueno, si?"

Jose lifted his eyes and saw Andrea looking at him expectantly from across the room. Her irritated façade had been replaced by a genuine look of concern, which he could only assume was brought on by the apprehension in his own voice. He focused on her now, trying to decide what to do.

With his eyes set on Andrea, he began talking himself down. If Alejandro had apprehended his aunt, and if she was hurt in any way, he could cure her. He could mend broken bones and heal lacerations, just as he'd done for her when he was younger. The problem was going to be getting her back alive.

"Where are you?" he asked.

The man laughed. "Oh, we're close. Very close, mi amigo. In fact, we picked up Aunt Carla at her apartment. Guess she just couldn't live without this ugly sweater she had to come back for. The problem is now she won't tell us where you're hiding with that little girlfriend of yours. I was just gonna chop her up and dump her in the harbor, but Alejandro thought she might be of more use to us alive. As part of an exchange."

He drew out the last word, exchange, as though he was offering up the holy grail. Jose's kneejerk reaction was to be offended – who did this guy think he was? Until he realized just who Alejandro intended to involve as the other half of the exchange.

He wanted to swap Carla for Andrea.

A series of disjointed thoughts ricocheted painfully around his head:

The primeval allegiance of blood over water.

The disappointment in his aunt's reckless behavior.

The obligation he felt to involve the police.

His inclination to remedy the situation himself.

How badly he wanted to deck Alejandro for his psychotic obsession with Andrea.

He needed time to sort through his thoughts, but he knew every moment he wasted in silent contemplation was a moment Alejandro retained the upper hand.

"Where do you want to meet?" he asked.

"You can meet us at the corner of Holabird and Broening, down by the shipyard. There's a vacant lot there were you can drop off Andrea. And I'm sure you know better than to involve any cops. We see anything suspicious, the deal's off. Tu comprendes?"

His mouth was so dry he could barely speak. "And what about my aunt Carla?"

"We'll leave her somewhere else, and she can call you to tell you where she is once we have Andrea."

He knew immediately he couldn't trust them to keep up their end of the bargain. He needed more information. "Before I agree, I want to talk to Carla."

"That's not gonna happen," he said.

Without missing a beat, Jose replied, "Then I'm not making the deal. For all I know you've tossed her in the harbor already." He tried his best to sound convincing, assuming the stifled cries he'd initially heard belonged to her.

He heard a hand being placed across the mouth of the receiver and the hushed conversation of two distinct voices. He assumed the second one was Alejandro's. A moment later, Aunt Carla's hurried voice came across the line.

"Jose, you must go to the police. Please, I beg you. Don't give Andrea to them, whatever you…"

She was cut off then, and he winced involuntarily as he heard her fighting back against her captors. Andrea was beside him now, nestled against his chest in an attempt to hear the other half of the conversation. He could feel her heart thudding heavily in her chest and knew she understood what was going on.

"Tomorrow. 4pm. By the docks."

And with that the line went dead.

CHAPTER

45

LANYING

Tuesday, October 11
Shanghai

As the credits began rolling at the end of the documentary, Lanying muted the sound and turned to her grandfather, who appeared to have dozed off for the third time. "It's hard to believe one man will treat another man that way," she said, rousing him awake.

His eyelids lifted briefly but closed again – the effort too much for him. "Every generation feels as though the next will be far worse off than their own, but truly, that this sort of horror exists in today's world can only mean one thing. The end is growing near."

They had just finished watching a four-part series on African genocides - Burundi, Liberia and Sierra Leone, Darfur, Rwanda, and Uganda, among others. Thinking about Salomon, living in such conditions, where the culture not only allowed the spread of annihilation, but encouraged it, tore at her heart. Before reaching out to him, she wouldn't have believed two people who had never shared the same space could bond so quickly, but their connection was clearly precipitated by the prophecy, providing a solid foundation on which their friendship was built.

Since their last conversation, she'd been trying to concoct a plan to secure a visa and funding for his trip to the States. Thomas had volunteered to help with obtaining a travel visa to the United States for him, but the airfare alone would cost over $1000. Between that and the price of travel documents, she wasn't sure how she was going to come up with enough cash to cover his expenses. Not to mention, if and when he did secure passage to the US, she wanted to be there herself to greet him, which would require additional funding.

"I wonder how hard it will be for Salomon to leave?" she asked her grandfather, although the question was mostly rhetorical, as she didn't expect him to have an answer. "And I don't just mean emotionally, but there's no guarantee the Democratic Republic of Congo will even let him go. Or that the US will let him in. And the cost alone may prevent any of it from happening."

He slid himself beneath his covers, as if he was preparing to sleep, but he didn't send her away. Instead he beckoned her closer, motioning with his hand. "You both need to go to Baltimore," he murmured. "And I will send you."

She assumed she'd misunderstood him. He'd depended on her parents for over a decade. They provided his meals, clothes, and a roof over his head. He didn't have his own money. "How will you send us?" she asked, moving closer to assure she could hear him properly, as his speech seemed particularly garbled.

"In the trunk, on the left-hand-side, is a latch. If you flip the latch, a panel will open up on the bottom. In the bottom is a satchel. In the satchel you will find account numbers belonging to a series of bank accounts which contain enough money to pay for your travels. And Salomon's travels. And his documentation if he can secure it."

She didn't move. How could it be after so many years that her grandfather was still surprising her? First with his knowledge of the prophecy, his trips to Africa, and now with the hidden money. But she wouldn't take it. She couldn't.

"No, Grandfather," she said. "I can't take your money."

With obvious determined effort, he opened his eyes and reached out to take her shoulder, bringing her ear to his face. "It's not my money. The money has been passed down over many generations, from mentor to mentor, keeper to keeper. Invested and reinvested over the course of many years before it came to me. Now I pass it on to you because time is growing short. And you will be the one to use it for its intended purpose – the fulfillment of the prophecy."

She pulled out of his grasp, backing away from him. She'd already explained to him during their initial discussion of the prophecy that there would be no fulfillment, at least not by the light, which came as the result of Kate's death. How now did he expect her to use the money to save the world? He wasn't making any sense.

"It's not possible," she explained to him again. "One of the seven is no longer with us."

He surprised her then, doing something he'd never done before. Quietly, in a voice so small she could barely hear, he began to sing:

> "Soft as the voice of an angel,
> Breathing a lesson unheard,
> Hope with a gentle persuasion
> Whispers her comforting word:
> Wait till the darkness is over,
> Wait till the tempest is done,
> Hope for the sunshine tomorrow,
> After the shower is gone."

Speechless, she stared at him, like a ghost under a burial shroud. And then she realized the time he spoke of as 'growing short' referred not only to the prophecy but to him as well.

"Grandfather?"

"*Whispering Hope*," he answered. "Listen to the rest of the song. Carry it with you. Do what you were born to do. And promise me, promise me, you will never lose hope."

She nodded because she couldn't summon a verbal response. His voice was barely a whisper, and he struggled to choke out the words, taking long pauses between each rattled breath.

"Take the money, Lanying. Wire some of it to Salomon if you are able. You must both go to the others as quickly as you can. Promise me. Promise me you will go to them and convince Salomon to go as well. The prophecy is coming to pass. The time has finally arrived."

A moment later his eyes fluttered shut, and she watched helplessly as he took his final breath, slowly, peacefully. Both stunned and horrified, she reached across the space between them to shake him awake, to bring him back to her, but as tears began trickling from her chin onto his face, she was forced to acknowledge he was gone.

"No, please!" she sobbed. "What does all of it mean? What am I supposed to do with lyrics from a song I've never heard? How am I supposed to stay hopeful when one of the light psychics is no longer alive? What good will it do for the rest of us to be together in her absence?" Her hands shook as she raked them through her hair, anguish overtaking her. "Don't go, please," she said finally. "Not now. Not yet. I still need you."

She sat with him until her parents arrived home from work and forced her into the hall, locking her grandfather's bedroom door behind them until arrangements could be made. While they made phone calls to the emergency response line, she retreated to her room, disquieted by the silence of her isolation. As much as she wanted to give in to the grief which accompanied the devastating loss of her grandfather, she knew he wanted her to keep going. To remain hopeful. To fulfil her destiny.

To save the world.

And so, despite her overwhelming sorrow, she logged onto her computer, yearning to fulfill her grandfather's dying wish. The least she could do now was to search for a liaison with the ability to transfer funds to Salomon.

She knew the money had the power to bring them together.

Beyond that, the only power she had left was hope.

CHAPTER

46

LILLIAN

Tuesday, October 11
Saint Tropez

Lillian felt her skin cooking. Her shoulders, her calves, baking into a deep, golden brown. She recognized the distinction between the sensation of a tan and a burn and wanted to avoid the latter, which is why she chose this exact moment to nimbly slip her bikini straps over her arms and turn over on the chaise. She'd been enjoying her uninterrupted time in the French Riviera, sunning and sipping mimosas without the constant annoyance of having to be at Patrick's beck and call. She tolerated him, of course, and in some ways even liked him, but his obsession with the prophecy in recent months had grown out of hand, and she'd been relieved when the others persuaded him to give them all some breathing room. The others didn't realize the toll biolocating took on her – placing stress on her mind as it struggled to focus on two places at once. Although, she thought now as she smoothed tanning oil on her thighs, they probably had no idea she seldom left her home in Saint Tropez, choosing instead to biolocate when she met with them.

The days had been growing cooler over the last several weeks, and Lillian was enjoying an unseasonably warm morning on the beach. The air was slightly brisk, causing gooseflesh to rise on her skin when it blew, but the sun was still warm, reminding her of the many years she spent basking under the hazy skies of Texas. She tried not to think of Texas, the first place in the world she felt truly vulnerable. The only place in the world she would never voluntarily return to.

She had no idea how much time had passed when her phone began to chime from the bag beneath her chaise, startling her from her repose.

"Hold your horses," she said as she fumbled to find her phone amongst the bottled waters, sunglasses, and various lotions strewn throughout her bag.

"Hello," she said breathlessly once she found it.

"Well, there you are," Javier said curtly in his thick Spanish accent. "I've been calling you for days."

"Oh, Darling," she replied. "I had no idea. Did you leave me a message?"

"That's hard to do when your mailbox is full."

Lillian remembered the numerous phone calls from her mother she'd failed to respond to. She tried to recall just how many there'd been. Enough to fill her voicemail?

"Well, you have me now," she said to Javier. "What's so pressing. I thought we weren't supposed to be in contact with one another. We're supposed to be taking a break, remember? Or is it that you just can't stand to be away from me any longer?"

He ignored her innuendo. "We may have found Number Seven."

Lillian bolted upright in her chair. "How? Does Patrick know?"

"No. Not yet. I decided not to call him until we're certain this man's a match. And right now Wesley's still searching for his exact location."

"Where?"

"In Pakistan."

"So Eshanti's drawings were right after all."

"Yes. We're lucky Patrick had the foresight to send a memo to the research team asking them to run the drawings against known locations using image matching software before he left. Even after Wesley wrote them off when he was unable to glean any useful information from them, Patrick didn't give up."

"And they're of Pakistan," Lillian interrupted.

"It appears so. Once the team had that information, they began to search exclusively for birthday matches within the Pakistani database. They called me two days ago with a hit."

Lillian's heart leapt. It was happening. She was finally going to live in a world where the revenge she sought would be not only justified but celebrated.

"Should I come to London?" she asked.

"Not yet. Just stay where you are for now. I'll be in touch with any news but it might not be a bad idea to have a bag packed. And Lillian?"

"Yes?"

"When the time comes, you're actually going to have to be here, physically here. You can't just biolocate. You know that, right?"

Lillian realized immediately he knew about her mild agoraphobia. And why wouldn't he? He would've been a fool not to have suspected there were many times she chose not to leave Saint Tropez in favor of biolocating to the others instead. She doubted, however, that he knew why.

"I understand," she told him, just before the line disconnected.

She sat there, the tanning oil beading on the unblemished surface of her thighs, reflecting on the plan she'd been concocting in her own mind for many, many years. Preparing for the day when there would be no punishment for the retribution she planned to undertake against her father. A day when she could reclaim the power he'd taken from her so many years before.

She'd been eleven years old the first time he'd come to her, alone in her bedroom in the middle of the night. She'd thought he was coming in to soothe her, to assuage her fears that despite the latest round of teasing she'd endured about her expanding bust line, everything was going to be okay.

But comforting her had been the last thing on his mind.

Her mother referred to her as their 'budding rose,' and as the juvenile boys in her sixth grade class were fond of pointing out, even the blossoms were bigger in Texas. The girls were no kinder, and she heard them making fun of her, calling her a whore as she hid from them, crouched in an empty bathroom stall. Seemingly overnight, her body had metamorphosed from a little girl everyone adored into a sideshow exhibit to be gawked at and insulted. In an effort to conceal the volume of her breasts, she secured them with ace bandages during the day under oversized t-shirts from her father's closet. But it was no use. The other kids saw them. Her teachers saw them. She saw them.

Her father saw them.

During that first night, as he groped and fondled her under the silky fabric of her Spice Girls nightgown, she'd instinctively imagined herself somewhere else – Saint Tropez. Earlier in the week, she'd come across one of her mother's many travel brochures, potential locales for her next getaway with her old sorority sisters. She'd mindlessly flipped through the one on top, of exotic Saint Tropez in the south of France, and imagined what it would be like to escape there, away from her classmates' judgment and scorn. As she lay beneath her father's heavy frame, her mind recalled the images of the city – terra cotta roofs, expansive white sand beaches, marinas with yachts the size of houses. And in an instant, she was there.

For a moment, she'd thought she was dreaming. That her father, as well as the warmth of the sun she now felt on her cheeks, were merely the products of her overactive imagination. But she was not asleep. She was wide awake and perfectly aware of what was happening in both places.

She heard her father moaning softly above her as clearly as the cry of a seagull overhead. In an attempt to block out the horror of what was taking place in Texas, she began to focus solely on Saint Tropez, on the extended line at which the horizon met the sea. Her bedroom fell away as she began to walk, testing out her legs as she felt the heat of the sand between her toes.

That beach became a place of refuge for her in the years that followed. On the nights of her father's visits she would biolocate to Saint Tropez the moment she heard the tell-tale click of the doorknob. Sadly, she was never completely unaware of what was happening to her back in Texas, and those memories drove her close to madness.

Until the day Patrick and the prophecy rescued her, providing her with an alternative to insanity.

Clouds began moving in. It was October, after all. The rainy season. Lillian packed up her belongings and started for her house, a two-story contemporary just beyond the closest dune. As she strolled through the sand, it occurred to her that she should delete some of the messages from her voice mailbox in the event Javier was unable to reach her. She was surprised to find eleven recordings from her mother and wasted no time deleting them, indifferent to whatever the woman had to say. She hesitated, however, her finger hovering over the delete button of the last message. Curiosity got the better of her, and as she reached the top of the dune, she pressed 'listen'.

"Lillian? This is your mother. Again. This is the last time I'm going to contact you about this. There's a man named Thomas Pritchett who's been calling and emailing the house nonstop for over a week. He's looking for you. He's interested in speaking with you about your abilities. I'm just letting you know because I'm tired of being harassed by one of your lunatic admirers. I expect you to take care of this problem immediately."

Lillian saved the message. And then she called Patrick.

CHAPTER
47

PATRICK

Tuesday, October 11
South Africa

Patrick maneuvered along the rocky coast of his native South Africa, stepping carefully from one weathered rock to another, checking to be sure each stone was secured to the surface below before trusting his weight upon it. Over two weeks had passed since the dark psychics had parted ways from his estate in London, when they agreed to limited contact with one another until such time that he felt the sixth psychic join the light side's growing ranks.

"Take some time to relax and refocus," Javier had counseled him. "Your abilities might be stronger if you give yourself a break."

Now, as he checked and rechecked his footing before venturing further along his path, he felt as if the last thing he needed was a break. There was no room in his life for leisure, not when there was so much at stake. But the others could not be assuaged. In the end, it was him who was forced to succumb to their wishes and not the other way around.

For Patrick, though, agreeing to their arrangement wasn't the worst part of the ordeal. Eshanti's tirade over his lack of abilities ground at his confidence more intensely than he was initially willing to admit. That night, he'd spent hours poring over his finances and corporate holdings, consoling himself with the knowledge that his abilities were responsible for the majority of his wealth and power. In the end, however, he finally admitted to himself that no matter how hard he tried, he had never been able to glean any valuable information about the prophetic psychics using his gift.

He came to a sandy stretch of beach and sat upon the cool, packed shore. Toward the horizon, sailboats swept along the jagged surface of the water and for an instant, Patrick longed to be as carefree as the ships' inhabitants. He had spent so many years chasing the idea of utopia – a world in which he would be free to do as he pleased without the unwarranted reproach of others. Now, although he was as close as he'd ever come to fulfilling the dream, he felt, for the first time in his life, as though the utopian ideal was undeniably beyond his grasp.

Patrick watched the boats for the better part of an hour, imagining what his life might have been like if he had never been chosen as part of the prophecy. If instead, he had just lived as any other man, unsuspecting of the world to come. Could he have been happy, sailing from port to port, without a care for what came next?

No, he decided. His life demanded purpose. A purpose the prophecy had given him long ago. A purpose he could not now abandon. He was done feeling sorry for himself, and as he listened to the steady pulse of the waves crashing upon the rocks, felt a renewed sense of certainty that the world would end up as the utopian society he always imagined it could be, devoid of the pompous sanctimony responsible for the moral code. He knew the principles of civilized society were a joke, often cast aside when adhering to them proved impossible to the masses. In times of war, famine, plague – the rules changed. Good and bad. Right and wrong. They were all very fluid. Which is why he knew he was no monster, simply an evolution of the species chosen to usher in the new order.

He was still watching the boats when his phone began chiming in his pocket. He stood up, fishing it out by the third ring.

"This is Patrick," he said, unaccustomed to answering his own calls.

"It's Lillian," said a familiar voice. "You were right all along. We need to get back to London right away. All of us."

CHAPTER

48

SALOMON

Wednesday, October 12
Democratic Republic of Congo

The trip to the city of Kamina was long and hot. Petia and Merveille clung to Salomon in the back of Marceau's truck, wrapping their sticky arms and legs around him as they bumped along the narrow, dirt road, away from Buganga and on toward new beginnings. They wept as if he were their own flesh and bone when he delivered them into the welcoming arms of a neighboring village, and it was all he could do not to remain with them. Certainly, they could use his planting expertise and harvesting techniques, but no. He knew now that staying would be like placing a dressing over a festering wound. Just covering such an injury wouldn't prevent it from causing death. His purpose was greater now. He needed to cure the infection at the source.

He left the girls, along with the others, and he and Marceau continued toward Kamina. The roar of the engine and rumble of the gravel under the heavily-treaded tires kept their conversation to a minimum, which suited Salomon and apparently Marceau as well. With nothing left to discuss but the tragic demise of his village, it was far easier saying nothing at all.

Upon their arrival to the city, their first stop was the University. Outside the stark, white, two-story cement building with contrasting green trim and bar covered windows, the head of the Agricultural Sciences department, Dr. Nyembo Musoya, waited.

"Salomon, my son, it's so good to see your face," the man gushed, hurrying to greet Salomon as he clambered out of the truck. "But under such unfortunate circumstances, I'm afraid. I'm so sorry for your loss."

Salomon welcomed his mentor's embrace, acknowledging his kindness. It wasn't going to be easy leaving him behind. "Thank you, Professor. I wish I could say I was shocked by what occurred, but how can I be when we live in a society such as this?"

Musoya nodded thoughtfully and beckoned Salomon and Marceau to follow him into the building where he led them through the narrow halls to his rudimentary office space.

After taking a seat with the others at the professor's desk and accepting a slice of coconut pie, Salomon wasted no time broaching the reason for his visit. "Professor, I've come because I need your help."

Worry lines crinkled the aging man's forehead as he swallowed the first bite of his pie. "Marceau warned me you have plans to leave the country, even when there is so much work left to be done. Please don't let this recent tragedy cause such a drastic change of heart. We need you here."

Salomon had no intention of telling either man about the prophecy, as he feared their scorn would bring about more resistance to his cause. Instead, he asked for their assistance in obtaining a student visa, with the promise to return to his homeland with the skills necessary to affect greater change.

"In order to obtain a student visa to the United States, you must first be accepted into a university. You haven't been accepted anywhere at this time, I assume?"

Salomon shook his head. He knew getting out of the country was going to be difficult, he just hadn't anticipated hitting an immediate brick wall. "No. I haven't. But you must understand that time is of the essence for me. My spirit is broken. There must be another way."

His aging professor rocked back on his chair and pulled at his greying beard. Although it was obvious he wanted Salomon to stay, he could see the man warming to the idea. "You would only need a class B-2 visitor visa if you want to take classes but aren't officially enrolled in a program. You'll need to schedule an interview at the US embassy in Kinshasa, and it usually takes about seven days to receive an appointment date."

If he applied the next day, he could have his interview in a week. "How much does it cost?"

"If I remember correctly there's a $160 nonrefundable visa application fee, as well as a $150 fee for the visa itself and another $250 for the DRC fee."

He quickly calculated the total in his head. "$560 altogether."

"Plus airfare, tuition, and room and board when you get there."

Salomon bowed his head, unable to face the improbability of what he wanted to accomplish staring back at him through Musoya's eyes. How naïve and idealistic he'd been to think it was possible to fulfill this destiny, lying alone in the charred remains of his village the week before.

"'Where we love is home - home that our feet may leave, but not our hearts.'"

He looked up at his professor. "Sir?"

"Oliver Wendell Holmes, a famous American poet said that, about leaving home." He took off his glasses, pinching the bridge of his nose as he leaned across the desk toward Salomon. "I can understand wanting to leave. It's a difficult thing, being an educated man, living in an uneducated world. It'll break your heart. So I won't try to stop you from leaving if you think distance and perspective might do you some good." He turned his attention to Marceau. "Do you wish to tell him or shall I?"

Marceau cut his eyes to Salomon. His friend's sadness was unmistakable. "You can tell him," he told the professor.

Salomon was confused. Tell him what? What had these two men been conspiring about behind his back?

"When the university scouts brought you here, all those years ago, I knew immediately there was something special about you, Salomon. To be fair, there's something special about all the men who attend this university, which is why they're brought here and not left like so many others to bear the burden of a life without hope. Because truly, that is what we teach here, in so much as anything else. More than law and biology, we teach young men to hope."

He took the last bite of his pie and chewed it slowly. Deliberately. Until he was ready to begin again. "Unfortunately, the problem which arises when we send you boys away from this place back into the world is that you carry that hope like a shield, as if it can protect you from all the ugliness. And when you discover the ugliness has a way of finding you, regardless of that hope, it can destroy even the purest of souls." Musoya locked eyes with him and Salomon could not look away. "Promise me hope will not leave your heart. Promise you will return to us. And promise you won't let what has happened to you destroy your soul."

He wasn't sure whether Musoya's words were meant as a blessing or farewell, but regardless, he was certainly no closer to fulfilling the prophecy than he'd been at his arrival. "I promise," he told his professor, because it seemed the only appropriate thing to say.

Musoya nodded his approval and reached inside his desk drawer, producing a sealed envelope. He slid it across the desk to Salomon. "Inside the envelope you will find two checks. One is already made out to the US Department of State in the amount of $560, enough to secure your travel documentation. The other check is made out to you for

$1500. It should be more than enough to cover your flight. You can thank Marceau for the checks."

His friend was smiling at him for the first time since before the rebel attack. "You're probably not going to believe this, but I received an email from a Chinese woman yesterday completely out of the blue. At first I was certain it was a scam, but I swear that she knew you. Knew everything about your situation and insisted on wiring the money necessary for both your travel documentation and the airfare to the United States. Believe me when I tell you she was adamant that I procure these checks for you." Marceau sighed heavily as he shook his head. "I must be honest though when I say, I don't want you to go. I'm going to miss you."

He couldn't believe what he was hearing – that Lanying had somehow obtained the funding for his trip and that his friends were encouraging him to go despite their personal inclination for him to stay. He looked between them, from the professor to Marceau and back again, blinking back tears of joy. "I don't know how to thank you both," he said at last.

"No man should have to witness the brutality you've seen. You deserve this opportunity to become the man you were born to be. I just pray when you've found yourself out there, you'll be strong enough to come back here."

He saw the anguish in his mentor's eyes and wanted desperately to tell him that yes, things were going to be better for all the hard-working, defenseless villagers throughout the Congo and throughout Africa. Because the end was coming and he was going to be there for it, alongside the six other light psychics who would usher in the new world.

And when the dark was overcome, he would return.

49

Wednesday, October 12
Baltimore

Jose was pacing. If there hadn't already been a worn path in what passed as a carpet on the floor of the motel room, he'd have made one on his own. He hadn't slept at all overnight, although Andrea had forced him to lie down beside her for several hours 'to rest for the day ahead.'

She looked up now from her phone and said, "You've gotta call Officer Rosetti, Jose. You need to let the police know they have Carla." When he didn't respond, she continued. "If you don't, I will."

While staring at the water stain on the ceiling above the bed overnight, he'd mulled over various scenarios to decide their best course of action. Of course, none of them included handing over Andrea outright, but he'd considered the possibility she might have to go along with him, at least for appearances. What he couldn't work out was how he was going to uncover Carla's whereabouts from Alejandro before he was forced to confront them.

"They specifically said no police," he reminded her.

She rolled her eyes in exasperation. "What do you think they're gonna do if the cops show up? Shoot her right in front of them? You're not making any sense. The only logical thing to do is call them."

He didn't want to involve the police. He no longer felt he could depend on them to solve the case. The two of them had been locked away in the motel room for over two weeks and in that time, the police had given them nothing – no viable leads, no end in sight. "What if we got someone else to go pick up Carla?"

"They're not gonna tell you where Carla is unless you hand me over."

They locked eyes with one another.

"You have got to be kidding me. We've gone through all this…" Andrea's hands flailed above her head defiantly as she stood to face him. "Shipping me across the country, hiding me away like some princess in a tower, and *now* you're gonna hand me over to him?"

She was in front of him, inches away, anger radiating from every pore of her body. He reached out to brush a tendril of hair from her face but she recoiled.

"I don't want to hand you over. But I don't know if we have any other options." He reached out to her again. "Just hear me out. What if, after they tell me where Carla is, I call a taxi to pick her up and then follow them to wherever they take you to get you back?"

She stared at him incredulously. "How long do you think it'll take him to kill me, Jose? Five minutes? Ten?"

She was right, of course. By the time he followed them to wherever they were planning on taking her, she might already be dead. There was no way of knowing for sure what Alejandro's intentions were, and he knew in his heart he couldn't risk losing her. Frustrated with the entire situation, he threw his hands in the air and began retracing his path across the room. "I don't know what else to do, Andrea! None of this was supposed to happen. You were supposed to come here to get well, and I was supposed to have Alejandro arrested back home. That was it. An easy plan. And I'm so sorry it didn't work out. And I'm so sorry this happened. But I need to figure out a way to get my aunt back and…" He glanced at his phone. "We only have five hours left."

"Call. The. Cops."

"So they can do what? The same nothing they've been doing this whole time?"

Without responding, she turned her back on him, her shoulders slumped, her chin lowered. It was the very same posture she'd been displaying the first time he'd seen her, waiting in the ER for the attending physician to stitch her wounds. And that was when he realized…

He wasn't helping her.

He wasn't saving her.

He wasn't making any difference at all.

"Fine," he said at last. "Let's call the cops."

An hour later, Rosetti and Anderson were caught up on Carla's abduction and the proposed exchange. Jose and Andrea sat beside one another on the far mattress while the officers sat across from them on the one closest to the door. Everyone leaned forward, their heads together.

"They said not to involve any police," Jose was reiterating.

Rosetti scoffed. "They always say that. You were smart to call us; I just wish you'd done it sooner so we would have had more time to put something together that resembled a decent strategy."

"You still have time though, right? You think you'll be able to get her without having to give me up?" Jose heard the fear in Andrea's voice and although it tore at his emotions, he was reassured by her sense of self-preservation. Perhaps she was healing after all.

"We're not giving you over," Anderson reassured her. "We just need to figure out where they might have Carla stashed and get to her before Jose's supposed to make the exchange." He looked at Rosetti, and Jose caught an unspoken understanding pass between them.

"What?" Jose asked.

"You're thinking they're hiding Carla wherever they're hiding the cars?" Rosetti asked her partner.

Jose was lost. "What cars?"

"We've recently discovered that a few of the guys Alejandro's been hanging out with here in Baltimore are running a car theft operation. We assumed they might be hiding some of the stolen cars down by the harbor since there's a good chance they're smuggling them out of the city on freightliners. Seems like more than a coincidence that they've asked you to meet them near the shipyard."

"So you think they've hidden my aunt with the cars?"

Rosetti nodded thoughtfully. "It makes sense, we just don't know exactly where they might be."

"We have the list of recently missing cars from Carson," Anderson added. "I think our best bet is to spend the next few hours canvassing the docks and shipyard for the cars. We find a car, we might find your aunt." He turned then to Rosetti. "Two squad cars aren't gonna cut it though. You might need to pull out the daughter card on this one to get us some more boots on the ground."

She smiled at Jose and explained. "My dad's the chief of police. Sometimes it helps. He's already familiar with your case against Alejandro, so it shouldn't be a hard sell for him to divert a few other officers in our direction this afternoon." She stood up and pulled her walkie off her shoulder harness. "I'll see if I can reach him now."

As he watched her walk out the door to make her appeal in private, he felt the strangest sensation, as if he knew her far better than he actually did. Or perhaps that one day he would. He must have gawked after her far longer than was appropriate because without warning, Andrea shoved him with both hands, rousing him from his contemplation.

"Stare much?" she whispered.

Embarrassed, he ignored her insinuation and turned to Anderson. "When you two leave, I want to come with you."

Anderson shook his head, chuckling. "Not a chance, buddy. And don't bother to ask Officer Rosetti. Trust me when I tell you she's been down that road before, and it didn't end well. There's no way she'll let a civilian ride along on this one."

He couldn't stand the thought of being left behind. Waiting. Not knowing what was happening. It was one of the many reasons he hadn't wanted to involve the police in the first place. Now they were effectively shutting him out of his own responsibility. "She's my aunt," Jose protested. "It's my fault she's involved in any of this to begin with."

Andrea took his hand. "No. It's way more my fault than it is yours."

Anderson hoisted himself off the sagging mattress and started for the door. "Neither one of you are responsible for the behavior of these men. But you need to let the professionals handle them. We're trained to deal with people who would rather shoot you than talk to you."

"Not that we enjoy getting shot at," Rosetti added, returning from outside. She turned to her partner. "Dad's sending three other units to the area, and he thinks we should bring Jose with us."

Anderson raised his eyebrows in shock and disbelief. "You've got to be kidding. Why the hell would he want us to do that?"

"He's not convinced we're gonna be able to find any of those cars in such a short amount of time. Jose is plan B." Her eyes cut to him, gauging his reaction. "Are you good with that?"

Before he could respond, Anderson interrupted. "I just got through telling him there was no way you were gonna let him go along." His eyes were pleading, and Jose could tell there was history between them neither wanted to discuss in front of him. "There's got to be another way."

Rosetti shot her partner a look that was the police equivalent of 'Not in front of the kids, let's talk about his later,' and returned her attention to Jose. "We're going to keep you safe, but we might need you to meet with them. Is that something you're willing to do?"

"Yeah, of course," he replied, without hesitation. "Just tell me what you need me to do."

50

Wednesday, October 12
Baltimore

It was just after three o'clock, and they hadn't found any of the stolen cars from the list. Mia clung desperately to the last rays of hope as the sun set on their original plan. The last thing she wanted was to involve Jose in the operation.

"Unit 136, this is 214." It was Carson, checking in on their progress.

"136. Go ahead," Jack responded.

"214 reporting a code G on the stolen vehicles."

Mia sighed, resting her head against the window as Jack responded. "10-4. 136 reporting a code G on the stolen vehicles."

"10-4. Request 10-19 to the station."

"Received. 15 08."

In the mirror, Mia saw Jose lean forward, slipping his fingers between the metal bars which separated him from the front of the cruiser. "What's going on?" he asked.

Jack shook his head. "The others haven't found any of the cars either. We're gonna meet up with them back at the station so we can get you set up for plan B."

278

Ten minutes later, Mia was fitting Jose with both a wire and a vest while she explained the logistics of what they expected him to do. As she carefully taped the hidden microphone just below his collarbone, she couldn't help but think of Kate, the other civilian life she'd risked, and prayed this operation would have a more favorable outcome.

"You don't have to do this," she said, feeling obligated to give him one last chance to change his mind.

He scowled at her. "You said it was our best chance of catching Alejandro and getting Carla back."

"It probably is. But there's still no shame in backing out."

He shook his head, resolutely. "I coulda backed out a long time ago," he said. "But I didn't then, and I won't now. Not when I finally feel like things are gonna get better."

As she tightened the vest around his chest, there was no mistaking just how much she liked Jose. If they'd met under different circumstances, in high school or through a mutual acquaintance instead of as part of an assignment, she was sure they would've been friends. The last thing she wanted was to see him hurt. "Now this vest is really thin and will only offer minimal protection. But they'll know immediately if you're wearing a heavier one so this'll have to do. I promise it's better than nothing."

"I'll be fine," he told her, with a level of conviction she couldn't help but admire.

She nodded but was too nervous to agree aloud. It was best not to tempt fate. "So here's what's gonna happen after we head out. We've got a couple of guys stationed at the meeting place already, watching to let us know when Alejandro gets there. Once we have confirmation, you'll drive my car the rest of the way, park along Holabird, and then walk over to where they'll be waiting for you. I'll be sitting in the backseat listening to everything."

"And you think Alejandro's gonna buy that you're Andrea?"

"I'll be wearing her clothes and leaning forward so my hair covers my face. We're the same basic size and shape and our hair is practically the same color."

"You do look a lot alike," Jose agreed.

"It's the only lucky break we've gotten, so we'll take it and cross our fingers." She smiled at him as he buttoned his shirt back over the vest. "Your only job is to get them to tell you where Carla is. Hopefully when they see me in the back seat they'll be willing to tell you the drop off location. Once we have an address, hand them the keys to the car and walk away. Just get outta there and we'll do the rest."

"What if Alejandro's not there?"

She was convinced Alejandro was the type of predator who would want to be on site to see Andrea for himself. Over the years, she'd spent enough time with profilers to know Alejandro wouldn't leave the job to someone else. She was banking on it.

"He'll be there, but even if for some reason he's not, the only other place he'd be is with your aunt, and we'll find him when we get there." She hoped she was bolstering Jose's confidence since she couldn't help but notice the way his foot had begun tapping nervously against the floor. "Okay?" she asked.

He smoothed his shirt over the vest and raised and lowered his arms to adjust the fit. "Okay," he said. "Let's do this."

Eleven men and women were assembled in the staging room, just inside the back entrance of the station. Mia was wearing Andrea's favorite bright pink tank top with her hair draped casually around her face. Four other officers were also in civilian attire while the other five remained in uniform.

"Carson, you're taking your crew to get Carla as soon as we have a location. Suarez, Dickson, Houston, and Briggs, you're coming with me and Jack to pick up whoever shows up to make this trade." Mia paused, glancing around the room and then at her watch. "We've only got 25 minutes. Where the hell is Jack?"

"Saw him about five minutes ago, heading the opposite direction down the hall. He looked upset. I think he got a personal call or something."

Mia pushed past Carter and Suarez into the hallway, sprinting as fast as she could up the stairs to her office. Jack was there, receiver wedged against his ear as he bent over, lacing his sneakers.

"Are you sure you don't want me to come?" he was saying, his voice worried, heavy with emotion. "Yes, but what did they say?" he continued. "How many hours? Three? Six? Nine?"

Mia tried to get his attention, but his back was still toward her, blocking her entry into the room.

"I can be there in fifteen minutes, Stella. I swear to God if this baby comes and I'm not there, I'll never forgive myself." There was a long pause and Mia felt like an intruder as Jack listened to his wife on the other end of the line. "Fine. I'll go. But as soon as this is resolved, I'm on my way. Don't have her. Promise you'll wait for me." Another pause. "I love you too. Both of you."

Jack set the receiver down and turned to Mia. "Damn stubborn, that woman," he said, ushering her out into the hall. "Her water broke this morning, but instead of calling me or going to the hospital, she stopped into work to drop off some papers. Apparently she didn't want to alarm me until she spoke with a doctor and now he says she's only one centimeter dilated and 5% effaced, so it'll probably be six to ten hours before the baby's born."

"I don't even know what you just said, but it sounds to me like she didn't want you to race over there."

"No! She wants me to 'serve and protect' and only go to the hospital once we've got Carla back and Alejandro down in lock up."

They took the stairs together two at a time and rounded the corner to where the others were waiting. "At least someone believes in us," Mia laughed thinly.

"Wish I shared her sentiments."

CHAPTER

51

JOSE

Wednesday, October 12
Baltimore

Jose eased the car against the curb and put the transmission in park. He took a deep breath.

"You good?" Officer Rosetti asked from the back seat.

He nodded but his mouth was too dry to respond. More emotionally spent than scared, he just wanted the whole ordeal to be over. He wanted Aunt Carla to be safe. He wanted Andrea to be safe. And he wanted to go back to his job at the hospital with his patients in the ICU. That was where he belonged. He was a healer, not a fighter.

"Do you see them?" she asked.

He glanced out the window without turning his head. "Yeah. Three of them. And I think one is Alejandro." He listened, unmoving while she delivered a message to the other officers. When she finished, her voice softened, from no-nonsense officer to concerned friend.

"Okay. You've got this. Just tell them Andrea's locked in the car waiting and you'll give them the keys as soon as they tell you Carla's location. I'll be listening, so don't worry about trying to remember."

He could barely hear her over the beating of his own heart. "What if they lie to me? What if she's not where they send us?"

She was quiet for a moment, and he could tell she had concerns of her own. Finally, she spoke. "I don't have a crystal ball, Jose. And neither do you. All we can do in this life is make the best decisions we can based on the information we have. I think it works out pretty well most of the time. And the rest of the time..." She paused then, as if to swallow down something difficult. "We go on blind faith," she continued. "It's up to you now, though. You can choose to get out of the car or keep driving. I'm good either way. It's your call."

He knew what he needed to do. He'd known all along. It was the same choice he made as a boy with the dog in the homeless village. The same choice he made every time he healed a patient who would never survive without his healing touch. The same choice he made the moment he'd gotten involved with Andrea.

He cracked open the door.

"See you in a few," Rosetti said.

Jose strolled across the vacant lot, hoping to appear casual. Confident. He knew there were five plain clothes officers watching from various locations around the block. He also knew none of them would get to him in time if one of the three men who now stood before him shot him from point blank range.

Alejandro was there along with two other Hispanic men he didn't recognize. He spoke to him in Spanish, without an ounce of apprehension. "You must be Jose."

"Where's my aunt?" Jose asked as steadily as he could.

Alejandro smiled pointedly at the men to his left and right. "Not even a hello from this one. So rude. Maybe we oughta teach him some manners, huh, boys?"

Jose raised his hands in front of his chest and resisted the urge to scoot back. "I don't want any trouble. I did what you asked." He nodded with his head in the direction of the car. "Andrea's sitting over there, locked up in the backseat of the car. Just tell me where Carla is, and I'll give you the keys. She's all yours. That girl's been nothing but trouble, and I've learned my lesson. I never shoulda gotten involved."

Alejandro took a step forward, flexing his upper body. "You think? No reason she would want somebody like you when she's already got somebody like me. So hand over the keys." He thrust his hand forward and for an instant, Jose was sure he was going to be sucker punched, but when he opened his eyes, there was merely an open palm, waiting for the key.

"Where is my aunt?"

Alejandro sighed heavily, annoyed by Jose's persistence. "We'll leave her at the corner of Beckley and Van Deman. And you better go alone. Now gimme the damn keys or we'll just take a crowbar to the windows."

"No," Jose countered, sounding braver than he felt. "Call them now. I want to hear you tell them."

Alejandro squinted into the sunlight over Jose's shoulder in the direction of the car, causing the hairs on the back of his neck to stand on end. *Please don't realize it's not Andrea*, he thought to himself. A moment later, seemingly assuaged, the man licked his lips and pulled his phone from his jean's pocket.

"Esto es Alejandro. Llevar a la mujer al dejar y dejarla. Sí. Sí. Adiós."

Satisfied the second team of police officers would be able to find his aunt, it was time to make his escape, but at that moment, Jose caught movement out of the corner of his eye and unintentionally glanced to the right, in the direction of the ally. He immediately realized his mistake when he recognized Officer Anderson strolling casually along the side of the building. All three men turned to follow his gaze and spotted Anderson as well.

"Never seen any wedos in this neighborhood," the man on Alejandro's left said.

"Naw, man, that ain't right," said the other, backing away from Jose.

Alejandro pulled a handgun from behind his back where it had been tucked into his waistband. "Walk. Slowly," he instructed, pointing in the direction of the car. "I swear to God if you try anything, I will shoot you in the back."

As a child, Jose had attended mass faithfully with his abuela, but once he began working as a teen, his schedule often prevented him from making it to church most Sunday mornings. As he shuffled toward Officer Rosetti, still hunched in the backseat of her Civic, he could hear his grandmother's voice in his head, praying to God and all the saints for intercession. If there was a time in his life when he needed divine intervention, this was most certainly it.

He kept his eyes down, to avoid making any inadvertent glances, either at Anderson or Rosetti, and as he continued across the vacant lot, he prayed the police were not only on their way to rescue his aunt but were also prepared to intervene now on his behalf. Because when it came to having a clue about what to do next, he was completely at a loss.

Less than twenty feet from the car, Alejandro froze and Jose's heart stopped.

He knew.

"Who the hell is that?" he cried, jamming the barrel of the handgun into Jose's back. "Because it ain't Andrea, you lying piece of crap."

"Police! Put down your weapon!" Anderson called from where he was now standing at the corner of the lot.

Jose, Alejandro, and the other two men turned in unison at the sound of Anderson's voice, and before he knew what was happening, a shot rang out. A second shot immediately followed. Jose dropped to the ground, ears ringing, and crawled underneath the car. From beneath the vehicle, he saw feet on the opposite side and realized Officer Rosetti was on the move. His instinct was to call to her, to warn her of the danger, but before he could cry out, he heard more gunfire. In his periphery, he could see two men running across the lot, even as Rosetti called after them but didn't give chase. Alejandro lay motionless in a small pool of blood, his firearm still in his hand. Without thinking, Jose scrambled from beneath the car and lunged toward him, kicking the gun from his grasp, across the dirt and gravel. Alejandro's accomplices were rounding the corner at the far side of the lot, and he considered running after them until he recognized several of the other plain clothes officers closing in.

On the sidewalk just beyond the car, Anderson was on the ground. Rosetti was bent over him, talking into the walkie-talkie secured to her shoulder, but between the ringing in his ears and the thundering of his own heart, he couldn't hear what she was saying.

Jose glanced down once again at Alejandro and realized the man was still breathing. As he examined the gaping gunshot wound and ever-widening bloodstain, which now saturated the surrounding shirt, Alejandro's eyes fluttered open and his lips began to move.

"Help me," he mouthed.

Over the course of his career, Jose had saved many patients. People he assumed were good, honest citizens, worthy of his gift. During that same time, he'd also had to let many others die. He couldn't save them all lest he give himself away. It was the part of his gift he hated the most, having to decide who to heal and who to let suffer on their own.

He crouched beside Alejandro, a man who was unworthy in every sense of the word. And yet, death was almost more than he deserved.

He reached down, placing his own hands over the wound and felt the immediate sensation of heat spreading through his body. He allowed the warmth to spread into

Alejandro, but only briefly. Just long enough to ensure, with proper medical intervention, he would survive.

When he finished, he peeled off his own shirt to wipe the blood off his hands and used it to pick up Alejandro's discarded gun. Then he sprinted, as fast as he could, across the lot to where Rosetti still hovered over Anderson.

His hearing was returning and as he approached, she hollered, "That bastard got him in the leg. Must have nicked an artery. He's bleeding out fast, and I can't get it to stop."

Jose's emergency room training kicked in, and he instructed Rosetti to help elevate his hips by wedging herself beneath him as he applied pressure. "How long 'til an ambulance arrives?"

She shook her head. "Two minutes. Maybe three. He's unresponsive already and his pulse is really weak."

Jose knew what he had to do and knew he had to do it quickly, but there was no way he was going to be able to heal Anderson without Rosetti watching. Seconds later, Anderson stopped breathing.

He had no other choice.

He cleared his mind, concentrating on his hands and the wound and the life force he felt slipping away. Slowly, steadily, the heat spread through the gunshot wound and surrounding tissue, making its way into the bloodstream and throughout the officer's entire system. A moment later, Anderson came to, taking a huge gulp of air before opening his eyes.

"Jack?" Rosetti sputtered in disbelief.

"I'm here," he moaned.

She pulled herself from beneath him and crawled toward his head, cradling his face in her hands. "Oh, my God, I thought you were dead."

"Me too," he said.

She sat with him, brushing the hair from his face in quiet contemplation. Jose could see her reflecting on what had just transpired, piecing it all together. Anticipating an interrogation, he scrambled to his feet and began walking away. He didn't want to be forced into an explanation.

"Wait, Jose," she called. "What just happened? What did you just do?"

His back was to her. He didn't know what to say. Certainly not the truth.

"You healed him. With your hands. I saw you do it."

He didn't turn around. She would never understand. His mind raced, searching his training for another possible rationalization for what had just transpired. He could feel her staring at the back of his head as the ambulance sirens sliced through the silence.

He took a step, intent on seeing himself out of the chaos which was about to ensue when he heard her speak, more to herself than to him.

"Oh, my God, Jose. Are you one of us?"

Thursday, October 13
Baltimore

"Is Stella going to be able to meet us?" Thomas asked Mia as she pulled into a parking spot in the garage at GBMC hospital the next morning.

"As far as I know. She and the baby are in the Postpartum Patient Care Unit on the second floor. And I didn't have a chance to call and find out where they moved Jack after he left the ER late last night. I feel awful for her that Jack never made it to the birth, but at least we were able to convince the EMTs to take him to the same hospital so they could be together today."

He hated the thought that Mia could have easily been in the line of fire instead of Jack. He didn't think he would ever get used to the idea of losing her. "I bet he wishes he would have ignored Stella and gone to the hospital right away instead of going on the assignment with you."

She unbuckled her seatbelt and gathered the balloons and teddy bear from the back seat. "At least it all worked out in the end. Especially with Jose. That he was there with this amazing gift just when we needed him. That his relationship with Andrea brought him to Baltimore to be here with us in the first place." She shook her head in disbelief. "It's all pretty spectacular when you think about it. Our prophecy sure works in mysterious ways."

Thomas thought it was interesting that she should choose the same phrase Mildred often used about God to describe the prophecy. He reached for her hand as they entered the hospital, something he always felt very grateful to be able to do. Mia was safe. Mia was alive. He never took it for granted.

They checked in at the front desk to find out where Jack had been relocated after his surgery the night before.

"Officer Anderson's on the fifth floor, room 5435," the receptionist told them.

On the elevator to the recovery rooms, Thomas couldn't help giving her a hard time.

"I can't believe you spent the last three weeks working on an assignment for a guy who ended up being one of the light psychics. He was under your nose the whole time and you didn't even know it. I met Lanying and had it figured out in ten minutes."

She nudged him playfully. "How was I supposed to know Jose was a psychic healer? It's not like he was wearing a t-shirt, 'Ask Me How I Can Heal You With My Hands.' I did get a strange feeling about him though, from the first day I met him. His aura was light. Really light. And it was almost as if I'd known him for a very long time, like we'd grown up together or something. When he told me his birthday, I swear they almost needed to carry me away in the ambulance too."

Thomas didn't like that her confession left him feeling the tiniest bit jealous. "Would you say you felt more connected to him when you met than you did to me after that first lineup?"

"Not even close," she replied, kissing him on the cheek for good measure. "Still, it's pretty disappointing to know that if Lanying's island woman turns out to be one of us,

Jose would've made number seven. That is, if we hadn't lost Kate."

Thomas let the weight of her declaration wash over him. It was true. The rippling effects of Kate's death continued to lap at their feet. But it was too late to dwell on the past. Now, they could only look to the future, continuing on with their plan of keeping the dark psychics apart.

To have come so close though…

"Well, look what the cat dragged in," Jack laughed as he and Mia entered the room.

Mia sailed across the room, hurrying to embrace her partner who was propped up in his hospital bed. "It's good to see you too," she said. They held each other for a long moment, and Thomas realized how lucky he was that Mia had such an amazing support system.

"And look who else is here," she gushed, turning to Stella, who looked exhausted but grateful in the seat beside the window, a tiny bundle cradled in her arms. "Oh my God. You have to let me see her."

"Him," Jack corrected, laughing. "My daughter turned out to be a son. We've named him Owen."

"You're kidding," Mia said as Stella handed her the infant. "He's beautiful, just the same." She held the baby to her face, breathing him in and snuck a glance at Thomas. "Maybe someday, huh?"

It was the first time she'd ever mentioned the possibility of wanting children. He felt himself blushing. "Maybe someday," he agreed, tying Jack's 'Get Well' balloons on the bed rail before perching himself atop the small table in the corner.

After handing Owen back to Stella, Mia returned her attention to Jack. "So tell me, besides having a son instead of a daughter, what other news do you have for us?"

"Well, I think they're actually gonna let me bust outta here tonight, since they only really kept me this long for observation. They thought initially I was going to need major surgery, but I didn't. The doctors said it was the strangest thing that the bullet tore through my quad and lodged itself in my hamstring but somehow missed the femoral artery it should have gone right through. I have a couple stitches where they took the bullet out, but other than that, there was nothing to see. Based on what they saw at the scene, the EMTs told the doctors they estimated I lost about five pints of blood, but there was no evidence of much blood loss at all when I was examined." He looked to Stella and held out his hand which she willingly took. "I can't believe how lucky we got."

Mia had already shared Jose's request for them to keep their knowledge of his abilities private, so Thomas knew it wasn't something she would reveal to Jack now. "Sounds like a serious miracle," she said to Jack. "You definitely used up one of your nine lives."

Jack chuckled, caressing the top of Owen's head. "No kidding. I gotta be more careful with the other eight, especially now that I'm someone's daddy." He shifted wearily under the white cotton sheet and looked again to Mia. "So I'm dying to know, what happened after they took me away? Please tell me Carson's guys got Jose's Aunt Carla back."

"They did, as a matter of fact," she told him. "Found her right where they told us she'd be. And you'll never guess the best part. Those idiots didn't have the sense to dump her more than two blocks away from the warehouse where they'd been keeping her. Carson and Harris canvassed the surrounding area on foot for less than 20 minutes and found the abandoned warehouse where they were storing the stolen cars."

"No kidding," Jack said.

"A happy ending all around."

"And Jose and Andrea?"

"They're planning to stay with Carla for a couple days at her place – she was seriously shaken up, as you can imagine.

Then I think they're heading back to Phoenix by the end of the week."

Jack nodded thoughtfully and then, seemingly out of nowhere, smacked himself on the head. "And wait, what about Alejandro? Jesus, I'd forgotten all about that SOB."

"You shot him, just under the rib cage on his right hand side. Through and through. Lots of blood, but last I heard, he's gonna survive."

Thomas watched a series of emotions wash across Jack's face - first disbelief, then anger, and finally acceptance, all within the span of five seconds. "Kinda wish I woulda taken the bastard out, but there'll be a lot less paperwork this way. As long as you think we have enough to put him away. This douchebag isn't gonna be out on the streets again if I have anything to say about it."

Mia held up her hands. "While you were in here convalescing, I took it upon myself to have a nice long conversation with the officer in Phoenix who was working his case. Between what they already had and what we have now, he won't see the light of day from behind bars ever again."

"Shooting a cop didn't hurt our cause," Jack said.

"I think we probably had enough without that, but thanks for taking one for the team anyway."

The baby began to whimper, and Stella announced that she needed to try to feed him. Thomas and Mia took the opportunity to see themselves out, promising to stop by the Andersons' house the following night with supper.

As they strolled together across the hospital courtyard to the parking garage, Thomas was overcome with a sense of relief. It was similar to the sensation he typically felt when something dreadful was about to happen, but instead of feeling the urge to get away, he understood somehow that he needed to go on because they were already traveling along the right path.

"It's all going to be okay," he told Mia, reaching out to take her hand, smooth and warm in his own.

"Jack and Stella and Owen?"

He searched his heart and found the stillness he was looking for. "Yes. But not just them."

"Jose and Andrea?"

"Yes. Them too."

She squeezed his hand. "You and me?"

"All of us," he told her. "I can feel it, in my gut, just like with the bad stuff."

She turned to him. "Like with your ability?"

He smiled. "Yeah. I've been practicing, feeling for the good stuff, and it's there now. I don't know how we're gonna do it, but I feel like we have a chance."

"A chance to what?"

"A chance to save the world," he said.

What if a group of psychic strangers came together to save the world?

Please enjoy this sneak peek of

beyond the

sanctified

book three of the sevens prophecy series

CHAPTER

1

AKANTHA

Friday, October 14
London

Akantha heard the chains rattling inside the wall, alerting her that a meal was coming. They'd been feeding her using this pulley system for many days. So long in fact that she had given up trying to get their attention. She snatched the new plate of food as soon as it appeared in the wall niche. This time it was a fish filet and cooked vegetables. For days she'd sent flames up the chute, hoping her show of power would hasten her release, but no one had come to get her. At one point she'd returned her plate engulfed in flames, but the meals kept arriving at regular intervals regardless of her provocation, so she'd given up.

She had no memory of how she came to be in the stone room, without windows or doors. There was a hatch in the ceiling but she couldn't jump high enough to reach it. Her last memory of the outside world was at the one they called Patrick's estate where she'd been given a room with a bed and something called a television. She'd spent hours watching the pictures flash across the screen and was even beginning to learn some of the language that was spoken in her strange new world. She liked it there. It wasn't hot like it was in the jungle and there were no bugs biting at her skin. She was grateful to her deliverer Patrick for bringing her there and considered him a friend. Especially since he hadn't even punished her when she'd accidentally set a corner of her room on fire the week before.

He'd taken her out of his house a few times, around the city he called London, to places where she could set fires. They'd snuck away together in the middle of the night without her interpreter to abandoned places where he allowed her to light as many fires as she liked. Once, when another person crept unexpectedly from the shadows and caught her burning things, Patrick allowed her to set him on fire as well.

She'd thought perhaps they were going to set fires again on the night she was asked, via her new interpreter, to join the other gods downstairs. This was the first time she'd been with them all at the same time, as part of their group. She liked them much more than she had ever liked anyone in her tribe. They didn't shun her or throw rocks at her; they treated her with respect and kindness.

In the sitting room she was offered something flaky, like bread, which she was surprised to find was sweet and delicious. So much better than any tortilla she'd eaten among her people.

But no, she had thought, correcting herself. *These are my people now.*

After she finished eating the sweet treat Lillian called a 'pastry,' one of Patrick's servants began passing around a tray of beverages in tall, silver mugs. Upon reaching Akantha, only one remained and she plucked it greedily from the tray. The last thing she recalled before waking up on the floor of the stone room was the pleasant warmth of the liquid on the back of her throat as she swallowed it down.

She'd spent days going back and forth in her mind about whether one of the members of her new tribe was responsible for her imprisonment. Some moments she was convinced Lillian or the brutish-looking man was to blame; other times she was convinced of their innocence. Today, she was certain they could be trusted. If Patrick believed in them, she could too. They'd given her no reason to believe otherwise. She just couldn't wrap her head around what had happened or why.

She was still finishing her vegetables, wondering how to escape, when she heard a sound she didn't recognize. She realized the sound was coming from above her head and glanced up in time to see the ceiling panel lifting open.

Javier appeared in the opening and beside him was her interpreter, Irene.

"Akantha," Irene called to her in her native tongue. "We've been sent by Patrick to rescue you." Javier lowered a ladder into the room. "Climb up quickly! The time has come and we need you! The prophecy is about to be fulfilled."

Dearest Reader,

When I decided to write the *Sevens Prophecy Series*, I knew I wanted to give a voice to some of the larger issues in our world which are difficult to discuss - the thousands of women and children who have been forced into sexual slavery, the pain and indignity of domestic violence, the tragedy of third world poverty and first world body shaming. Please know that although I've written works of fiction, there's nothing fictional about the real-life anguish actual men and women facing these issues experience each and every day.

Here are some of the facts:

"An estimated 2.5 million people are in forced labor (including sexual exploitation) at any given time as a result of trafficking, the majority of these trafficking victims are between 18 and 24 years of age, and 98% of those used for forced commercial sexual exploitation are women and girls.

Worldwide, almost one third (30%) of women who have been in a relationship report that they have experienced some form of physical and/or sexual violence by their intimate partner, and globally, as many as 38% of murders of women are committed by an intimate partner.

Some 795 million people in the world do not have enough food to lead a healthy, active life. That's about one in nine people on earth. Sub-Saharan Africa is the region with the highest prevalence of hunger. One person in four there is undernourished. However, if women farmers had the same access to resources as men, the number of hungry in the world could be reduced by up to 150 million.

In the United States, 20 million women and 10 million men suffer from a clinically significant eating disorder at some time in their life. The best-known contributor to the development of anorexia nervosa and bulimia nervosa is the body dissatisfaction (40-60%) of elementary school girls (ages 6-12) who are concerned about their weight or about becoming too fat. This concern endures through life."

I implore you to learn more about what you can do to increase awareness or help put an end to these issues by taking a few minutes of your day to read the information on the following websites which served as my fact sources:

www.ungift.org   www.nationaleatingdisorders.org
www.unodc.org   www.wfp.org/hunger/stats
www.who.int   www.unglobalcompact.org

In the words of the great 18th century abolitionist William Wilberforce:
"You may choose to look the other way but you can never say again that you did not know."

Sincerely,
Amalie Jahn

About the Author

Amalie Jahn is the author of the *Sevens Prophecy Series*,
The Clay Lion Series, and many, many to-do lists.
Visit her online at www.amaliejahn.com.

www.ingramcontent.com/pod-product-compliance
Lightning Source LLC
Chambersburg PA
CBHW021311250626
47155CB00002B/490